"That's ... of asking if you are free,"

Brad said.

Lili's heart skipped a beat. "You mean, as in marriage? Yes. I'm free. Now."

"You mean there *was* a Mr. . . . someone?"

Lili nodded. That seemed, somehow, less devious than a spoken yes. "But there hasn't been for some time." That, at least, was true.

"Any kids?"

The big one. The A-plus, top-of-the-line, state-of-the-art question. It required an answer, so what was she going to say? The truth—to a point. "Yes, one boy."

"Does he look like you?"

"Not really." He was, in fact, a small clone of the man sitting across from her. From the day he was born, Donny had been a living, breathing reminder of Brad.

"I envy you," Brad said. "How I'd love to have a son."

Lili's heart, still only semihealed from its eleven-year-old trauma, contracted with pain.

Dear Reader,

Welcome to **Silhouette Special Edition** . . . welcome to romance. Each month, **Silhouette Special Edition** publishes six novels with you in mind—stories of love and life, tales that you can identify with—romance with that little "something special" added in.

This month, **Silhouette Special Edition** has some wonderful stories on their way to you. A "delivery" you may want to keep an eye out for is *Navy Baby,* by Debbie Macomber. It's full steam ahead for a delightful story that shouldn't be missed!

Rounding out October are winning tales by more of your favorite authors: Tracy Sinclair, Natalie Bishop, Mary Curtis, Christine Rimmer and Diana Whitney. A good time will be had by all!

In each **Silhouette Special Edition** novel, we're dedicated to bringing you the romances that you dream about—the type of stories that delight as well as bring a tear to the eye. And that's what **Silhouette Special Edition** is all about—special books by special authors for special readers!

I hope you enjoy this book and all of the stories to come.

Sincerely,

Tara Gavin
Senior Editor

MARY CURTIS
Top of the Mountain

Silhouette Special Edition

Published by Silhouette Books New York

America's Publisher of Contemporary Romance

SILHOUETTE BOOKS
300 East 42nd St., New York, N.Y. 10017

TOP OF THE MOUNTAIN

ISBN: 0-373-09699-2

First Silhouette Books printing October 1991

Printed in the U.S.A.

Books by Mary Curtis

Silhouette Special Edition

Love Lyrics #424
Cliffhanger #526
Top of the Mountain #699

MARY CURTIS,

a former Californian who now resides in Massachusetts, divides her artistic energy between writing projects and work in community theater. This author of a dozen romance novels and mother of three daughters also finds time to play the heroine herself, in musicals such as *Guys and Dolls, Kiss Me, Kate* and *The King and I.* When not performing, directing or writing, Mary is likely to be traveling with her husband, gathering new story and setting ideas along the way. She is also known to romance fans as Mary Haskell.

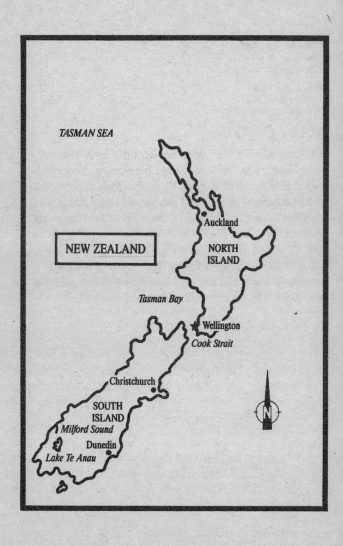

TASMAN SEA

NEW ZEALAND

Auckland

NORTH ISLAND

Tasman Bay

Wellington

Cook Strait

Christchurch

SOUTH ISLAND

Milford Sound

Dunedin

Lake Te Anau

N

Chapter One

As Lili hurried across the patio between her cottage and the main building of the Te Anau Hotel, she cast a baleful glance at the sky. Her stomach clenched at the sight of heavy gray clouds forming a solid cover over the fast-disappearing blue. *Okay, stomach,* she ordered, *stop your lurching about. We're doing this hike . . . rain, shine or typhoon.* Her stomach gave one last rebellious roll before settling into uneasy acquiescence. It was a familiar battle of will over organs.

"Rain, rain, go away, don't come back till a week from today." The childhood incantation was worth a shot. Maybe an outside vote could sway the Supreme Weather Director's decision.

The moment she stepped into the lobby, Lili saw the board listing the Milford Track orientation meeting. She followed its arrow down a long hallway. A set of double doors opened into a large rectangular room that held rows of chairs facing a display of boots, sturdy clothing, backpacks and various other mountain-hiking paraphernalia.

People milled about, wineglasses in hand, nibbling on cheese and crackers and chatting in the animated tones of those on the brink of adventure.

Lili walked to the refreshment table, filled one of the plastic glasses with white wine and looked around for someone to talk to. Her eyes met the twinkling blue gaze of a young woman about her own age, so Lili returned the welcoming smile and headed her way.

"Hi." She shifted her wineglass to shake the hand that extended to meet hers. "I'm Lili Jamison. I'm hoping you're on your own, as I am."

"My name is Gillian. Gillian Greene. And yes, I'm alone."

Lili grinned. "You're either from New Zealand or England, and I'm embarrassed to say I can't tell the difference."

"I'm a Kiwi, from Auckland. No mistaking you. You're a Yank. How long have you been here?"

"I arrived in New Zealand yesterday. Actually, I've been in Australia for three weeks, but I'm afraid my body is still trying to decide which end is up."

Gillian laughed. "Better settle that before you get on the trail, or you'll be in trouble, right enough." She raised the plastic glass, giving it a rueful look. "Not exactly posh crystal. Do you think they're trying to tell us something?"

"I'm sure. This is probably as fancy as it gets for the next five days."

"Is this something you've wanted to do for a long time? The Milford Track, I mean."

Lili grimaced. "Well . . . Not exactly. You see, it happens to fit into a childhood dream."

"Really? Tell me about it. I'm a aficionado of childhood dreams."

"I read a book when I was little, called *A Boy, a Dog, and 20,000 Sheep*—"

"Oh, yes! Benjamin Potter! The perennial twelve-year-old boy! Grew up on his adventures!"

"Did you really?" Lili smiled. "I felt right away we had something in common! Anyway, I loved that story. And from then on, I longed to come to New Zealand and retrace Benjamin's adventures. Which just happened, if you remember that book, to include hiking the Milford Track."

"Of course! So here you are, and dreams do come true!"

Lili's laugh was a tiny bit forced. "Well, Gillian, I hope so. I sort of forgot it was this twenty-eight-year-old out-of-condition body that has to do the walking."

"Listen, you'll do fine. Why, I bet—" Gillian fell silent and her mouth formed a silent whistle. "Oh, my."

"What's up?"

"At the moment, my antenna. The most beautiful example of 'maledom' I've set eyes upon in many a moon just entered. Has to be one of yours."

Lili cocked her head and frowned. "Excuse me?"

"An American. Something about his carriage. All that self-assurance. Steal a peek, Lili. We'll flip for him."

Lili laughed. "If he's that gorgeous, he's probably married and has five kids."

"If so, they're not with him. So we'll still flip for him."

Still grinning, Lili turned her head to "steal a peek," and had to reach for the edge of the table to steady herself. She felt the blood drain from her face. The world, already upside down, did a double flip and settled at a hazardous tilt. "Oh, my God."

"Are you all right?" Gillian reached out to grasp her arm. You look like you've seen a ghost!"

A ghost. It might as well be. He was the last person Lili had expected to see again in her whole life. Yet here he was, in a remote corner of New Zealand, on the other side of the world from where he belonged. He stood just inside the door, looking ten feet tall, his powerful body dominating its space, his face wearing that expression of pleased expectation she'd so often seen in her dreams.

"Lili?"

Momentarily dazed, she refocused her eyes on Gillian's concerned face. "Oh, sorry. Just a bad moment." Lili fumbled with her purse, hitching it higher on her shoulder, taking the opportunity to turn her back toward the door. He mustn't see her! But how could she avoid him in here? The room seemed suddenly to have shrunk radically. "I..." Lili reached behind Gillian for the wine bottle and refilled her glass. "I haven't quite adjusted to the change—" she gave her new friend a sick smile and took a gulp of the wine "—of latitude." Between Australia and New Zealand? Gillian must think she was crazy. She hazarded another glance over her shoulder. Maybe she was crazy.

"Someone you know?"

Lili moved her head up and down, feeling as if it were slightly loose on its "hinge." "Yes. Sort of."

"Sort of." The other woman's face displayed her skepticism. "That is *not* a 'sort of' expression." She looked around. "I suppose I ought to mingle... get to know some of the others."

"Oh, no! I mean...don't rush off. Uh, I'll go with you." She knew her smile must be weak, but it was the best she could muster. "To circulate, I mean."

Gillian gave her a pat on the arm that was clearly intended to be encouraging. "Why not go over and say hello to your 'sort of' friend?" She heaved an exaggerated sigh. "I have a feeling I'll lose the toss." She cast a regretful glance in the direction of the American "hunk," then gave Lili a nod that urged action before moving away. Lili stood in the deserted space, feeling like a kangaroo trying to hide inside a backpack.

Was it possible—oh, no!—that he also was going on the Milford Track hike? She hazarded another peek. Of course, it was possible. Why else would he be here, sipping wine and talking to the couple clutching handfuls of brochures? She longed to turn around and study him, to see if he'd changed. But she didn't dare. If, by some mean trick of fate, he still turned her insides to mush the way he used to, she'd better compose herself, get a good grip on her inventive abilities before he asked, "And what's happened in your life since the last time I saw you?"

Lili was so rattled that she'd unintentionally shut out the sounds in the room around her, and it wasn't until one of the men standing nearby tapped her on the shoulder and said, "We're supposed to sit down now," that she noticed most of the people had settled into the chairs. She nodded her thanks and headed for a seat, frantically searching for *him*, so she could sit on the other side of the room. She needed a little breathing space, some time to pull herself together. But a thorough perusal failed to reveal him. Maybe he *wasn't* one of the hikers; maybe he'd just drifted into the room to see what was going on. Maybe he was simply stopping in New Zealand on his way to Australia—her pattern in reverse. But, she had to ask herself, did anyone just "drop by" Te Anau? It wasn't exactly on the jet run.

She found a seat near the back and slid quickly into it, trying to stop the wild spiraling of her mind. Brad. Bradford Andrew Hollingsworth III. He had been the walking, talking, breathing embodiment of every component of Lili's dream man, the unknowing object of her worshipful ardor, the unwitting owner of her heart. Lili had fallen desperately in love with him the first time they'd met, when she was twelve and Brad was seventeen. She had never wavered in her affections until that last time she'd been with him, when he'd escorted her to her high-school senior prom. No. To be honest, long past then: until her memories of him had faded and the hard realities of everyday life had made daydreams a bygone luxury.

It was hard to concentrate on what was being said, with frantic speculations racing about in her head and her heart thumping a rat-a-tat rhythm in her chest. Brad. Dear God. Was that glimpse all she was to get? And if so, was it a blessing, or what it felt like inside: a calamitous blow from spiteful fate?

" . . . Come pick up your pack first thing in the morning so you'll have plenty of time to assemble everything." The man in front was giving instructions, and she'd already missed part of what he'd said. "You'll be given a bed sheet at the first hut to carry with you. We also loan you one of these." He held up a rain slicker. "Don't leave without it. Our average rainfall is about two hundred and fifty inches a year, which should give you a clue about how hard it can come down. Nothing but a good old PVC will protect you. Now, these are the other things you need . . ."

Someone slid into the chair next to hers, and she knew, instinctively, that it was Brad. Her antennae had picked up his presence, had registered its intrusion on her senses. She kept her head turned away, postponing the moment of recognition. On second thought, maybe he wouldn't remember her; after all, it *had* been eleven years. How could she stand it if he didn't even know who she was? Given the dimension of the changes, not to mention the *problems* he had brought into her life, the possibility seemed unbearable.

"The Milford Track has been described as the most beautiful trek in the world, and you'll all have plenty of spectacular memories to carry out with you. . . ."

"Is that Robert Romauch?"

Lili almost turned toward him, remembering at the last second to keep her head down. "Pardon?"

"Robert Romauch, the track manager. Is he the man who's talking?"

"Uh, yes . . . I think so." She hadn't the foggiest notion. But one question was answered. The instant he spoke, her stomach turned to Jell-O. God, she wasn't a seventeen-year-old kid anymore; she was a grown woman, a working mother, who had dealt with a lot more trouble than he'd probably ever seen. She couldn't afford this foolish reaction. She had too much at stake to risk a muddled head.

Lili was overwhelmed. In just these short minutes, her childhood daydream had been turned into a cross between her most flamboyant fantasy and her worst nightmare. For a moment, she resented having her lifelong dream invaded. But the enticing force of his presence made resentment impossible to sustain. She wished she could hold on to it. It might be a useful buffer against some of the other emotions bombarding her senses.

"...You'll want to have a lot of film with you. I hope you all brought a good camera—it's one of the things that's worth its weight. But, speaking of weight, if an item isn't on the list you received, you probably shouldn't take it. Your pack will get heavier with each mile, so keep it under eleven pounds."

Brad shifted in his seat, his arm brushing Lili's. She couldn't believe the tingling waves that skittered through her. The reaction belonged in her past. What was it doing here, today, in a world so far removed from the one in which she'd known him? She tried to edge away, but it was impossible, given the closeness of the chairs and the breadth of his shoulders.

"...should include long underwear, a wool cap, a wool sweater and mittens. It could be hot, like today, or change to rain and sleet by the time you hit the Mackinnon Pass."

"Sounds like we may slide over the top." His voice, low and humorous, tickled her ear. *Please,* she wanted to beg, *don't get so close!*

"The first day is easy...."

"Getting excited?"

Lili jumped. She couldn't keep answering him with the back of her head in his face, but that first eye contact was looming in her mind as *the moment of truth.* Luckily she only had time to nod before the speaker continued.

"The second day is a pleasant ten-mile stroll through a rain forest, where you'll see a great variety of giant ferns and moss and exotic birds...." Ten miles! Was she out of her mind? Her legs were used to carrying her down busy streets, into subways, into elevators.... If only she'd used the stairs more often! "Then you'll reach Pompolona Hut, which is named for a type of scone made by Quintin Mackinnon, back in the days when he was charting the trail."

"Sounds pretty easy so far."

She turned her head slightly. "Maybe to you, it does."

"Uh-oh." His tone was full of sympathetic teasing. "Having a few second thoughts? You'll do fine. Just—" He broke off, then said in a voice suddenly filled with astonishment, "Lili?"

She raised her eyes to meet his. Even steeled for a jolt, as she was, it hit her with an impact for which she was unprepared. "Brad!" Her voice was weak enough to sound surprised. "What on earth are you doing here?" The question could finally be asked.

Someone had stopped the talk with a question, but now Robert was starting again. Brad leaned close to her. "What a shock to see you!" With a reluctant nod toward the front of the room, he said, "Guess we'd better wait until he's finished." She gulped and nodded, hoping her head was still attached.

"The third day... Well, let's be honest, that's the tough one. Pretty much uphill to Mackinnon Pass, about six miles, then another mile to Pass Hut, where you'll be greeted with soup and drinks to eat with your lunch. From there it's downhill for the last three miles, but steep and rocky. I guarantee you'll be mighty glad to see Quintin lodge." There was a tittering of laughter, some of it strained.

What can I do? Lili wondered. *Trapped here with a man I can't be close to without reverting to the emotional patterns of the teenage ninny I once was. And to meet him again on my first mountain hike.*

This was *not* a setting designed to display her finer abilities! But the wounding of her pride was nothing compared to the damage that could be done with one slip of the tongue. She glanced around, just now aware that something was missing. Where was Brad's wife, the oh-so-proper and prominent Esther Cahill? As a cascade of memories flooded her mind, she shivered.

Brad put his hand on her arm. "Don't be scared, Lili. It won't be all that bad, and I'll help you over the rough spots."

She wanted to turn and throw herself into his arms, to feel that incredible closeness she'd experienced just once, all too fleetingly. *And what then, you idiot? Ask him where he was through all the* really *rough spots?*

"Thank you," she whispered. "I'm going to need all the help I can get."

He chuckled—the same low, rich sound she had never been able to forget. "Ah, Lili, still the same honest girl you used to be."

Honest? What a laugh. You'll never know, Bradford Hollingsworth, the magnitude of the lies I once told.

"You'll want to drop your pack at Quintin, then take the walk to see Sutherland Falls—it's only about thirty minutes away, and you wouldn't want to miss it. It's the world's longest waterfall, drops over nineteen hundred feet from Lake Quill."

"We'll have to see that. Sounds too spectacular to miss!"

We. Did "we" mean him and her? This entire scene belonged in a storybook, out of the real world. She could scarcely breathe, thinking of that word *we.* How she had longed, prayed, yearned, pleaded with whatever powers willing to intercede, to bring about a permanent blending of that particular "we." Too late. The time had passed, and she'd given up belief in miracles.

"I doubt my legs will still work by then. Better find a more hardy walking chum." *That's right, Lili, keep it light. Never let him see the crack marks in your heart.*

"I'm seventeen thousand miles from home and run into Lili Jamison, and you tell me to find another chum? No way! This has to be destiny."

Oh, Brad. Please don't do this, she thought. *Don't make little "you and me, kid" jokes. I can't take it! And that makes me so damned mad! After all these years, I should be able to look right into your eyes and laugh and joke and feel nothing but the dim memory of a long-forgotten passion. Instead, the touch of your hand and the sound of your voice...* Something went *click* in her mind, and she remembered that was a line from an old song... What was the rest? Oh, yes—"makes me weak." The songwriters had captured it all, hadn't they? All so corny, and all so true!

Suddenly Lili felt terribly afraid. A strongbox of emotions had been broken into, releasing feelings she'd kept safely locked away all these years: passion, pain, fear, despair, hope—all scattering through her, shaking loose the constraints she'd built to keep her life under control. She wanted to run away, get out of here before any real damage could be done, before she could be hurt all over again. With enormous effort, she tore her eyes away and tried to focus on the man at the front of the room.

"The fourth day is steadily downhill and rocky. You'll find yourself checking all the mileage markers, wondering if you'll ever reach the end of the thirteen miles. But just hold on—you'll have such a high when you realize you've finished the whole hike!"

Hold on, hold on, hold on. She'd have to chant that with each step, if Brad were beside her.

"You'll meet the boat at Sandfly Point, which is aptly named, so bring plenty of insect repellent. We sell Dimp here, and if that won't keep them off, nothing will!"

The remark was met with laughter, and Lili took the opportunity to sneak a glance at Brad, except her furtive glance became eye-to-eye contact: he was watching her openly. She gave a nervous laugh. "I'm almost convinced I'm in the wrong place. This sounds like a mecca for jocks, which definitely doesn't include me."

He was, if anything, better-looking than she recalled. Maturity had honed his features, giving him the rugged, taut-muscled appearance of the consummate athlete. His dark blond hair was still thick and wavy. His eyes, deep-sea blue, had the sharp-focused expression that promised complete attention and displayed a keen intelligence. And his mind was as superior as his face and body, Lili knew. He had always been on the honors list, had been valedictorian of his graduating class at Harvard. That was as far as Lili had been able to follow his career. She didn't even know what kind of job he held, although probably he had followed his father into the banking business.

"And when you reach the hotel at Milford Sound..." Reluctantly, their gazes disengaged and returned to the front of the room. "There'll be time to freshen up and do some laundry before we meet for the celebration dinner and the awarding of the Milford Track certificates. And the fifth day? Pure gravy. A relaxed breakfast, and a two-hour cruise on Milford Sound."

As the talk ended, Brad asked, "Have you had dinner?"

The question caught Lili by surprise. Food? How could she think of food at a time like this? "No."

"Let's go to the dining room and get something to eat." He smiled, making a flagrant display of his perfect white teeth.

"Well..." She glanced around, then thought, *What am I looking for, a hook to yank me off this improbable stage? No such luck.* No matter how bad her performance, there was no reprieve. "All right."

They were stopped on the way out by Gillian, who said, "Did I just lose my single hiking companion?"

Lili gave her an apologetic smile. "I ran into an old friend."

Gillian looked from her to Brad and back to her. "So I see." As Lili made the introductions, Gillian's irrepressible smile overtook any disappointment she might feel. "Well, to the victor and all that."

Brad looked puzzled. "I beg your pardon?"

"Nothing. Forget I said it. Have a good evening. I'm sure we'll meet on the trail."

"You can count on it." Lili started to say that she was sure Brad would want to take a faster pace than hers, but unless Brad had changed completely, he'd stick with her, turtle or hare.

To Lili's relief, nothing more was said until they were seated in the sparsely populated dining room and had ordered a gin and tonic for Brad and a vodka and tonic for her. She wasn't much of a drinker, but tonight she felt in need of fortification. Brad moved, spoke, selected a table—not the first they were shown—and ordered, with that special, inexplicable manner of those born to privilege and educated at Eastern prep schools and ivy-covered colleges. It wasn't arrogance, but sureness; an absence of uncertainty. Lili recalled how envious she'd been of that elusive quality when she'd first encountered it in Brad's sister, Marcia.

The thought of Marcia brought up a handy and natural topic of conversation. "How's your sister?"

"Marcy?" He grinned. "Terrific. She's married to a neat guy named Carl Jackson, and has a son and two daughters."

"Marcy?" Lili was amazed. "But marriage and a family were always last on her list. Wasn't she dead set on being a veterinarian and saving all the beleaguered animals of the world?"

"She certainly was, until her second year at Smith, when she met Carl. Next thing any of us knew, she and Mom were planning a wedding, and the animals were on their own."

Lili laughed. She'd met Marcy when she was twelve, and had gone to tryout for one of two teenage parts in a play given by the Weston Players, a theater group in the town adjoining Lili's. Until the previous year, Lili had envisioned herself as a screen star or a Broadway actress, but all of those pie-in-the-sky ambitions had swooshed down the drain with the sudden death of her father. She'd had to learn something practical, something that afforded a reliable living. But her mother had encouraged her to audition for the play, knowing her daughter badly needed diversion from the premature onslaught of tough reality on her young life.

At that time, both Marcy and Lili lived in Massachusetts, but there the similarity ended. Lili and her mother lived in Wayland in a tiny house that was humble by any standards; Marcy lived in a section of Weston that was open only to the very rich.

Each of the girls had landed a part in the play, and, during the six-week period of rehearsal, struck up a friendship that—although Lili fully expected it to end with the last performance—somehow endured all their differences of background. The first time Lili was invited over to meet Marcy's parents, she'd been speechless with apprehension. Her mother had dropped her off, and after walking down the long, tree-lined driveway past gardens so neat they must require a small army of maintenance men, and up broad granite steps to a front door that looked like the entrance to a cathedral, it had taken every ounce of her courage to push the bell.

Her timidity had been swept away by the warmth and graciousness of Mr. and Mrs. Hollingsworth, who had welcomed her as though they could imagine no one they'd rather have visit their daughter. During the five years of her friendship with Marcy, Lili had bloomed under the kind attention of those two people, who had tried to afford her opportunities to experience things otherwise unavailable to her. She had grown to love them, and had missed them terribly when she and her mother moved away.

And of course, it was in that magic house that Lili had met Brad.

"Hey, have I lost you?"

Startled, she quickly lifted her gaze to Brad. "Oh, sorry. I was remembering when I met Marcy."

"Yeah. The two teenage terrors."

"We weren't terrors at all. We were sweet and well behaved."

"You, maybe. My sister pulled some doozies." He grinned. "Of course, I wasn't exactly a saint, myself."

"I know. I remember."

His face clouded. "Yes, I just bet you do."

The appearance of a waiter at their table came as a welcome distraction. "Are you ready to order?"

She gave a nervous laugh and shifted her eyes from Brad's compelling gaze. "I haven't even looked at the menu."

"Okay, take all the time you want." The waiter was a fine-looking young man with a sunny countenance. He glanced over their heads and said, "Uh-oh."

She stared up at him. "Uh-oh? What does that mean?"

"Look at that rain come down."

For the first time, she became aware that a storm had indeed started, and with serious intent. The rain fell straight and heavy, a curtain of water. "Good grief! If it's like that tomorrow, will we still go on the hike?"

The waiter laughed. "You kidding? They go in any weather. Fact is, most people get rained on when they do the Milford, so you might as well plan on it." He gave a bob of his head. "Be back in a few minutes."

Lili watched him leave, then turned to Brad. "The prospect of climbing a mountain is scary enough, but in heavy rain? That's terrifying!"

The rainfall, if possible, was intensifying and beginning to slant in at an angle. By the time they'd ordered their meals, it was blasting sideways at the building, leaking in around windows. Buckets were being placed at strategic spots.

"Hey—" Brad chortled "—this could get downright exciting!"

She gave him a look of disbelief. "You're one of them, aren't you?"

"One of who—whom?"

"Those jocks. You'd probably *enjoy* plowing through a rainstorm, slipping and sliding over rocks and boulders."

Brad threw back his head and laughed. "Okay. Guilty as charged. But just for you, I promise I'll pray for fair weather. I wouldn't want the tiniest cloud to invade your hemisphere!"

"That's not much help. This *isn't* my hemisphere."

"Your *temporary* hemisphere. And don't be so nit-picking when I'm trying to be gallant."

"All right, agreed. I'll gladly accept your prayers on my behalf." She wanted to add, *Put a few other items on your prayer list, please. Like we emerge from the next five days as friends who've had a nice time and bid each other a weepy goodbye, with all the phony promises to get in touch. And that I survive the whole experience without falling into a thousand pieces!*

"All right, down to business. What's been happening in your life since the last time I saw you?"

Lili almost choked on her shrimp cocktail. The conversation had taken such twists and turns, she'd forgotten the inevitability of that question. Couldn't they just talk about the now and hereafter, and skip yesterdays? "Mmm. Nothing monumentally exciting." *Oh no, just dull routine. Here I go again, good old honest Lili!* "I've had to work, so I've been getting my college degree by inches at night school. One more year should do it. Then I'll have that precious certificate." She managed a laugh. I doubt it'll shoot me straight to VP, but who knows?"

"That's doing it the hard way. Makes me realize how lucky I was. So, where do you work?"

"At Digital. I started part-time in high school, working summers, making tiny components for computers. I really liked the company, so, after Mom helped me get through a year at Katie Gibbs, I kept applying at Digital until I got a job as a secretary."

"So that's what you do now?"

She shook her head. "No. I was so lucky! I had a terrific boss, who kept handing me more and more responsibility. As fast as I could take it, he piled it on. I hardly did any secretarial work. Before I knew it, I was in the middle of writing a new system for the purchasing department. Now the system is being adapted by more and more branches of the company, and I'm the traveling expert, teaching its use.

That's how I got here. The head of purchasing in the Australian company requested that I come over for three weeks to instruct their people. And, since I got to fly over here at company expense, I took the opportunity and my meager savings to fulfill a lifelong dream—to come to New Zealand.''

"And do the Milford Track?"

She laughed. "Well, now. That's another story."

He ate the last of his mussels. "Lucky you were free to take the time." He cocked an eyebrow. "That's supposed to be a subtle way of asking if you *are* free."

Lili's heart skipped a beat. "You mean, as in marriage?"

"That's the question."

"Yes. I'm free." She pushed her empty shrimp-cocktail dish to one side, her mind spinning like a berserk clock spring. "Now."

"You mean there *was* a Mister... someone?"

She nodded. That seemed, somehow, less devious than a spoken yes. "But there hasn't been, for some time." That, at least, was true.

"Any kids?"

The big one. The A-plus, top-of-the-line, state-of-the-art question. It required an answer, so what in God's name was she going to say? The truth—to a point. "Yes, one boy."

"Lucky you."

She nodded enthusiastically. "Oh, yes, without reservation. He's the most wonderful part of my life."

"How old is he?"

Just a momentary hesitation. "Eight. He's eight years old. His name is Donald, after my father."

"Who's taking care of him?"

"Mother." She smiled. "Talk about a good sport!"

"I bet she doesn't mind. Your mother struck me as a woman just full of love. She must dote on her grandson."

Lili felt the tickle of tears at the backs of her eyes. "How sweet of you to remember her, and that way."

"I remember everything about you, Lili." Was he really saying that? And just an hour earlier, she'd wondered if he'd remember who she was! "You were such a cute kid. So naive about everything. It was fun to have you hanging around. My folks really enjoyed you, too. Said you were good for us, gave us a chance to kind of see things in a new light. So much we took for granted that you were so damn wide-eyed about. It was a kick."

A kick. Oh, yes. It was that.

He took a deep drink of his wine, regarding her thoughtfully through the clear liquid. "Then, of course, you grew up."

Lili's heart was thumping wildly. She *had* grown up, far too fast for her own good. "Yes. But that's inevitable, isn't it?"

"I suppose." He leaned forward. "What happened to you, Lili, where did you go? You and your mother just disappeared. When Marcy got back from her vacation the end of that summer, she tried to call you and found out you'd moved. She was terribly hurt, you know, that she never heard from you again." He paused. "And I was concerned, too." Another pause. "We all were."

It was a reprimand. Given in the soft-spoken, polite Hollingsworth manner, but a reprimand, nonetheless. Lili kept her eyes riveted on the water goblet that her fingers were turning around and around in a circle. "I know. I should have phoned Marcy, or dropped her a note. It's just... Well, it was a difficult period. Mom had to sell the house, to raise enough money to get by. And I was going to secretarial school and working. The time with Marcy seemed so far away, part of my life that was... just gone."

The Hollingsworths must have considered her the epitome of ingratitude. All their kindness, their love, rewarded by a quick disappearance with no communication. She glanced around the room, looking for some magic escape from this conversation, sighing with gratitude when the waiter appeared to put her main course in front of her.

Broiled red snapper. It looked delicious. She wondered how she'd manage to consume one single bite. "Now, come on. Enough about me. Tell me, where's your wife? Esther. Isn't that her name?"

His expression sobered, and his fork, headed for a piece of lamb, stopped in midair. "Esther is no longer my wife. The divorce became final two weeks before I left."

Lili's heart took such a leap of joyous hope that she feared it would pop out of her open mouth. "Really? I'm shocked. I thought you two were supposed to be perfect for each other. Hadn't you known her forever?"

"Close to. Since we entered preschool in the same class."

The same class. Ah, yes. "So, what happened?" Lili had to admit, her belief in miracles was undergoing a ressurection. After all, getting to New Zealand alone would qualify, and now?

"Well, if all the other stuff is shoved aside, I'd say our problem was we couldn't have what you have—a child." Lili swallowed twice in rapid succession to dislodge the fish stuck in her throat. "Children were very important to both of us," Brad continued. "We wanted them desperately. Plus, well, I'm the last male in the Hollingsworth line, and there was that unspoken expectation from all the relatives. Carry on the family name, you know. All that sort of thing."

No, she didn't know, not really. No one in her family ever gave such a consideration a thought. "Yes."

"After about four years passed, Esther found out she was the one who couldn't conceive, and she started going to all kinds of doctors. God, what an assortment! Best-qualified to craziest quack. It got to be an obsession. I kept telling her it didn't matter, we could adopt. It did matter, of course— I was damned disappointed. But hell, you accept things the way they are and make the best of it. Esther, though—she couldn't accept it." He ran his fingers across his forehead. "It became our own little nightmare. That the marriage lasted over ten years is a miracle."

And so much for miracles! The delectable snapper had, during his recitation, turned inedible, as the magnitude of issues grew higher, layer upon layer. The marriage, supposedly made in heaven, had failed because the wife couldn't produce an heir to the lofty family name. No new prince. Adoption wouldn't do, because the bloodline would be different. But what if an adoption had been possible, with the proper heritage included? Lili suddenly felt sick.

Her mother had taught her, from as far back as she could remember, that a lie, once told, multiplied; and that what goes around comes around to face you in its new, immensely magnified girth.

Oh, Momma, why didn't I listen to you?

Chapter Two

Brad reached across the table to touch Lili's arm. "Lili? Is something wrong? Fish no good?"

The gaze she returned seemed confused, he thought. "What?" she asked.

"The fish. You're not eating, and you look a little ill."

"Oh ... No."

Lili laughed, with a strained, forced sound that reminded Brad of an incident that had happened during one of Lili's visits to his home. The family was seated around the dinner table, and Lili accidentally knocked over a glass of water. She'd given the same nervous laugh then, and immediately apologized, her face red with embarrassment. "Gosh, I'm sorry." Her frantic attempts to sop up the water were quickly circumvented by Amy, their maid. Lili's discomfort had been palpable. "I didn't mean to laugh," she'd said. "It just comes out when I'm upset. My mom's always after me about it. Says I'm trying to cover up my feelings—" She had stopped then, obviously further humiliated by her gushing words. Brad frowned now, wondering what had made her uneasy.

She waved a hand at the window. "Just a shot of instant panic. We might be out in that tomorrow."

Brad smiled and hesitated just a moment before moving his hand. *Lili Jamison.* He still couldn't get over it, running into her in this remote corner of the world. She was just shy of beautiful, as he'd expected she would be when she grew into herself. Grew into herself—one of his grandmother's old-fashioned expressions. But it applied in Lili's case. She had been such a timid girl, like a skittish kitten hovering in the doorways, waiting to see if the inhabitants were friendly. As he'd gotten to know her, in those long-ago days, he'd grown protective, wanting to shield her from the rebuffs of the inhabitants who *weren't* friendly. And some of their snootier friends had been far from receptive toward this "outside waif." *Protective.* The word popped out of his thoughts to slap him in the face.

"What are you smiling about? The thought of me slipping and sliding down that mountain?"

He jumped, brought back to the present by her question. "Precisely. And the prospect of catching you en route."

Lili blanched. "Unfair thought patterns. If you're going to conjure up a vision, please make it of me tramping up that trail, strong and stout and valiant."

"Uh-uh. No fun. Wouldn't give me a shot at being the hero to the rescue. And you know how I always savored that role." An expression flicked across her face, too quickly gone to be accurately identified, but it had looked very like fear. He frowned. What could Lili be afraid of? Was the prospect of the hike really that daunting?

She moved her fork from one side of the plate to the other. The fish remained largely intact. "Such a surprise, seeing each other here, of all places."

"I can't imagine a nicer surprise. Kind of a second chance, isn't it? To pick up some loose ends, see if we can tie them into bows?" Brad grinned teasingly in an attempt to lighten the mood, urging her to smile back. It worked, and the tension eased.

Lili sat back in her chair. "God, that's beautiful, Brad. When did you become so poetic?"

"Now, now, no sarcasm. I'm doing my best. I majored in finance, not creative writing."

"That's right, so you did. Are you working in your father's bank?"

He laughed. "Dad would love *that* description! He doesn't really own it, though he does have a proprietary attitude toward it. And no, I'm with another bank."

"President?"

He nodded.

"What else? You always did rise to the top, as cream should."

"Now you're making fun of me."

"Not at all. Simply stating a fact. I can't exactly picture you serving burgers at McDonald's."

"Then you'd have faulty vision. I did just that."

Her eyes widened. "Come on. You're kidding!"

"No. Dad invested in a few of their franchises early on, and recently turned them over to me. I wanted a hands-on feel for it, so I spent several weekends behind the counter. It was a kick."

She grimaced. "I'm sure the other employees thought so, too, trying not to drop the French fries on the floor in front of the boss."

"No sweat. We got along fine. Even taught me how to make a first-class Big Mac."

She laughed aloud. "You always did want to try everything!" Her expression sobered, and she stabbed aimlessly at her fish.

He knew what had crossed her mind, and it was a subject better left alone. No use digging up an incident that must have been as troubling to her as it was to him. Time for a nice, safe, engrossing subject. "Tell me about your son." That should do it. All mothers loved to talk about their children. Fathers, too, for that matter. He sure wished he had one to talk about.

A sudden movement of Lili's fingers sent her knife clattering to the floor and she bent to retrieve it, struggling to compose her face into sanguine lines. Her son. Donny. A strong surge of love, bristling with protectiveness, shot through her. She straightened her spine and sorted through her thoughts, getting them in order. She was an intelligent, able adult, and it was time to start acting like one! "Well, he is, of course, superior in every way." The light tone was just right. The slight quaver wasn't.

"Naturally. Does he look like you?"

"Not really." He's a small clone of the man sitting across from me, she thought ruefully. Wiry, handsome, blond, blue-eyed, precocious, athletic, sweet, thoughtful. An achiever. "He has light brown hair, and his eyes are...hazel. He's cute and bright and does pretty well in school." Pretty well. He'd been in every accelerated program available since his first class.

"Does he like sports?"

"Yes. He's on a junior-league team. He likes playing, and enjoys all the kids." He was the star pitcher, and easily the most popular boy on the team. From the day he was born, Donny had been a living, breathing reminder of the man now sitting across the table from Lili. The day he'd been born—not eight years before, but almost eleven. A replica of his father.

"I envy you. God, I'd love to have a son."

Lili's heart, still only semihealed from its eleven-year-old trauma, contracted with pain.

"Funny, I never thought much about the structure of my life, when I was a kid. You know, all the tradition. Going to the same primary school my dad and his brothers attended, then following to St. Mark's, where his name is still on a couple of soccer plaques. Then, of course, Harvard and the B-school. It'd sure be something to watch my son doing the same thing." He shrugged. "Corny, huh? Following-in-the-old-man's-footsteps kind of bull? But, I have to admit, it *is* important. There's a sense of continuity, of really belonging to something special.''

St. Mark's, Harvard, Harvard's business school for his master's. The feeling of sickness was creeping back into her stomach. Tradition, privilege, opportunity. Maybe Donny could have had them all. Or would Brad have insisted on an abortion, so his ''special'' life wouldn't be disrupted? ''Not corny at all,'' she managed to say. ''Enviable. I wish I could offer Donny even a little of that.''

''But I'm sure you do, Lili. The most important thing for a child is being loved and nurtured. Your son must get a lot of that, between you and your mother.'' She could smell the next question. He hesitated a moment before asking it. ''How about his father? Does he spend much time with him?''

''His father is dead.'' Dear heaven, how had she become such an accomplished liar? She hated it; hated the way it made her feel. Truth beckoned, an enticingly clear, uncorrupted beacon of sanity. *Tell him, get it out. Deal with it. No more lies.*

She looked at the rain beating against the windows, tried to garner courage from the raw power of nature. But she couldn't. Dozens of what-ifs crammed into her mind. What if he got furious, which was almost a certainty, and she ended up in court fighting for custody? How could she defend her position against the Hollingsworth name and fortune and power, not to mention all the assets they could offer. Private schooling, college, travel, an extended family that would give him the cousins and aunts and uncles and grandparents he'd never had? A golden life, the sort every kid dreamed of, there for the taking. Donny couldn't help wanting it, could he?

''I'm sorry. How did it happen?''

How did what happen? Oh, yes. The death of Donny's father. ''An accident. He was in a car accident.'' Not very inventive, but easy to remember. She'd better go to her room and take notes, so she could remember all these lies she was telling. A sudden urge to flee overpowered her, and she pushed back her chair. "I'm sorry, Brad, I *am* feeling a little queasy. I put in some long hours while I was working in Australia, and it's catching up with me. Do you mind if I say good-night?"

He stood and walked around to hold her chair. Damn. He shouldn't have asked about her husband; obviously his loss still hurt. "Where's your room?"

"Over in one of the cottages, across the terrace. I can just make a dash."

"No way. We'll find some means of getting you there nice and dry. Hold on while I pay for dinner."

She couldn't but help feel sheepish. So much lovely food left untouched. "I'm sorry I couldn't eat more."

"Don't be. The food was incidental. It was being together that was important."

She watched him cross to the waiter, saw the instant response of the young man to Brad's friendliness, the quick summing up of the bill, the exchange of money, the smile of appreciation at what must have been a bountiful tip. Some Yankees were known to be tightwads. She'd never seen anything but abundant generosity in the Hollingsworth family.

The scenario that followed intensified all the feelings Lili already had: admiration, awe, overwhelming sadness at the absence from Donny's life of this man who would, on all counts, be an exceptional father. Soon Brad had borrowed parkas for both of them and had a van lined up to drive them as close as possible to her cottage. Despite her protests, he insisted on accompanying her, even though his room was right upstairs.

A smiling bellhop, sheltered under a poncho, held an umbrella for her between the entrance and the car. Brad, spurning shelter, made the dash after them, sliding in beside her. The bellhop got behind the wheel and reeled in the umbrella. "Fine storm, isn't it? Get a lot of them here."

"Great storm." Brad's face was alight with enjoyment. "That wind could push a hiker or two right over the top of the mountain and down the other side."

"That's right, mate. An' you'll have a chance for a go at it tomorrow." The "mates" had a good laugh, while Lili's stomach took another roll.

The van came to a stop two cottages away from hers. "'Fraid this is close as she'll come. Best to hunker down under the parkas and shoot for it. Umbrella'd be no use in the open in this wind."

Brad gave the bellhop's shoulder a friendly pat. "This is fine, and thanks."

Lili turned to him. "Why don't you stay in the van, Brad? You're going to get soaked if you walk back."

"No way. Have to see you to the door. Do you want me to toss all my upbringing out the window?"

"I don't think you'll have to. In this, it'll blow away."

"She's right, mate. I can wait for you, if you'd like."

"No, thanks. I'll be fine."

With some misgiving, Lili forced herself to slide across the seat and follow Brad outside into the howling wind and pelting rain. Her legs and feet were soaked in seconds, and water ran in rivulets down her face and under her collar. Brad grabbed her hand, and together they dashed to the shelter of the little porch of the cottage, where she pushed the hood of the parka off her head, an action that sent a miniwaterfall trickling down her back. She shivered. "Oh, yuck!"

Brad felt nearly oblivious to the water that had plastered his hair to his head and was running in streams down his face. He was too absorbed in the winsome sight of Lili, huddled against the elements, to be worried about his own slight discomfort. Time had accordioned, wiping out the eleven years just past, leaving them, once again, a seventeen-year-old girl of beguiling beauty, and a young man of twenty-two, unaccustomedly awkward and unsure of what to say. Well, when in doubt, try glib. "Wetness becomes you."

She lifted her face, and her damp cheeks caught the gleam of the overhead light. "Isn't that supposed to be moonlight?"

"Yeah, but that's hardly applicable at the moment. Maybe tomorrow night." A spark danced in her green eyes for a brief moment, then died. Something, he was sure, had deeply hurt Lili, had put her firmly on guard. Was it the loss of her husband? Still, why should she be wary with him? His grudging mind, always doggedly honest, recalled the long-ago incident he'd pushed aside earlier. Maybe his loss of control had kindled a distrust of his motives. Well, he had four more days to break through that not-quite-invisible shield, to try to mend trust and reestablish the easy, friendly rapport they'd once had. He had enjoyed his "big brother" role with Lili as well as Marcy, before he'd allowed his overactive hormones to move Lili out of the role of "sister." She seemed a little fragile now, as if she could use a good friend.

He took her face in his hands and touched his lips gently to her cheek. "Lili, I'm so glad to have found you again. I do look forward to the next few days."

Her eyes dropped, so her voice was scarcely audible. "So do I. But I'd better say a few prayers for better weather."

"Sunshine in the morning."

Her eyes, when they rose to meet his, were moist. Was that the rain? "Promise?"

"Promise." At the moment, he felt he could summon bright skies for Lili by the sheer strength of his desire to please her, a desire surprising in its intensity. After the door closed behind her, Brad ran for the main hotel, tempering speed with caution because of the slippery cement squares underfoot. The last thing he needed right now was a broken bone. He'd wanted to do the Milford Track for years, although his timing for the hike had been dictated largely by a desire to escape the very painful end of his marriage. But now, well, the anticipation was definitely heightened. His face broke into a smile. *Lili Jamison. What a kick!*

Lili stood under the stream of hot water, her mind roaming distant vistas. From the moment she'd written for her reservation, this hike had posed a challenge. Now it loomed like one of the glacial mountains that jutted above the Tasman Sea. After drying herself and putting on her pajamas, she laid her wet clothes over the backs of a couple of chairs and put them in front of the heater. All the things she would take on the trail were laid out on the extra bed, ready to put in the backpack when she picked it up in the morning. She sank onto the bed beside the stacked clothes as memory engulfed her.

The wonderment of being Marcy's "best friend" had been like a talisman that she wore inside her heart instead of around her neck. Looking back, it was hard to recall how they had found so many common bonds, considering the enormous gap separating their ways of life.

Marcy was transported to private school in a car pool; had tennis and golf lessons at an exclusive country club; had her own horse at a nearby riding stable; spent summers at the family "place" in Maine; took piano and dancing and flute; and knew exactly which utensil to pick up at the most elaborate dinner.

Lili got to the public school on the bus; couldn't participate in school sports because she had to do all the shopping and housekeeping due to her mother's long work hours; had never been on a horse or had a lesson or gone on a vacation. And the first time she had a "simple" supper at the Hollingsworths', the array of cutlery had stymied her—a dilemma that had been met with gentle humor and a bit of kindly instruction from Marcy's mother.

Until she became accustomed to the Hollingsworth home, Lili had never imagined that such a huge house could be termed "cozy." But that big, sunny living room filled her with a sense of well-being, as though the very wallpaper had absorbed the graciousness of the inhabitants. She had become a regular visitor at their house by the time she met Brad, who was away at prep school. The scene of their first encounter was emblazoned on her mind like a cattlebrand.

She and Marcy had attended a Friday-night rehearsal, after which Lili spent the night with her friend. They slept late, a treat that was not a regular occurrence in Lili's life. When they awoke to the sound of laughter and slamming doors, Marcy turned over in the other twin bed, stretched and groaned.

"Oh boy, I forgot. Brad's home. He must have his army with him."

"Army?"

"Yeah. Every time he's here, about six million of his closest friends show up. Getting to the refrigerator is like skiing the slalom."

Lili hesitated, wanting to ask what a slalom was, and decided against it. "It must be fun, though, having an older brother." It would be fun to have a brother or a sister of any age. A real family. Not just two isolated people, a mother and a daughter.

"I guess. Sometimes. Other times it's a real pain in the neck." Marcy slipped out of bed and into the pretty pink bathrobe with white trim that matched her nightgown. Lili didn't own a bathrobe. She went from pajamas to clothes, with no interim stages. It gave her great pleasure just to observe Marcy's wardrobe—in fact, to observe Marcy's life. It was a little like having a role in a finely staged fairy tale.

Just as she was about to get up, there was loud pounding on the door, followed by a male voice yelling, "Hey, sis! Are you decent?"

"Yes!"

Lili hastily pulled the covers up to her chin as the door banged open and the handsomest boy she'd ever seen in her whole life, including in the movies or on TV, barged into the room. Remembering, she smiled. Brad always made an entrance, he couldn't help it. His size and appearance commanded instant attention, and his exuberance abolished silence. Her body had stiffened, and her face turned hot, the first two of a succession of previously unknown sensations that rapidly permeated her young being. Lili's heretofore unawakened libido underwent a birthing process that may have been record setting.

The seventeen-year-old Adonis, tanned—how could someone be tanned in March?—vibrant with health and good nature, grinned, further dazzling the besotted young girl huddled under the covers. "How're you doing, kid?" Brad opened his arms to Marcy, who threw herself into their embrace. Lili had never experienced such jealousy. His gaze moved to Lili. "Hi. I'm Brad."

Lili made one attempt at speech, swallowed, cleared her throat and managed a wispy "Hi."

Marcy came to the rescue. "This is Lili, my friend."

"Greetings, friend Lili. Pretty name." Her heart whirled, did a pirouette and resettled, slightly askew. "Either of you want to get in on a tennis match?"

"With you guys? Are you nuts? We'd be killed!" Marcy was shuffling her feet under the side of her bed, searching for the fluffy slippers that matched the rest of her ensemble.

"How about you?" The radiant blue beacons had turned in Lili's direction, causing a tremor in her lower lip.

"I...I don't play tennis." Why did that feel like an admission that she didn't read, or that she ate with her fingers?

"Oh?" His face registered genuine surprise. "Pity."

"Anyway—" Marcy had found her slippers and sat down on the side of her bed to put them on "—Lili and I are going to study our scripts."

"Ah, that's right. Mom told me. You're in a *play*." He drew the word out, teasing them with it.

"Yes. And none of your smart-aleck cracks!"

He opened his mouth, looked at the expression on his sister's face and silenced the retort with a smile. "Okay, no cracks. Congratulations on getting a part. You, too."

It took a second for Lili to register that he was referring to her. "Oh. Thank you."

"Don't work too hard!" With that, he was gone as abruptly as he had appeared.

Later, when Lili told her mother about meeting Brad, her eyes agleam with the wonder of it all, Louise Jamison had studied her daughter with an expression of amusement tinged with a dollop of sadness. "My, my," she had said, putting her arm around Lili's shoulders. "Your first case of puppy love."

It had seemed a silly, inadequate description for such a huge emotion. Even at twelve, Lili had known, somehow, it was more important than that.

Now, as Lili lay in her bed in the cottage in Te Anau, so many miles and years away from those events of her youth, she almost allowed that other memory to emerge—the one that had hovered on the edge of her conscious mind for so many years, just waiting for the chance to leap to life, to unwind its tantalizing scenario yet again. But eleven years of practice at the art of suppression won out. If that golden night hadn't produced Donny, if it had been simply—another silly, inadequate word—the culmination of five years of daydreams and steadily escalating physical longings, she'd have had that memory on Replay over and over and over. Without question, it had been the emotional highlight of her life. But it had become weighted, as so many of her dreams had, by a reality encumbered by immense difficulties. She shifted on the hard mattress. And now, this New Zealand daydream had fallen victim to the same fate.

She squeezed her eyes shut, searching her imagination for the scenes she had played there often in her youth, of a Lili lithe and trouble-free, running up a sunny mountainside with a little boy named Benjamin Potter, laughing aloud as his clever dogs ran the sheep to pasture, gazing out over the

wonderland of New Zealand. Well, here she was, and that
dream and the dream embodied in the person of Bradford
Hollingsworth had somehow, mysteriously, converged. And
reality, as always fraught with problems, sat heavily in the
midst of both.

What was she to do? It was very tempting to make up an
excuse, a reason for "chickening out." But she had paid in
advance—a whopping seven hundred and seventy-five dollars of nonrefundable American dollars to go on this hike.
No one in her financial position could afford to forfeit such
a sum. Besides, she'd spent her adult life facing and conquering challenges—she wasn't about to fold under this one!
Ah, Lili, she chided herself, be honest. It isn't just the
money. Nor is it your indomitable spirit. There is no way,
regardless of the dangers, that you could turn away from a
chance to spend four days with Brad. You'd climb the
highest mountain, swim the roughest ocean, cross the dri-
est desert—all for such an opportunity. How could you de-
prive yourself of four days, *four whole days* of his
company! The answer was swift and irrefutable.

She couldn't.

Lili stirred, opened her eyes and sat up. What on earth
was that banging? It took a few seconds to orient herself, to
remember where she was, then to ascertain that the pounding was an assault on the door of her cabin. "Just a minute!" She got quickly out of bed and crossed to the door.
"Who is it?"

"Me. Brad."

Lili opened the door a few inches and peered out at him.
"Are you trying to break down the door, or just scare me to
death?"

"Neither. I have our morning planned, and you have to
get cracking or we won't have time to eat breakfast and
check in at the track office and get to the glowworm caves
in time for the nine-thirty tour."

Lili squinted her eyes and stared at him. "What are you talking about?"

"Come on, Lili. Get dressed and I'll explain it over coffee and crumpets. Trust me, it's too good to miss!"

Trust me. Funny thing was, she did. "Give me five minutes." Her clothes were laid out, ready to slip into. Lili was compulsively neat. The combination of crowded living quarters and crammed schedules had left no room for clutter in her life.

The rain had stopped, but the sky was heavy with gray clouds, a circumstance that in no way diminished Lili's sunny mood. Swinging along beside Brad, trying to match his long stride, sneaking glances at the tall marvel of a man, provided ample brilliance for any day.

The office didn't open until eight-thirty, so they headed across to Henry's Restaurant for breakfast. The place was nearly full, and they spotted a number of the people who had been at the wine reception. Lili started to detour toward Gillian, who sat with three of the other hikers, but Brad put a hand on her elbow and steered her toward another table. She settled for a wave and a smile at Gillian. When they were seated, she leaned toward him and, keeping her voice low, asked, "What's the antisocial bit?"

"Glowworms."

"Glowworms?"

"Uh-huh." Reaching into his pocket, he extracted a brochure and slid it across the table. "One of my friends told me they were a must-see. And this will be our only chance." A quick glance through the pamphlet was enough to pique her interest, so they hurried through breakfast, picked up their packs and parkas at the office and dropped off the equipment in their rooms before rushing down the road to catch the boat to the glowworm caves.

Brad bought the tickets, and they joined the line to board the small launch tied up at the pier. Lili sighed with pleasure. "You know, for the first time, I feel like a full-fledged, 'bonny-fidey' tourist!"

"How come? You were in Australia for what...three weeks? Surely you didn't spend all your time staring at a computer terminal."

"No. But it *was* different." She paused. Feelings did not translate easily into words. Maybe that's why, so often, she didn't even try to talk about them, instead putting them off with a shrug and an "Oh, I don't know, nothing really." Somehow, with Brad, sharing them was important. "Going to Australia was terribly exciting, and it was certainly the big 'first.' You know—flying across the ocean—" she laughed "—or anywhere, for that matter."

"Don't tell me you'd never flown before?"

"No. Where would I have gone?" Seeing the look of incredulity on his face, she didn't wait for an answer. "It was awesome, being in a foreign country for the first time in my life, listening to the wonderful Australian accents. And everyone was terrific about showing me around when we could break free, which wasn't often. But it was, well, business. There was a legitimate reason for my being there. It wasn't frivolous...just for pleasure." She looked up at him. "Does that make any sense?"

The little girl was still there, looking at him out of eyes bright with anticipation, still agog at things that, for him, were taken for granted. Brad took Lili's hand and twined his fingers through hers. "Yes. Of course it does." He shook his head. "At least part of it does."

"But?"

"But frivolous? Just for pleasure? Dear God, Lili, where did you get the idea that doing something just for pleasure was frivolous? Don't you know how important it is to have fun? To do something nice for yourself? No, not important, that's too tame. *Vital!* I do believe I've come back into your life just in time."

Lili's throat tightened with emotion. Had she ever been so happy? Just now, at this precise moment, anything seemed possible. Easy. Even the hike. Why, there was no reason for fear—she'd sail right up those trails and over those mountains. So engrossed was she in the vision of herself, daintily airlifted above lofty peaks, that she stumbled on the railing and would have fallen smack into the boat if Brad hadn't caught her.

"How about that! Not even on the mountain yet, and I get my first chance to rescue the fair maiden!"

The "fair maiden," feeling like a pigeon-toed hippo, sank onto the nearest bench seat, too embarrassed to glance around at her fellow passengers. Better scratch mountain-skimming and concentrate on standing erect.

The ride across the stretch of Lake Te Anau was chilly, and Lili was thankful for the sweater and windbreaker she'd worn, as well as for her decision to wear slacks instead of shorts. Even more, she was grateful for the warmth of Brad's body pressed against hers. Right then she made a vow. For the next few days, she would tuck away doubts and misgivings and guilt, and enjoy sharing the rarefied air that surrounded this special man. He took her hand, tucking it into the curve of his palm. It felt warm there, warm and safe and cared for. Why not? Why not enjoy each and every moment of the experience and make a mental scrapbook to be perused at her leisure? When they parted in Milford Sound, she'd probably never see him again, so these days should be cherished like the one-of-a-kind treasures they were.

When they reached the curve of lushly forested land that held the Cavern House, they disembarked and went inside for an introductory lecture, after which the guide led them along a path that wound through the surrounding grounds, while he pointed out the rich display of flora and fauna. Unfortunately the famed sand flies came along on the tour, and proceeded to make a late breakfast of the tourists. About halfway through, Lili gave up and joined a small clutch of refugees in a dash back to the shelter, where she applied a liberal coating of Dimp over what small areas of her flesh were exposed to the nibbling of the voracious insects.

When Brad returned with the hardier contingent, he appeared to be untouched by fly bites, and disdained her offer of the bug repellent. She tucked it back into her pocket, trying to stifle her irritation. Superiority in most things was all well and good, but he could at least be vulnerable to *insects,* for pete's sake!

The journey through the caves was a combination of walking along dimly lighted stone paths with sturdy iron railings and traveling by punt over the water. Brad, ever the gentleman, insisted Lili stay behind him when they were on foot. "It's pretty dark in here, and you don't want to hit your head."

"What, mine's more tender than yours?"

"No question. My father always told me I was hardheaded. "Ouch!" His dialogue with Lili had prevented his hearing the guide call out "Duck!"

Lili was enchanted by the enormous caverns. A cascade of rushing water rolled alongside the walkways, throwing up wisps of spray, forming waterfalls that ranged from playful, dancing dropoffs to thundering cascades. The guide informed them that this was the only "living cave" in the Southern Hemisphere that was open to the public. It was considered "living" because the powerful underground stream from Lake Orbell continued to hollow out the limestone cliffs of the Murchison Mountains, in whose womblike caves the glowworms completed the whole of their unique life cycle.

When they reached the spot of entry into the glowworm caves, they were helped, one by one, into a punt. Brad handed Lili down into the boat. "Don't fall here, Lili. You'll disappear down the waterfall and become part of the glowworm culture."

"Don't be a wiseguy."

The guide stood in the bow of the punt to pole them through water now stilled to mirrorlike calm. Their surroundings grew steadily darker as they approached an opening beyond which nothing was visible save a wall of blackness. "Careful of your heads, and don't use any flash cameras—it disturbs the cycle of the worms. Are there any questions? We'll have to be very quiet, once we're inside."

A woman at the back spoke up. "Sorry to be a pain, but I missed the talk you gave earlier. In the loo, you know."

Everyone laughed, including the guide. "Could you give just a quick version, so I'll know what to look for?"

"Sure, glad to. As you can see, the caves are very dark, cut off completely from any source of outside light. The worms attach themselves to the ceiling of the cave, then let themselves down on webs. The whole thing, webs and worms, lights up—very colorfully. The purpose is to attract insects for the worms to feed on. They stay in this condition for about nine months, at which point they turn into flies and mate and reproduce and die, all within a span of days. The flies have no mouths, so they literally die of starvation."

Lili shuddered. It seemed a harsh destiny. How come those poor flies got no mouths at all while the sand flies outside had such big, greedy ones? Where was the fairness in that? But all speculations vanished as they entered an enormous cavern, where the only light came from what looked like thousands of brightly colored webs dangling in different lengths from the top of the black cave. Despite the caution for silence, Lili couldn't suppress a gasp. It was unlike anything she'd ever seen or imagined. The surreal scene, its unearthly quiet broken only by a muffled gurgle of water, engulfed them in a different dimension, a dream state far removed from the normal perception of earth, sky and water that formed the usual human environment.

She huddled closer to Brad, grateful when his arm went around her shoulders and held her close. Everyone in the boat was still, either too observant of the rule of silence or too awed by their surroundings to speak. Lili cast a mental vote for awe.

When they emerged from the cave, the sun had broken through, and the brightness of daylight brought forth a combined sigh of relief from the occupants of the punt. Lili thought of the worms, back there in the dark caverns, locked into the rigid regularity of their life cycle. Nourish, shine, reproduce, die. No decisions, no traumas, no disruptions to the plan. The ultimate security. Somehow the experience had subtly changed her. Security didn't seem quite as alluring as it had.

A short time later, as they stood on the spit of land, watching the approach of the launch that would carry them back to the pier, Lili said, "You were right, Brad, that was a 'must-see'! I'm so glad I didn't miss it. It's incredible, isn't it? All the different, unimaginable ways creatures find to survive."

He smiled at her and nodded. "Against all odds, in many cases. Speaking of survival, are you ready?"

"For what?"

"To challenge the mountain."

Lili gulped. Talk about odds! But then she thought of the glowworms, who never even had a chance to see the sun, let alone to try to wiggle their way up a mountain—a security that translated into confinement. She was out of shape and scared of heights and not much of an outdoor person. But when had she let the odds beat her?

She nodded. "Yes. I'm ready."

Chapter Three

Lili arrived at the Milford Track office, to the rear of the hotel, a few minutes ahead of the appointed time of twelve-thirty. Everything she would have with her for the next three days was in the pack slung over her shoulder. The rest of her luggage, including her purse and passport and most of her money, was in the hands of the hotel management and would be waiting for her in the Milford Sound hotel at the other end of the trail. *The other end.* She wished the words didn't have that slightly ominous ring.

She and Brad had grabbed a quick lunch at Henry's after packing and checking in their extra gear, then gone to their separate rooms to pick up their backpacks. The aura of make-believe moved with her from one event to the next. Here she was, on the vacation of her dreams with the man of her dreams. *Careful, careful,* she warned herself. *Don't try to turn any more dreams into reality.* It had spelled disaster before, and there was no reason to suspect happily-ever-after endings had become any more reachable in eleven years.

Gillian was standing with a young man Lili hadn't met, and she waved her over. "Lili, meet Jonathan Barnes. He's another Aucklander." Gillian's cheery smile led Lili to suspect that Jonathan was unattached and, in her new friend's view, available.

Lili readjusted her pack to free her hand for a shake. "Good to meet you, Jonathan." She glanced around. "Looks like quite a group."

Jonathan was a slight man, very fair, with an engaging grin that looked at home on his face. "About thirty-seven, I understand. Almost the limit." The size of the hiking groups were strictly controlled by the Tourist Hotel Corporation, and though a new group departed daily, no more than forty were allowed at once.

"This should be an . . . interesting experience."

His grin widened. "A bit queasy, are you? Don't worry. My seventy-year-old great-aunt did the trek. Had a grand time!"

Lili suppressed a groan. The only thing more depressing than witnessing effortless athletic achievements of people her own age was hearing about the ease with which the old and infirm accomplished feats that threatened her endurance.

"Where's your friend? Bradley, was that his name?"

Lili could tell by the light in Gillian's eyes that she had full recall of the name. "He should be here any minute. Just went to get his pack and check in the rest of his stuff."

Brad emerged from the hotel a few minutes later and saw that the group was being lined up for a picture. His eyes scanned the faces, looking for Lili. He was surprised by the jump of pleasure he felt when he saw her. What was happening here? A mere meeting of old friends? Or the renewal of something born on an evening eleven years before? He shook his head in a futile effort to dislodge the unwelcome thought. He sure as hell wasn't in the market for any further assaults on his emotions. He'd come here feeling tattered, and he had every intention of returning home rested, relaxed, with a renewed optimism and his newly acquired freedom intact. So it had to be friendship. Period.

He walked over and squatted next to Lili at the end of the second row. "Just in time," he whispered. "Wouldn't want to be missing from the photo. Have to be right here at your side from now on. The friend in need." His slight emphasis on the word *friend* would, he hoped, put both of them more at ease.

"Forget need. I intend to dazzle you with my footwork." God, what a wonderful smile he had! And he and his smile would be right at her side until the end of the trail. Which, in this case, was too close in time and too far in miles and altitude, Lili thought.

Following directions, she looked at the photographer and smiled. The picture would probably end up in one of those massive Hollingsworth family albums. She could imagine him, years from now, showing it to his children. "This was in February of 1990, the time I hiked the Milford Track—" or more likely, "the *first* time." Darndest thing, I ran into an old friend of your Aunt Marcy's. What was her name? Lili something."

She stood after the second flash of the camera, turning her mind away from the mental picture. It hurt to think of Brad with his own family, separate from her, not knowing, or caring, where she was or what she was doing. But wasn't that just what she was aiming for? To get all the way through this hike without a slipup, without letting him know of the permanent link that joined them? She'd better stop letting her mind wander, and concentrate. It was all too easy to say the wrong thing and foolhardy to forget the degree of Brad's intelligence. One hint could set him to putting the pieces together.

They had already covered the subjects of her son and her supposed marriage, so she would steer away from those. There were many things she'd like to know about Brad's life, and the trail would provide a lot of interesting things to discuss. Besides, part of the fun would be getting to know the other people on the hike and immersing herself, through them, in the culture of the New Zealanders. The pep talk sounded good, running through her brain, but she knew it would be darned hard to concentrate on anyone else with Brad around. Gillian was right: he was an exquisite specimen of the male animal. The problem was the way he stirred up the female animal in her. She'd have to post a few Caution signs in her brain. About one a mile, like the markers for the trail.

It was cruel of fate to drop him back into her life, and even more cruel that he still roused passions and longings and dreams with no possibility of fulfillment. What about her vow, made only this morning, to enjoy these few short days, then let go, with no regrets? Vows, like New Year resolutions, were far easier to make than to keep. She wanted him so much. Wanted to be the wife sitting next to him as they showed their children the pictures in the scrapbook. She'd even be willing to come back, to do the trail again at the age of seventy, like Jonathan's great-aunt, if Brad were by her side. What fun it would be to gather their grandchildren around, to show them pictures of their intrepid grandparents standing at the top of the pass, smiling for the camera. She shook her head to clear it of the silliness. Stop it, Lili. You're setting yourself up for another fall.

"Are you a birder?"

"I beg your pardon?"

Jonathan was standing next to her, adjusting a pair of binoculars that hung around his neck. "Do you do any bird-watching?"

"Uh, no."

"Too bad. Some rare ones here. Should see a yellow-breasted black-backed tomtit. And I'm determined to spot a fantail. May be my only chance." It had taken a second or two to reenter the present, but the gleam of anticipation in Jonathan's eyes was most beguiling.

"Is it fun bird-watching?"

"Oh, yes, great fun. Gets to be a compulsion. Check off a couple and go after the ones that are left."

"They're wonderful creatures, aren't they? So much freedom. My mother put up a bird feeder once, outside our house in Dorchester, but it didn't seem to have much of a draw. Considering what's happening to the neighborhood, the birds were probably scared of being mugged." They both laughed. She was sure Jonathan thought she was kidding. Americans weren't supposed to live in crummy neighborhoods where you had to bar the doors and windows after dark. Or, more recently, during the day. "Will you point them out to me, if I'm close by?"

"Sure. There're several others on the trek that I know of. Birders, that is. I'll let them know you're interested."

"Thank you."

Brad, seeing that Lili was occupied, stopped on his way out of the office to talk to a couple he'd spotted the night before. "Hi. You'll probably think I'm nuts, but you both look very familiar. My name is Brad Hollingsworth."

Ed Grainger, a big man with massive shoulders and that air of solid dependability that often accompanies an English accent, laughed and held out his hand. "Not nuts at all. You just solved a mystery for Josie and me. We were saying the same thing, that we were sure we knew you, but couldn't quite recall how. But Hollingsworth—that's the ticket. No wonder we couldn't quite place the face, it's much higher up now!" His jovial laugh rang out once more. "We met you when you were a boy—about ten, I'd say."

Lili glanced up in time to see Brad wave her over. She excused herself from Jonathan and went to join them. "Lili, did you meet Ed and Josie Grainger? Ed went to Harvard with Dad, and my folks have visited them several times in England. And, they were just reminding me, they spent a week at our house when I was a kid."

"What a coincidence!"

"Isn't it? Go off to the other side of the world and renew old friendships." He beamed at her. "Lili and I go way back, too. She was my kid sister's best friend. Used to hang around the house with Marcy." He raised his eyebrows. "Grew up to be quite a dish, wouldn't you agree?"

They both nodded—Ed a little more enthusiastically than Josie, who asked, "Did you go to school with Marcy?"

"No. We met when we were in a play together, in a little-theater group in Weston."

"Oh, what fun! I didn't realize Marcy enjoyed acting. Her parents were always bragging about how adept she was in sports, especially horsemanship. Do you ride?"

Sure. Elevators, street cars, automobiles. "No. I'm not much of a sportswoman." Sounded great, like she could be, if she wanted to. "In fact, Brad has promised to hike behind me and push." The sound of laughter did, at times, deflect further questions, but in this case it didn't work.

Josie, in an effort to establish rapport, tried a few other avenues of mutuality. Had Lili attended one of the seven-sister colleges? Did she belong to the Junior League? A member of the Vincent Club, perhaps? Lili's head kept going back and forth. Was she about to be handed a report card, all F's? This niggling tad of defensiveness about her poor background was one hurdle Lili hadn't quite mastered yet. It shouldn't matter. It didn't make her any less valuable. She truly believed that, in her head. But in her heart? Still some work to do, some barriers to overcome.

Happily, the trail manager chose that moment to call, "Okay, everyone load up on the coach!"

"Here we go, Lili." Brad touched her arm and they moved toward the bus. "Off on an adventure!"

The seventeen-mile trip went by swiftly, with all of them scenery-watching, exchanging weather predictions and relaying tales told by other hikers of the coming track. By the time the coach parked in a wide, graveled area on the bank of Lake Te Anau, the sun had come out full force, and most of the clouds had disappeared, leaving only a few wispy stragglers to decorate the brilliant sky.

"All right, ladies and gents—" the driver stood in the front of the bus "—be sure you have everything with you. The MV *Tawera* is at the dock, ready to board, and I advise you to step sprightly, because a busload of free hikers is just behind us, and they have their big packs with them, so you'll want to secure your space!"

"What are free hikers?" someone asked.

"Well, mate, they're the ones who do it the hard way. Carry their own food and sleeping bags and the lot. Stay in rustic huts along the way that offer only shelter and a loo. Cheaper, you know. But tougher."

Lili leaned close to Brad. "How come you're not part of the tough-guy pack?"

He grinned. "Too much gear to lug from home. This was kind of a last-minute decision. I had some time freed up and I needed to get away. Badly." He looked at her, his smile broadening. "I was lucky they'd had a couple of cancellations in this group. Isn't it great that it worked out the way it did?"

"Yes. Great." *Great, wonderful, miraculous, splendiferous—and scary as all hell.*

The boat captain, a short, rotund man with gray whiskers and a jaunty navy blue yachting cap complete with a gold-braided insignia of unknown designation, greeted them as they boarded the launch. He was standing inside a wooden cubicle, serving hot tea and biscuits. Brad and Lili went inside the cabin to lay their packs on a bench, then returned to avail themselves of his offerings. "Looks like you may be lucky," he commented. "Sun's out. Course, never can tell. Storms whip themselves up out of nothing. Cross a dry stream in the morning and rope across a torrent in the afternoon." That bit of information was passed along with a benign smile.

Lili wished he'd forgo any further comments. She was beginning to suspect these rugged New Zealanders of having a little fun at the expense of city-bred tourists who might be less than well prepared for the rigors of the mountains. She also suspected they could spot her coming—an American pigeon. Jonathan might want to add her to his list of birds.

They were barely settled when the free hikers showed up and were soon on board, stowing their bulging packs, at least three times the size of Brad's and Lili's, wherever a space was available. They were a blatantly hardy-looking bunch. One of them, a man somewhere in the middle span of life, sat on the floor opposite them and immediately struck up a conversation. "Americans, then, the two of you?"

Lili raised her brows. "Good grief! Does it show?"

He laughed—a nice, hearty bellow of good will. "Sure enough. Air about you. Privilege, I think it is."

She was about to dispute that, then decided it wasn't worth the effort. Besides, she hated a "poor me" line.

"Have you done the track before?" Brad's cultured voice instantly verified the New Zealander's assessment.

"Sure enough. Number of times. Beautiful. Your first?"

"'Fraid so. But I hope not my last." Brad nodded toward the man's backpack. "I'd like to try it your way next time."

"Well, I'll trade places with you!" The bellow sounded forth again. "Too rich for my blood, mate. Most of us natives can't afford the tariff, you know." Though bluntly stated, his remark seemed to contain no asperity. Spotting the refreshments that had been abandoned by the captain, who now had the duty of running the boat, the New Zealander jumped up and, with a bob of his head, went over to serve himself.

The boat pulled away from the dock, and despite any trepidations about her physical prowess, Lili felt a lift of her spirits. "I can't believe this is real. That I'm here in New Zealand, about to hike the Milford Track. It has been a fantasy for so many years!"

"Fantasies do sometimes come true," Brad responded.

She looked over at him, wondering what his fantasies had been, or if he'd ever felt a need for any. "Rarely."

"I'll tell you one thing, Lili. This is one of the premier hikes in the world. A dream of backpackers everywhere. You'll be able to drop the name in the midst of any bunch of jocks and be instantly included. 'Hey,' they'll say, 'come meet Lili. She did the Milford!' "

"That's good to know. Believe me, I will make full use of it. If I survive."

"Well, if you don't, at least your obituary will be colorful."

"Thanks a bunch." She reached for his empty cup and took both of them forward to drop into the trash can. When she returned, she suggested, "Let's go up above where we can be outside."

"Ah. The true Lili begins to emerge. Outdoor girl. Nature woman."

"Bull . . . puckey." Brad laughed and stood to follow her up the stairs.

The upper deck was already crowded, and they joined the happy group, their hair blowing in the breeze generated by the boat's movement, faces lifted to the warm sun. Lili pulled her camera from where it hung around her neck. "Will you walk up front and let me take your picture?"

"Walk? You mean fight my way through?"

"You can do it. Just use those fullback shoulders."

"I played quarterback."

"Picky, picky."

When he reached the curve of the bow and turned around to smile at her, she pressed the shutter release, waited for the film to wind to the next exposure and shot another for good measure. *There, I've got you on film*, she gloated. *I'll take lots of pictures on this hike and get you into as many as possible. Preservation of valuable memories. Top priority.*

A tall, gangly man in shorts, boots and a pullover sweater stepped up next to her. "Very pleasant day, isn't it?" The

natives used a hard *e,* so pleasant come out as "pleesant."
"My name is Glynne. Glynne Vernon. I'll be tramping with
you."

"Hi, Glynne. I'm Lili Jamison. I'm glad to be meeting
some New Zealanders. I was told in Australia that I'd be
lucky to talk to anyone who wasn't another tourist."

"Been to Australia, then? You're on a nice long vacation?"

"Not exactly." She explained the circumstances of her
business trip, and the chance it had given her to visit his
country. When she told him about reading *A Boy, a Dog,
and 20,000 Sheep,* he hooted in delight.

"Of course! Great book! Grew up on it myself. There was
a series of them, you know. Benjamin Potter stories."

"Oh, really? I only had the one. I read it so often it's
practically in shreds."

"You must leave me your address. I'll see you get another copy."

Brad, making his way back to Lili, spotted a tall, attractive man beside her, his head bent in rapt attention. He
didn't like the cozy picture one bit, and even more, disliked
the fact that it bothered him. *Come on,* he chided himself,
*Lili's beautiful. Why wouldn't any guy in his right mind be
interested in her? Like me. My reaction to Lili is perfectly
normal. I just have to hold it in check.* Just. *What a word.*

Before Lili could thank Glynne for his kind offer, Brad
had returned, and the two men were soon deep into comparisons of skiing, white-water rafting and, of course, *serious* backpacking. She sighed. Well, if she insisted on
putting herself in jock country, she had to expect the population to be made up of jocks!

The boat trip afforded a beautiful first glimpse of the
towering mountains and rushing waterfalls that were such a
trademark of the land. Lili leaned against the bulkhead,
lulled by the *plop-plop* of the hull and the soothing touch of
warm breezes on her cheeks. Brad stood close to her, so although he was engrossed in conversation with Glynne, the

intoxicating pleasure of his arm around hers filled her with an all-pervasive contentment. She wished the ride could go on forever; that she, like Peter Pan, could stay in Never-Never Land and refuse to grow up and return to the real world.

She looked around, sucking in the beauty, storing it for future enjoyment. Everything was so... untainted; the sky so clear it redefined the color blue. Sun reflections danced across water pure enough, she had been told, to scoop up and drink. And this was air as air should be: nourishment for lungs, rather than a lethal assault.

It seemed impossible that two and a half hours had passed when the launch pulled up to the wharf. Lili hoisted her pack to her shoulders, feeling the pull of its eleven pounds. As she watched in astonishment, a girl more slight than she flipped one of the large backpacks into place and clipped the latch at her waist. How in the world did she do it? It probably weighed thirty-five pounds. Maybe she should join a gym when she got home, lift weights. Lili sighed. When? In her spare time, between work and mothering and going to night school and doing homework? She never had a free moment as it was. In fact, if it weren't for her mother...

"Lili? All set?"

"Oh... Yes, I'm ready."

They followed the scattered group, its members still sticking close to the people they knew, along a wide, level path that led into an idyllic, sun-filtered beech forest. The path forked just after a large sign that read, Milford Track Fiordland National Park.

"Brad, will you stand by the sign so I can take your picture?"

"Lili, the point of this trip is the scenery. Take pictures of the trees."

We all have different priorities, Bradford, she said silently. *You stick to yours and I'll stick to mine.* Aloud, she retorted, "Signs are very important for orientation, and they look better with someone standing beside them."

"Here—" Gillian came up and lowered her pack to the ground. "Let me take one of both of you."

"Thanks, I'd appreciate it." Lili showed her how to shoot it, then joined Brad. He put his arm around her shoulders and she slid hers around his waist, while Gillian called out the inevitable "Smile!" She'd start a whole new album for these pictures, Lili thought. One that was reserved for New Zealand. For a moment, her smile died. Would her friends notice Brad's remarkable resemblance to Donny? Would Donny? One more Caution sign wedged itself firmly in place.

The trail was flat and wide and easy, and when it took a turn to the right, providing their first view of the Clinton River, Brad said, "Not too tough so far, is it?"

"If I think this is hard, I'd better head back for the boat. But this nice, easy stroll can't fool me. I'll not be lulled into a false sense of security. I read the description in the book. It's day after tomorrow that will do me in. Until then, my chances for survival are excellent."

"They're looking even better. There's the Glade House."

Sure enough, ahead of them was the first hut, where they would spend the night. "Gee, that's almost *too* soon," Lili remarked. "Seems like we should walk a little farther, get some of the mileage behind us while we're fresh."

"We could do that. Of course we'd have to pass up dinner and sleep outside. But we'd have a jump on the rest of them."

Somehow the appeal of getting a head start didn't compete with the lure of hot running water, prepared meals and toilets that flushed. "We'd better stick with the others. Wouldn't want to be antisocial."

He threw her a teasing look. "What a sport."

The hut was pine-paneled-rustic, homey and comfortable. Gillian called out to Lili, "Come stake out a bed while we have a choice." They went into the women's dorm and positioned their gear on two of the lower bunks. Gillian asked, "You don't snore, do you?"

"Well, if I do, my mother and my son have failed to mention it."

The other woman's eyebrows rose. "And those are the only two who would know? My, you've led a sheltered life." She unpacked a nightgown and slippers, which she set on the bed. "How about the husband. Or is he an ex, like mine?"

"He's an ex. In a way." Lili hoped it would stop there. It would be so much more comfortable if she didn't have to embellish the story. But her past experience led her to expect the next question.

"Oh. Is he . . . I mean . . ." Gillian's face flushed as she searched for the right words. "Are you a widow?"

"Yes."

"I'm sorry. Didn't intend to be such a clod."

Lili forced a smile. "You weren't. In today's world, your assumption makes more sense. Come on. I understand they're serving tea and scones."

"You don't have to twist my arm. Not where food is concerned!"

On a long, screened porch with benches running down the inner wall, a couple of tables were laden with coffee and tea and homemade scones, butter, jam and cookies. "If this is roughing it," Lili quipped, "I could get used to it."

"Welcome to Glade House." A man of about thirty-five, tan and slim and fit, came forward, his hand extended. "I'm Brian, and I'm the manager here, at least through tonight."

They shook hands and Lili asked, "Why just tonight? Are you leaving?"

"Yes. Been here three seasons, and it's time for a turnabout."

"Getting cabin fever?"

He laughed. "No. I'll miss this place terribly." He glanced around, his gaze lovingly taking in the hut and lingering on the river and the forest beyond. "But, I got a very good offer to manage a catering service, and my wife and I want to start laying up a nest egg. Might want to build a nest one day—" he laughed "—so to speak."

"Has your wife been here at the Glade House, too?"

"Yes. This is where we met. In fact, she's staying on."

Lili was surprised. "Won't that create problems, being separated?"

"I don't think so. We're pretty steady." He waved a hand toward the repast. "Here now, dig in. Then you'll want to take the climb up the mountain out back, to see the waterfall. Really one of the hidden treasures of the trail."

One of the women she'd met briefly at the reception appeared out of an adjoining room, followed by her husband. "Oh, my, doesn't this look scrumptious! How can I be so famished? We haven't really done much in the way of exercise yet." She stopped in front of Lili and Gillian. "I'm Margy, and this is my husband, Doug. I believe we met the other night, but I must admit to forgetting names easily."

When Gillian and Lili had refreshed her memory, Margy said, "This place is very cozy. Have you looked around? No? Well, I'd advise waiting until after tea to do so—" she nodded toward the people spilling out of the two dorms "—judging from the size of the advancing hordes."

Lili had tea and a buttered, jam-laden scone in hand by the time Brad appeared. "Hey, what am I missing here? This looks delicious!" He helped himself to coffee and a scone, then tucked a couple of cookies on his plate, for good measure. "I understand there's a waterfall to be seen out back. Are you game?"

"Sure. Nothing like a hike to warm up for the hike."

"You said you wanted to get going." Lili just nodded and kept on chewing. Someone like Brad wouldn't see the vast difference between wanting to "get going" and wanting to put some of the mileage behind her. "Gie... the guy from France... was telling me about seeing some bungy jumpers. Sounds like a blast."

"Bungy jumpers?"

"Yeah. There's a bridge over a river just outside Queenstown. About two hundred feet or so high." One side of his mouth twitched. "The bridge, not the river. Anyway, they tie a bungy cord, which is like a long series of rubber bands, around the jumper's ankles, then he dives out off the bridge and keeps bouncing back up until the rubber settles. Then they lower him to a raft in the river and take him out. God. I'd love to have a shot at it!"

She stared at him, her mouth agape. "Are you crazy?"

"What do you mean? That would be a real experience!"

"Probably your last!"

"Lili, Lili. You have no spirit of adventure."

"What I have is a son and a mother to support. I can't afford to end up bashed on a rock in a river. Even if it is in New Zealand. I have a feeling you can be just as dead here as in the good old U.S."

"Well, no problem. There are no bungy cords on Milford Track. That I know of." One eyebrow lifted. "Just a twelve-second drop."

Her hand shot up. "Don't tell me—I don't want to know." Opting for what had begun to sound both safe and sane, she suggested, "Let's go see the waterfall."

"Sounds like a good idea."

Jonathan met them at the door. "On your way up the mountain, by chance?"

"Yes, we are."

"Mind if I join you?"

"We'd be delighted. Brad, have you met Jonathan? He's a bird-watcher. He's promised to point out a few of the New Zealand species to me."

"If I spot any, that is." Jonathan glanced over toward the river, where Brian stood surrounded by a group of their fellow hikers. "They must be feeding the eels. Shall we have a look?"

"Eels?" Lili couldn't hide a tone of distaste. "There are eels in this river?"

"Sure. And trout, of course. Lots of those."

Lili carefully avoided the edge while they watched the eels, big eels, six to ten feet long and a half-dozen inches in diameter, churn up the water in front of Brian, fighting for the chunks of bread he was tossing into the river. The feeding ritual, he explained, was a regular routine, and the eels had learned to show up at this time every morning.

"I'll be damned!" Brad exclaimed. "Trained eels. That's remarkable! Hell, if an eel can be trained, might even be possible to train a woman!" He dodged out of the way barely in time to avoid being pushed in to join the slithery creatures.

The ascent up the mountain, despite the "easy" label, was steep and slick, and Lili had to keep biting her tongue to avoid gasps, groans and other betrayals of her unsure footing. *I can, I can, I can,* she chanted in her head, like the little engine that could, a favorite story of Donny's in his younger years. Brad was in front of her, and at a couple of junctures, her hand shot out to clutch at his belt. "Step in my footprints, and dig in," he told her. She did, and, as promised, reached the top of the path safely.

A group that had preceded them had already begun the descent, and Jonathan, in pursuit of a bird with a high, trilling sound, disappeared around a grouping of rocks on a narrow side trail, leaving Brad and Lili alone in the densely forested glade. Water, awesome in its might, cascaded past them, sending up flumes of spray as it bounced across rocks and over a couple of fallen trees. The air was rich with the scent of damp peat and pine. They leaned against a large tree trunk, and Brad took her hand in his. "What a spot. Listen, Lili. What do you hear?"

She lifted her head, alert to the sounds around her. "Water, and that one little bird song." She shook her head. "And that's all. What a difference."

"Between what and what?"

"This . . . and Dorchester."

"Dorchester?" He looked down at her, a frown on his face. "Is that where you're living? *Dorchester?*" The name of the town was often on the evening news and in the paper. Teenage gangs and shootings and drugs. He couldn't imagine Lili there. In fact, the picture filled him with apprehension.

Error, error, error, the computer of her mind bleeped. If he still lived in Boston, it would be easy for him to "drop by," to see how she was doing. "Well...for the moment. I'm looking for another place, something we can afford in a little better area."

"God almighty, I should hope so."

"It isn't that bad, really. Parts of the town are nice. It's just, well, the news only shows the bad sections." Change the subject, quickly. "How about you? Still in the Boston area?"

"No. I'm living in a condo outside Hartford."

"And Esther? Where's she?"

Brad felt his whole body tense at the sound of his ex-wife's name. Trying to deal with Esther had become difficult; living with her was impossible. Still, the failure of the marriage was painful. "Still living in our house in Simsbury," he said. "I don't know whether she'll stay there. I doubt it. Her parents have moved to a big family home in Philadelphia, and they want her to come live with them for a while."

"Will you move back into the house, if she leaves it?"

"Hell, no. I want no part of it. It's too big and it holds a lot of memories. Besides, it's hers now, to keep or dispose of as she sees fit." He turned away, his face set, a deep furrow between his eyes.

"I'm sorry. I didn't mean to bring up a hurtful subject."

"It's okay. After all, those are the ones we usually need to talk about."

"You sound like my mother. She's always telling me I keep things too bottled up."

"And is she right?"

"Yes. I suppose she is."

"And what would it take to uncork the bottle?" His head was bent toward hers, and the tree-filtered sun highlighted the golden streaks in his dark blond hair. His eyes asked for answers she longed to give, but didn't dare.

"I don't know. A small charge of nitroglycerin might do it."

"Sorry, none on me. How about a little dynamite? We should be able to generate enough of that to have some effect." Brad tried to keep his tone light, teasing. But here, in this quiet, sylvan setting, looking down at her lovely face, his tone unwillingly turned serious—as did his intent. Encased in nature's arboretum, displaced from his everyday reality, the emotions rising within felt natural, reliable, inevitable. He cupped her cheek with the palm of his hand and tilted her face to his.

Lili's heart pounded in concert with the crashing crescendo of the waterfall as his lips came closer to hers. *Stop this,* she told herself, *before it gets out of hand.* But the words of caution were drowned in a flood of longing too powerful to withstand mere reason. His mouth touched hers, gently inquisitive. Brad, Brad! The call, though silent, raced through her body, bending it to his.

The contact galvanized their defense systems at the same instant of contact, and they pulled away quickly, both flustered, both apologetic.

"Lili, I didn't mean to—"

"Brad, this isn't—"

"I found him! I did!"

Startled, they turned to see Jonathan, who had just emerged from the woods and stood beside them, a triumphant grin on his face. "My first coup!"

Brad, regaining his shaken poise, declared, "Well done! Guess we'd better go with you from now on!" The moment passed.

Lili, too rattled to do more than smile foolishly, followed the two men down the trail, musing on those words "from now on." The "from now on" in her life was changing from moment to moment. How was she to keep up, keep her defenses in place? She watched the easy swing of Brad's tall body as he descended the steep incline, the quick, instinctive dip of his head to avoid tree branches, the sure placement of his feet. What a man! The judgment of the twelve-year-old girl concerning the seventeen-year-old boy still held true. Only now, they were grown. A man and a woman with responsibilities and commitments. And at the head of both of those categories—for her—was her son. Born as a result of this same passion. And it was for the protection of her son that she must not yield to the burning need that had, once again, been ignited. Life wasn't fair. It just wasn't. But then, nobody had ever said it was.

Before she could burrow too deeply into her glum musings, she was halted on the downward trek by a hushed "Stop!" from Jonathan. "See? Right over there." His voice was a bare whisper. "A yellow-breasted black-headed tomtit! Stand very still. Let's see if he'll come closer."

The three of them froze, six eyes staring through the dark underbrush at a tiny bird standing on a twig, who, in turn, was watching them with like intensity.

"Oh, Jonathan," Lili breathed, "he's adorable." Evidently encouraged by her kind words, the tomtit hopped over and jumped onto the toe of her boot. Lili sucked in her breath so she wouldn't make a sound. The bird pecked at her socks, then jumped up to take a stab at her leg with his beak. Lili glanced over at Jonathan. "What's he doing?"

"Catching insects."

"On me?"

"Yes." He laughed softly as he positioned his camera and took a series of shots. "Very small insects. But then, he's a very small bird."

Lili managed to hand her camera to Brad without interrupting the bird's feast, so he could get a few snaps of the impromptu snack. When the tomtit had had his fill, he gave a bob of his head, jumped to the ground and was quickly lost in the dense foliage. "Oh, my," she said, "that was such fun! To think I helped Jonathan get a picture of one of the birds on his list. Will wonders never cease?"

Brad gave her a long, probing look that had nothing whatever to do with tomtits. "No. It appears not," he said softly.

Dinner that evening turned into a festive affair. The new manager, Wayne, had arrived, along with several of the trail guides, and they produced, with great fanfare, a goodly supply of champagne.

After gathering everyone to the front of the dining room, Wayne popped the cork on one of the bottles. "Ladies and gentlemen, you are about to participate in a very unusual event—cocktail hour at Glade House!" A rousing cheer went up from the willing about-to-be-participants. "I'd like everyone to get a full glass in hand. If you can't, or won't, drink the bubbly, there's plenty of grape juice on the front table. We have a few dozen toasts to raise to our departing friend. And to his wife, who is staying with us." He arched his eyebrows and tried for a sinister leer. "We assure you, Brian, we will take *very* good care of her!"

Brian didn't look at all fazed. "Gail's always been able to take very good care of *herself*. So, good luck to you!" Another cheer was led by the jovial group of guides.

Brad handed Lili a full glass and got one for himself before settling beside her on a wooden bench. "Looks like we picked a good first night for our hike."

"I know. I must admit, I never expected to be served champagne on the Milford Track!"

A series of tributes, sincere to teasing, was raised and toasted, and the noise level and affability ratio rose with each tilt of the glass. When dinner was ready, they all got in line to heap plates with well-done beef, mashed potatoes, string beans, tossed salad and dinner rolls.

Lili piled her plate high, commenting to Gillian and Brad as she sat down at the long, communal table, "Here I expected to lose a few pounds on this hike, so I could overindulge on the rest of my trip. All this food! And look at me, about to stuff myself like a sausage!"

Gillian took a gulp of the cold milk that was served by the pitcherful. "You'll work it off."

"I was afraid you'd say that."

Brad shrugged. "From what I hear about New Zealand food, this may be the height of their cuisine, so you may as well eat up."

The person at the end of each table was given the duty of carrying the dishes to the kitchen window and serving dessert, which was plum pudding or truffles, or both, and coffee. When everyone was well stuffed, Brian asked each person to stand and give his name and nationality. There were hikers from England, the U.S. and Canada, Australia, Switzerland, Austria and France, and five from New Zealand.

Dinner was followed by games. Brad was drafted for the first, which entailed hooking a looped string over one ear. The other end was tied to the hollow ring of a mason-jar lid, and his object was to try, with both hands behind his neck, to get the lid over the top of an empty beer bottle. The sight of tall, muscular Brad, head tilted to one side, desperately trying to hoop the elusive bottle sent Lili into gales of laughter. When he returned, she and Gillian gave him a hardy burst of applause despite his loss to a tiny slip of a girl from Idaho. The two of them teamed up for a "blow the Ping-Pong ball across the table" game, and won their round, a feat that won them an extra serving of dessert, which they both declined.

When they all headed for bed, tired and happy, Brad touched Lili's elbow and tilted his head toward the outside door. She followed him, her heart pounding with a combination of anticipation and misgiving. She was beginning to feel like the original spineless wonder: too entranced to say no and too fearful to say yes.

He took her hand and they walked down the path to the edge of the river, where it was too dark now to see anything but an occasional reflection of the sliver of a moon. He was quiet during the brief journey and for a few minutes after they reached the water. When he did speak, his voice was low and very serious. "Lili, what happened up by the waterfall—"

"Brad..." She didn't want to talk about it, afraid it would make it too real, something they couldn't ignore. But it *was* real, and Brad had never been one to ignore reality. She said nothing more, afraid that any comment would be the wrong one. Wrong for what? She was far too confused to know.

"We got carried away once, you and I, and it might have had disastrous results."

Disastrous. So now she knew, with that one word, how he'd have reacted, all those years ago, if she had told him. Lili's stomach knotted, twisted by the secret she held so tightly inside.

"I have no idea how you feel, but I want to be very, very honest about where I am. I came here to escape from the bitter end of a relationship that has torn me to pieces. I'm far from ready to get involved again. With anyone." He lowered his head, and took a deep breath. "This probably sounds awfully presumptuous. I mean, you've done everything but slam a door in my face, so it isn't like I'm trying to warn you off." He stopped. "God, Lili, why am I running on like this?" He turned, taking her shoulders in his hands. "I've never forgotten you, Lili. If I hadn't been...bespoken..." He gave a mocking laugh at the sound of the old-fashioned word. "Hell, I don't know. I guess I'm just expressing my own frustration at a matched set of bad timing. Then and now." He dropped his hands, feeling like a damned fool. Who was he trying to protect? Himself, obviously. She was awakening feelings in him that raised havoc with his determination to avoid, at all costs, any type of entanglement.

They returned to the cabin in silence, and Lili felt submerged in a pool of deceit that she had filled, drop by drop, herself.

Chapter Four

The bustling activity that had prevailed in the cabin when they left had completely vanished, and the place was vacant and still and black. They hesitated just inside the door to let their eyes grow accustomed to a darkness that was more dense inside than out. Brad took Lili's arm to guide her down the length of the porch. The dark was broken only by a couple of low-wattage bulbs, strategically placed between the men's and women's dorms and the toilets.

"Damn." Lili jammed her toe into a table leg. It didn't really hurt through her sneaker, but the crash of the table against the wall sounded like a gunshot in the absolute quiet. Brad's fingers tightened around her arm, accelerating the flights of fancy that had invaded her mind the moment he'd touched her when they stepped inside—visions of crawling into one of the narrow bunks together, of spending the night wrapped in each other's arms. She struggled with her errant mind, searching for a sane thought. Just one. Anything to shove the insistent fantasy from her head. "I forgot to put the sheet on my bed. I hope I can figure it out." It wasn't much, but it was mundane enough to do for now.

Brad eased his grip but kept hold of Lili's arm. He told himself it was to prevent her colliding with any more furniture, but a part of him had to admit the truth: he wanted to keep her close, to postpone the inevitable moment of separation. Crazy, how a simple reference to a bed sheet could cause the blood to run faster in his veins. "Well, it'll be a little complicated in the dark." His fingers unwillingly forfeited their hold. "It's one unit, sewed together. The bottom part goes on the mattress like a regular fitted sheet, so be sure you get the right side down." He wanted to make love to her, not give housekeeping instructions! She moved, and the sweet scent of her hair teased his nostrils. "At least you've taken your shower. You smell—" *delicious, inviting, sexy* "—fresh."

Lili scuffed the rubber toe of one shoe against the wooden floor, aware, too late, it was the gesture of a befuddled teenager in love. "Had to. I couldn't bear the thought of sitting down to dinner with insects all over me. Even if they *were* tiny."

"Even if they were a feast for a tomtit?"

"Even then."

"I goofed it. Got into a gabfest with a few of the other men right up till dinner call." His hand moved toward her, close enough to feel the heat of her skin, then dropped. "So, I shall head for the head. At least the showers won't be crowded." He tried for a light, joking tone—"How about coming along to wash my back?"—aware, too late, of the sexual yearning that ran through.

Oh, yes, yes. She'd love to. "Tch-tch. Such a suggestion! Why, think of the scandal if I were found in the men's bath!"

He touched her arm, unable to discipline his hand. "Better say good-night and let you go. Long day tomorrow."

Lili felt the welling of tears in her eyes. She had no idea what they were about, but she didn't want Brad to see them.

"Yes. Long day." She wiped them quickly away. There *were* advantages to the dark.

Brad allowed his lips to brush her cheek, a "brotherly" salute, gentle and undemanding—and unbelievably difficult to manage. Brad couldn't understand the strength of the longings engulfing him. What was it? The dark? The distance from home and reality? No. It was Lili, and the implications of that were troubling. They both had been emotionally wounded, and needed plenty of time and space. While Brad's mind carefully acknowledged the rational factors of their situation, his groin ached with need of her. What he wanted to do was scoop her up and bear her off the deserted living room, where they could make purposeful use of the lumpy couch. He stepped away, irritated with his overzealous hormones. "Well, off to the shower." He laughed softly. "Better make it cold."

Lili watched him go. A cold shower might be just the thing for her, too. With great care, she felt her way into the dorm and to her bunk. She took off her sneakers and was about to feel around for the bed sheet when she heard a whispered "Lili!"

She turned around. "What?"

"It's me. Gillian. I made up your bed." There was a stifled giggle. "Figured you'd miss lights-out."

Lili sank onto her bunk. "Oh, Gillian, thanks. What a pal!"

"What are friends for? See you in the morning." There were the sounds of turning over, and a deep presleep sigh.

Lili, infinitely grateful for Gillian's kindness, managed the transition from clothes to nightgown with minimum difficulty and slid into the clean, welcome enclosures of sheet and blanket. The silence was absolute, a soundless hymn of praise to untrammeled nature. Then, from far off, came the muted hoot of an owl. Lili smiled. She must remember to tell Jonathan. Although she fully expected to lie awake, sleeplessly pondering the swiftly altering circumstances of her life, she fell asleep almost instantly.

* * *

Brad was awakened by the *thump* of Ed Grainger's head against the bottom of his mattress. Brad leaned over from his top bunk. "You okay?"

"Yes. Perfectly all right. Rather a surprise, waking up in a dormitory. Haven't done so since college." Ed had a marvelous laugh—low and rumbly and full of goodwill. "But, takes a bit to injure this hard pate." He stood. "Good morning, my lad. I must commend you on your quiet ascent up the ladder last night. Hardly heard you a'tall."

Brad chuckled. "Hope not. I was trying to be quiet, but I'd forgotten just where my bunk was located."

"Well, perhaps we can stake out our berths the same way tonight. Then, if you wish to do a bit of after-hours trekking, I can signal you with my flashlight."

"What a sport!" Brad pulled on his clothes and headed for the john. This time he had to wait in line for a chance to shave. It seemed the bearded outdoor look was not highly coveted by this crowd.

The bunk room was bustling with activity when he returned, with all the men packing up for the day before heading out for breakfast. Ed put the last of his belongings into his pack and placed it on his bunk. "Brad, don't mean to trespass on your privacy, but I did want to express our, well, concern, Josie's and mine. Your mother wrote us about the divorce. We're so sorry. Must be a damned painful business."

Brad finished tucking his bed sheet into his pack, then faced the other man. "Yes, no question. It's been a bitch. But it's over. And it needed to be over."

"So your mother says. This other girl, this Lili. Seems a fine sort. May be just the ticket, so to speak."

"Little early for anything like that." Brad grinned. "So to speak." The statement sounded perfectly reasonable this morning, in the sobering light of day, and not too difficult to toss off. Last night? A bit of moonlight madness, nothing more. He hoped.

He hurried to the dining room, aware of an unwarranted degree of hunger. Lili was sitting next to Gillian, and the two of them leaning across the table in conversation with Jonathan and Glynne. The back of Brad's neck bristled at the look in Glynne's eyes as he bent toward Lili. Damn, where was the calm detachment of a few minutes ago? When he reached the table, he greeted them all as he slid in beside Lili. "Everyone set for the trail?"

"Ready to go!" Jonathan had his binoculars in place, as though on alert in case of a fly-through. "This should be quite a day for birding. Rain forest, you know. Birds love them."

Glynne pulled a dog-eared book out of his pocket and began to flip through the pages. "So, you spotted the tomtit and the tui. Well, I can top you. Took an early stroll out through the fields, and damned if I didn't see a native falcon." Jonathan's eyes widened in envy. "I stood about for a half hour, hoping to see him go after a rodent in the grass. They move like a shot, you know. But he finally just flew away. Made my day though, I'll tell you. Before it even started!"

"Attention!" Wayne, now fully in charge, stood at the front of the room. "Let's get cracking! Come up one table at a time, starting at the back. The two people at this end of each table get cleanup duty. As soon as you're through, you can hit the trail. There will always be a guide in front of you and a guide behind, in case anyone has trouble. You can pick up your sandwich and fruit and cookies over on that table to take along for lunch. Cold drinks and hot tea will be served at the lunch hut. Have a fine day. It's been good having you with us!" There was a scattered applause and calls of "Good luck, Wayne" and "Thanks for the champagne." The general mood was very cheerful.

Brad turned to Lili. "Sleep well?"

She smiled at him. "Yes. And you?"

"Great."

Gillian stretched. "Been a while since I slept in a room full of women. At least the rest of it no longer bothers me. The sleeping alone. Having a warm body to snuggle up to was the only thing I missed about my husband when we split."

Jonathan laughed. "Seems we've a lot in common. Glynne, Gillian and I, and now you, Brad, survivors of the divorce court."

Brad nodded, his face set. There was nothing about divorce he found humorous. But it was good to think he might, someday.

Glynne's eyes were on Lili, as usual. "Of course, we're all single, but Lili had to arrive at that state in a more painful manner." He paused. "Although I wonder if that's true. At least there's no rejection involved in death. The person doesn't leave you of his or her own free will."

A brief discussion followed on which was worse emotionally, with Lili adding nothing but a few nods, monosyllabic retorts and shakings of the head. This charade of falsehood was so hard. Bad enough with the others, but with Brad it was unbearable. It was clear that he thought her reticence was based on the pain of loss. He was going to want to know more about her "husband," and she'd have to invent still more stories. Just as her mother had said, layer upon layer, a pancake platter of lies. But what else could she do? Ever since she'd awakened at a little after five this morning, her mind had been a maelstrom of conflicting arguments. "Tell him." "I can't." "What if he wants to get together back home, suggests renewing your ties with his folks, with Marcy?" "Impossible." "So how will you avoid it?" "I don't know." And to top it, all the shoulds and cannots and carefuls she'd set firmly in place simply faded into oblivion the moment he sat down at her side. Had she ever stopped loving him? She doubted it. There was certainly no disguising her feelings now. She ached with wanting. And she wanted all of him. For the rest of her life.

"Lili? I think we're up."

Startled back to awareness, she stood and joined the food line. When she slid back into her seat and put her plate in front of her, she had to laugh. "I never eat anything but a bowl of cereal for breakfast, and look at this! Eggs, bacon, fried potatoes, toast. How am I going to convince my friends at home that I barely survived the rigors of this hike if I come home looking like the side of the mountain I supposedly climbed?"

Glynne, whose plate outdid hers, grinned. "Never fear. We'll set you a lively clip, so all those calories will just melt off. Besides, a few more pounds would do you no harm."

Jonathan nodded his agreement. "He's right. And we're all eating just as much."

Lili swallowed a mouthful, washing it down with the orange juice Brad had thoughtfully poured for her. Heaven forbid she should miss anything! "Thank you. But why do I get the feeling both of you could eat that and seconds and never show an ounce of it?" The food, plain fare as it was, tasted more delicious than any meal she could recall. If the small amount of exercise she'd already had could do this to her appetite, what would it be like at the end of the toughest section of the trail tomorrow? Or *was* it the exercise that made her feel so alive and ravenous?

It was amazing, considering the large portions of food consumed by almost everyone, how quickly the group finished up, donned their packs and struck out for the trail.

Gillian had gone ahead with Glynne and Jonathan by the time Brad and Lili set out on the track that led from behind the hut. The sun, already high in the sky, radiated a welcome early-morning warmth. All the doubts and fears and misgivings of dawn had abandoned Lili's mind, driven out by the sheer beauty that surrounded her—and by the intoxicating presence of Brad, striding along just behind her on the narrow path.

He called out, "Looks like the first thing on the docket is getting across that suspension bridge!"

Sure enough, right ahead, a bridge over the Clinton River—made of rope and strips of wood planking—swung crazily, stirred to motion by those presently executing the crossing. Lili gulped. "It looks pretty...precarious."

"Piece of cake." They reached the river and halted in front of a sign that cautioned no more than one person at a time on the bridge. "Want me to go first?" Brad was bouncing on the balls of his feet, full of eagerness to test the bridge.

"Are you kidding? Look at you. You'd probably have it swaying back and forth like a crazed hammock! Why don't you stand here and steady it while I cross?"

"Steady it?" Brad cast a skeptical eye on the lengthy suspension. "Well, all right. Step sprightly now, give it a bit of a go." His imitation of Ed Grainger was remarkably close. "First bloke in the drink is eel dinner."

Lili glared at him. "Not funny. Not funny at all." She leaned over, scanning the water for the slithery creatures, relieved not to see any. With great trepidation, she set one foot on the bridge, then the other. Gaining confidence at the absence of anything but a minor sway, she tried for the free, loose gait suggested by Wayne in the morning briefing. A regular rhythm was supposed to prevent wild swinging. She was almost to the one-third mark when the real bobbing and weaving began, producing a sensation similar to her one experience of being in a small boat on the ocean in a gale. "Oh, my God," she muttered. "Oh, my God!"

"How're you doing?"

"Great! Terrific! No prob!" Her teeth set in an ivory clench of true grit, she hung on to the wire cables that supported the bridge with all her strength. Her whole body felt like Wednesday-night supper in the North End—spaghetti heaven. Where were her bones, for crying out loud? The swaying accelerated, and the cable got higher, so she had to clutch desperately at the loops of rope. Somewhere, far behind, from the safe plateau of the shore, the sound of laughter goaded her. "All right, damn it," she grunted at herself. *"Stride!"* Somehow, with very little grace from heaven or bodily parts, she made it to the other side, where she leaned weakly against a tree. A nice, solidly planted tree. With roots. In the ground. She gave its bark a pat. She loved trees.

Brad, naturally, swung across the bridge as if he spent his life walking on water beds. Maybe, if she kept watching performances like this along the way, she could grow to dislike him. But then he reached her side, his face shining with exuberance, and announced, "If you're the prize, lead on to the alligator pits! I'm ready for any obstacle to win this delicious morsel of femininity! Lead on, fair damsel!" Any chance for dislike withered and died. She liked everything about him, even his abominable agility.

He braced one hand on the side of the tree, bringing his magnificent body close enough that she could feel his warmth. "Of course, on the other hand, we shouldn't rush this experience. Wouldn't want to miss any of the scenic splendors." His proximity sent shivers through her overheated body. "For instance, off in the distance—" he swung his arm out in a random direction "—are the Disappearing Peaks."

"Why are they called—"

"Please. Questions later." The truth was, he didn't know. "And in that direction, madam—" the arm swung again and his hand brushed against her arm "—feast your eyes on Mount Skelmorlie and Mount Lang." He leaned against the tree, so close, so close. "And farther on, Sentinel Peak stands guard over the Clinton Canyon."

"What did you do, get up at the crack of dawn to memorize the guidebook?"

"Yes, that's just what I did. And at the end of the trail there will be a quiz, so perk up your ears, because there is a penalty for missing any of the answers."

Lili's eyes met his, and the endless possibilities of the nature of the "penalty" hung between them. He had laid out his determination for no involvement, had erected a wall to match her own; but the look in his eyes contradicted all of it—and, she knew, matched the look in her own. The attraction was not one-sided, and that knowledge was enough to imbue her spirit with dancing feet.

They both perked up their ears at the shouts of hilarity when the next person on the trail began to traverse the bridge. "Guess we'd better move." Brad took off, setting a sprightly pace.

Lili matched her stride to his, throwing in a few running steps here and there to keep up, filled with a happiness that made no sense and had a life of its own. Not far into the beech forest, they were joined by two robins, who hopped alongside for quite a spell, as though drawn to these two members of the tall, featherless species by the special radiance they exuded. It didn't seem strange to Lili to have these tiny winged companions supplying their guidance on the trek. At the moment, she felt attuned to all things beautiful and natural and free.

After a while, the trail widened and flattened, enabling Brad and Lili to walk side by side. "Lili, I assume the death of your husband must have been fairly recent."

She stopped, thrown off guard by the abrupt change from their bantering of a few minutes before. "Why would you assume that?"

"Because it's still a very touchy subject."

Lili kicked at a pile of twigs in the middle of the sandy trail. "As a matter of fact, it was a long time ago."

"Oh?" They resumed walking, but at a much slower pace.

"Yes." Lili had told this story many times before. She refused to risk exposing Donny to any of the stigma attached to being a fatherless son, so right from the beginning, she had pretended to be a widow. But telling it now, to Brad, was infinitely more difficult than any previous recital. The certainty she'd had of the wisdom of the decision she'd made eleven years before was wavering badly. Even so, she took a deep breath and plunged in. "The marriage was a mistake. A dumb mistake. I was very young. I was—" she did some fast calculations "—nineteen and he barely twenty. He was funny and exciting and bright, and I thought I was in love with him. We'd only known each other a short time." She was beginning to sweat under the cool canopy of trees. "We were married just a few months when I realized I'd made a mistake, but I didn't have time to do anything about it before he was killed. I found out I was pregnant a week after his car skidded on a patch of ice and went into a tree."

It had the stilted cadence of a memorized script, which was understandable. It was. Brad was still waiting, probably for some sort of ending.

"Such a waste," she added. It *was* a waste, this whole sickening charade.

"I'm sorry," Brad said automatically, but he felt puzzled. If the guy had been dead for such a long time, why the pained reaction whenever the subject came up? Especially if she had already decided the marriage was a mistake?

Lili, sensing his confusion, decided to tell enough of the truth to add some plausibility. And, hopefully, to put the subject to rest. "It was a terribly difficult time for me. I hadn't intended to get pregnant, and it put an end to my plans to attend college. In a way, it felt like the end of my whole future. And I'd brought it on myself, which always makes things worse."

"I don't suppose you considered abortion?"

"Yes. I did. But I couldn't do it. I guess that's something you just can't know until you face the dilemma. But I couldn't." She shuffled her feet in the soft ground-cover, remembering the all-too-real trauma of that series of decisions. "I also considered letting someone adopt the child. Someone more mature and financially capable of raising it. But—"

"You couldn't do that, either."

"No. I...*we* had been living with Mom. It was supposed to be temporary, but money was so tight." Money. Brad probably had no concept of how money, or the lack of it, could dictate the choices of your life. "After Donny was born, we tried all sorts of things, Mom and I. Child-care centers and a neighbor woman. Mom working while I stayed home, then switching after I managed to finish secretarial school and land a job at Digital. At that point I could make more than she could. And that's pretty much how it's been since. I owe her more than I can ever repay."

"And your son, Donny? Are you glad—"

"That I had him...and kept him?" She had stopped again and faced him squarely, looking him straight in the eye. This was easy to answer. There were no deviations from the truth in this. "Oh, yes. More than I could ever express! I love him more than I've ever loved anyone. He's worth all of it. And more!" His gaze lowered, and she was sure he was thinking of his own desire for a son.

"I'm sure you're a wonderful mother."

"I do my best. Time is such a problem. Between work and night school and homework, it's hard to get enough hours with Donny."

The walk resumed, and Lili felt relieved. Maybe that would be the end of the questions and she could relax and just enjoy the experience. All of it. Her gaze kept drifting sideways, searching Brad's profile for hints of his thoughts. Despite his innate self-assurance and native buoyant optimism, there were shadows in his face, signs of sadness. She wanted to pummel him with questions, but was afraid to reopen any doors.

They were a little farther along the trail when he asked the next question. "And since? Has there been anyone special? *Is* there anyone special?"

"Not really. My life is complicated. Any single mother's is. There are a lot of factors involved in a relationship beyond just the man. For one thing, I owe a tremendous debt to my mother. She has given up a lot to help us. I know she'd hate hearing me say that. She doesn't believe in martyrdom. She says that what she's done was her own free choice, and she doesn't expect or want me to feel obligated."

"But you do."

"Sure. How could I not? Mom was only—" Lili caught herself just in time. She and Marcy had baked her mother a birthday cake on her thirty-sixth birthday, and Brad, who came over to drive Marcy home, had thoughtfully brought a bouquet of flowers. That was when Lili was sixteen. If she said how old her mother was at the time Donny was born, it wouldn't take long for the calculations to begin. God. Another layer. "Forty, when Donny was born, and, well, you remember her. She was still pretty and fun and full of life. And she was dating a couple of men fairly regularly. There was every chance for remarriage."

"Lili, you're carrying an awfully heavy load for such a young woman."

"Well, I suppose. But it's mine to carry."

"And what if someone wanted to share it?"

She looked over at him but continued to walk. If she stopped now, she might throw herself in his arms and start to cry. All the need, the longing, the fantasizing of having someone—no, not just someone, *him*—to share the load might spill out all over both of them. And what a flood that would be! "I don't know, Brad. Maybe. Someday. But I need to complete what I've started. I'm so close to getting my degree, and it's very important to me. My job is going so well—it's offered me opportunities I never anticipated. And Donny has to come first, always. And then there's Mom. I can't ask anyone to assume all that. I'm responsible, and I have to work it out."

"Wow. Quite a list. Conquering the Mackinnon Pass sounds like duck soup next to rising above all those obstacles."

She gave a cryptic laugh. "Yes. Not many takers, I assure you."

"And what if someone wanted to take on the lot? Share it all? Could you let go of some of the load?"

"That's a funny way to put it."

"Not really. A lot of it is tied up with guilt. Have to be careful of hair shirts."

Lili stopped dead and whirled to face him. "And what's *that* crack supposed to mean? That my problems are all in my head? I'm just a crybaby, sniffling over nothing?"

"For God's sake, of course not. Things have been damned tough for you. But if you insist on looking at it as your fault, something you brought on yourself and have to pay for, it's going to play hell with your life from now on."

"And how do you suggest I look at it? Like a bunch of insignificant trivia, to be tossed aside at the first prospect of a marriage proposal?"

He raised his eyebrows, studying her face intently. "No to the first, and maybe to the second. There are points of view to everything. For instance, it isn't automatically necessary to abandon all your plans in order to have some guy share your life. You don't have to *pay* for love. It just happens. Why couldn't you complete college and keep your job if you got married? And maybe Donny would like to have a father. And—" he tilted his head to one side "—your mother's only, what? About fifty? She might enjoy a little freedom."

"And maybe you don't know what the hell you're talking about! What do you know about problems, anyway? Or guilt?"

She started to walk away, but he reached out to grab her and swing her around to face him. "How do you think I feel about my own life, Lili? Like some great frigging success story? You had it rough from the beginning. There were very few advantages in your life. Naturally you'd be vulnerable to someone who promised some fun—a little relief from all the problems. You met some guy and fell for him and it turned out to be a mistake. Happens all the time. It wasn't your fault he was killed. Me? I had nothing *but* advantage. Esther and I knew each other forever. We had smooth sailing all our lives. If any marriage should've worked, ours should have!''

"But she's the one who got so paranoid—"

"Oh, come on. Things like that are never one-sided. I told her it didn't matter, that it wasn't her fault. I told her we could adopt, and that it didn't change the way I felt. But it was so much crap, and she knew it. You can't hide feelings, no matter how hard you try. I was disappointed as all hell at not being able to have my own kids, and I'm sure it showed in my face and the tone of my voice and my attitude. Which, at times, was lousy. I was a pretty spoiled kid, you know— used to getting what I wanted. And even though I was supposed to be a man, the kid hadn't quite grown up. It seemed so damned unfair, like I'd been singled out to be picked on.'' He dropped his hands and gave a short, humorless laugh. "Poor me. Couldn't have what I wanted for once in my life. What an ass.''

"So now who's wearing the hair shirt?''

"Me. I am. And have been for a long time. And it's time to take it off.'' He gave her a tentative grin. "I will if you will.'' There were messages flickering in his eyes; speculations, invitations. There were cracks in his heart, too, Lili realized. A heart she had supposed was perfect. But evidently perfection was a myth. Along with so many other things.

Lili's heart was sitting squarely in the back of her throat, blocking the normal flow of air. Brad was holding out a hand to her, offering...? The potential was wildly intoxicating. Maybe not only the chance for a friendly ally, but a shot at the realization of a sixteen-year-old dream. The only problem was, he was standing on the other side of a pool of quicksand, and she had no idea how to navigate the crossing without sinking. "I don't know, Brad. I don't know if it's removable.''

"Hey.'' He pulled her into his arms, laughing softly as he tried to encircle her backpack. "You're tough and I'm hardheaded. We can do anything, you and I.''

Their gazes were locked, their mouths slightly open as the impact of closeness hit them both at once. What had started as a comradely embrace changed, altered by a chemistry neither could control. He kissed her then, and this kiss held no indecision. It was demanding and full of passion, and it obliterated Lili's shaken defenses. She opened her lips to his, wanting, wanting. His tongue probed, moving deep into her mouth. Heat suffused her body, stirred by an eruption of joy and hope and anticipation. Mind-locks opened, flooding her brain with memories—memories of his hands touching her breasts, of his lips on her nipples, of the panorama of erotic sensations he had released in her so long ago. And now—oh, God, it was all reawakening. All those longings she had locked away eleven years before.

Brad raised his head to look down at her, his eyes misted with sentiment. "Lili, no wonder it took me so long to put you out of my mind." When his lips met hers again, it was with a need that echoed hers. He cupped the back of her head with his strong hand, tangling his fingers in her short, curly hair, pressing her closer, as though to ensure that this time nothing could separate them.

He lifted his head again, this time with a jerk. The sentimental gleam in his eyes had been replaced with an expression very close to alarm. He stepped back so suddenly that Lili was momentarily thrown off balance. "Jesus, Lili, what are we doing?"

The alarm transferred to her, infusing her mind. Crazy, crazy. Playing with fire, tempting fate, courting disaster—all the old clichés rang out, resonant with truth. She had spent her adult lifetime learning and honing the art of control, and now, in an instant, she had let go of it. She shook her head. "I don't know. But it has to stop here, Brad. It has to."

His hands took hold of her shoulders, his head bent toward hers. "God, this is confusing. We both want the same thing—" an ironic smile touched the corner of his mouth

"—obviously in more ways than one. We'll have to help each other, I guess, to keep our emotions in check."

"Hey, look! It's a fantail! Quick, focus your camera!" There was a pregnant pause. "Uh-oh. Bad timing?"

Brad and Lili stared at Jonathan, who stood just beyond a stand of silver beech trees, his face a mask of consternation. Behind him were Glynne and Gillian. Lili could feel the flush of embarrassment creeping up her cheeks. It was obvious they had seen the embrace. "No...no, not at all. Uh, just talking." She cleared her throat and blinked, trying to make the swimming figures settle into focus. "I thought—" Her voice cracked, and she had to try again. "I thought you were way ahead of us."

Gillian, obviously amused, tried for a contrite expression. "We took that side path back there to see the river." One corner of her mouth twitched. "Guess you missed it. Must have been thinking of something else."

Brad wasn't used to feeling gauche, but that certainly described his present discomfort. "Lili and I are...renewing an old friendship."

All three of them burst into laughter, which, after a second, Brad and Lili strained to join, neither wanting to give the incident too much significance. Glynne spluttered, "I'd say you were doing a right good job of it, mate! Although, if *I* had a chance to kiss a lady, I'd head for the bush."

Lili, trying to foster the impression of a moment's dalliance on the trail, unimportant, lighthearted, gave an exaggerated shudder. "No way. There may be snakes in there."

Jonathan shook his head. "No snakes in New Zealand. No predators or creepy-crawlies. Very benign topo, this. The bush is as safe as can be."

They all fell into a leisurely gait, making an unspoken decision to join forces, at least for the time being. "Are you sure? No poisonous spiders or wild boar?" Lili was delighted to have the conversation turn away from her and Brad and their "friendship renewal."

"None. No wild anything. Actually, there were no mammals at all on the island when it was first settled, with the exception of bats." Jonathan stopped and cocked his head to listen to the bell-like trill of a bird. He grinned. "Bellbird. Aptly named. Man brought in the animals and decimated the bird population. Damn it all."

"No animals. Really? How come?"

"Couple of ice ages and rapid changes in the topography. Rapid as in the formation of continents, you understand. Then the whole island was isolated by water, which cut off the possibility of migration."

Brad chuckled. "Tell Lili what the first animals were that the Maoris brought in."

"When they came over from Polynesia in outrigger canoes about a thousand, twelve hundred years ago," Jonathan supplied obligingly, "they imported dogs and rats."

"Rats! Why would anyone deliberately start a population of rats?"

"Pretty basic. That's what they ate."

"But that's disgusting!"

"See?" Brad said. "That's what happens when people get overcivilized. They grow picky."

"Listen to you. I can just picture you ordering rat stew for dinner."

"I've never seen it on a menu, so how could I?" He gave Lili's arm a playful tap, glad to be dropping back to the easy camaraderie that had preceded their kiss. "Just think of the problems it would solve in Boston if they could popularize the dish!"

They were getting deeper into the Black Forest, where black, red and hybrid beech trees joined the predominant silver beeches. Ferns of many varieties grew to heights well above their heads, and the air was filled with bird calls and songs and the flutter of wings, which had Jonathan and Glynne whipping binoculars to their eyes and sneaking off into the tall brush in search of yet another species to add to their growing list. Although the trail had veered off from the river, the sound of rushing water accompanied them, joining the other sweet songs of nature.

They passed under trees heavy-hung with lichen and moss, or "Grandfather's Beard" as it was called by the locals. The sun was almost shut out by the density of the trees' foliage, ferns and high bushes. This was the rain forest, where the trail was flat, well tended and easy to walk, and the sweet, heavy smells of wet earth and richly nourished greenery accompanied every step. As the forest deepened, the bark of the trees became darker, and their trunks and branches twisted and turned, forming a panoply of sinister eeriness that would have made a properly frightening background for the flight of terror for any Walt Disney hero.

Brad and Lili stuck with the others, enjoying the shared laughter and thrills of discovery, as well as seeking refuge in the old concept of "safety in numbers."

Part of Lili hated the protection. There was nothing on earth she'd rather do than make love.with Brad, and it would be all too easy to fall prey to the reasoning that there was no harm in it, that it would simply be another wonderful memory to tuck away. But here again reality reared its ugly head. She certainly had no form of birth control with her, and she couldn't imagine that Brad had come on this hike so equipped. The ultimate irony would be a repeat of the eleven-year-old drama. A single encounter, a goodbye, with another unexpected "dividend." The end of the trail meant just that, in more ways than one. She must, *must*, stick with the crowd! But the realization that Brad also was struggling with desire made it much more difficult to hold certain entrancing mental images at bay.

Shortly after the seven-mile marker, they walked around a lake that had been formed when a landslide dammed up a section of the Clinton River, and approached the Haruru Falls lunch hut. "Oh, boy," Lili breathed. "Lunch."

Brad bent to remove a branch that had attached itself to his boot. "How can I be hungry, after that longshoreman's breakfast I put away?"

Lili laughed. "Beats me, but so am I. I'm starved. I think the only way to lose weight on this trip is to join the free hikers and subsist on beef jerky."

Most of the group was gathered at the hut. Many of them had shed their boots to give tired feet a chance at some cool air. One of the guides from Glade House was handing out hot tea and cold lemonade. Brad and Lili both opted for the cool drink and found a place to drop their packs and settle down to eat.

Ed and Josie, who had reached the hut shortly after them, came over to sit on a stairstep just above the one Lili and Brad had chosen. As Ed unwrapped his sandwich, he motioned to the side yard with his head. "Don't leave your gear lying about, cameras or sweaters or such. Been told the kea birds will steal anything. Take right off with it."

"Kea birds?" Lili set down her paper cup of lemonade, then moved it closer to the side of her leg. At this juncture, she was unwilling to lose it, even if the robber was cute and feathered.

"Yes. They're South Island mountain parrots. Cheeky rascals. See? Right over there."

Sure enough, the raucous creatures were hopping about, making darting raids on carelessly placed sandwiches or catching tossed bits of food in midair. They were gaudily colorful, with large hooked beaks and a call that could match the most loudmouthed crow's.

Lili sat in the midst of this cushion of contentment, chewing on the thick chicken sandwich that, although it had been squashed in her backpack, rivaled any morsel she'd ever consumed. The midday sun warmed her bare legs, and the dance of the kea birds enchanted her. Laughter and spirited talk surrounded them, and Lili was full of affection for these companions of the trail, enthralled by the beauty around her. Most of all, with no contest for first place, she was filled to the brim with love and desire for the man who sat beside her. The problems inherent in his absence paled beside the delight of his company. She'd almost forgotten how much fun Brad was, how full of enthusiasm and interest and humor. The words he had spoken back on the trail, before he had pulled away from their embrace, crept back to mind, twirling in her brain with dizzying glee: *"No wonder it took me so long to put you out of my mind...."* He *had* thought of her, after that night! The knowledge heated her, stroked her—and consoled her, spreading a salve over the wounds of the years. Was there some way to suspend the movement of time? To bask forever in this temporary paradise?

One of the big kea birds hopped directly in front of her, cocked his head, and issued forth a demanding caw. Lili smiled, broke off a large chunk of her sandwich, and tossed it to him. Fair was fair. He was part of her pleasure, and should be rewarded for his contribution. He swiftly disposed of the food and jumped back and forth, as though to speed its journey to his stomach, then stared at her in expectation. *You're just like me,* she thought. *Not satisfied with one taste, you want more.* With a smile, she threw him the last piece of the bread. Maybe her largesse would be rewarded: maybe kea birds had a vote in the workings of fate.

Chapter Five

It was after the eight-mile marker that the forest opened to reveal the sheer-sided sweep of the Clinton Canyon to the left and, ahead, the awesome peaks of Mount Hart and Mount Balloon, towering against the sky. In the distance, Mackinnon Pass, where the two monoliths met, came into view. Because this was a fjord, formed from milleniums of glacial shifting, melting and breaking, the mountains rose straight up from the valleys, where streams and rivers had cut ancient swaths. It was a landscape of uncompromising angles, and it was breathtakingly beautiful.

Lili stopped, her eyes widening and her mouth dropping open. "Is that it?"

"Yep. Magnificent, isn't it?"

"We have to go *up* that thing?" she exclaimed.

Brad put his arm around her shoulders as he chuckled. "Now, Lili, the trail won't be straight up, you know. It zigzags. And look how well you're doing. Not a single sign of fatigue. You'll be fine. Just wait and see."

It sounded too much like a locker-room pep talk: "Okay, so the other team outweighs you by half. Don't worry if you get banged around a little. They're only bones—they mend!" Lili gulped, but the fear wouldn't be swallowed. "We can't go around?"

Her question brought a full-throated bellow of laughter from Brad. "I'm sorry, but the mountain can't be circumvented like an island. That's why it took so long for the explorers to find a route to Milford Sound. You have to climb up until you find a pass to go through. Of course, if you do it first, you get to name it after you—as Mr. Mackinnon did."

"Mr. Mackinnon must have been out of his skull. Why didn't he just stay home and eat scones?"

Lili was perfectly happy to plunge once again into the cover of the beech forest, where the hovering threat of the mountains was hidden from view. At least, she comforted herself, the weather was good, and she had to admit she felt fine—in fact, so fine that she surprised herself. And she was having fun. Brad had gone ahead with Glynne and Jonathan, the three of them ready to set a pace she and Gillian couldn't maintain. The two women settled into a comfortable stride, content to let the hotshots do their thing.

"So, Lili, you have that hazy look of a lady who's falling in love. And who can blame you? He's gorgeous, he's fun, he's nice and, as a lovely bit of frosting, he's rich! How did you get so lucky?"

It was one of the few times in her life when Lili was sorely tempted to spill the whole story. The true story. She'd held it in for so long. With the exception of her mother, no one knew—not even the doctor who'd delivered Donny. The tale of her dead husband, complete with phony names and dates and situations, had been in place and rehearsed well before the baby's birth, and nothing her mother could say had altered her determination to shield her unborn child from any negative labels. Over the years, Lili had badly needed a pal, a confidante, but her desire for secrecy had become obsessive, and the possibility of her trusting a friend increasingly remote.

"Well, of course Brad and I knew each other a long time ago. I had a terrific crush on him then, too. And it was no more feasible that it would work out the first time around than it is now."

"Hey, wait a minute." Gillian laid her hand on Lili's arm to slow her. "Why not? He's divorced. It's plain as can be he's attracted to you. So what's this 'feasibility' business?"

"He's barely divorced, and he's dead set on staying unencumbered. Divorce isn't easy for a man like Brad. It'll take time for him to mend."

"Oh, twaddle. A little well-directed temptation could hasten the process. It's not like you just met and have no history."

Lili gulped. "We're so different, Gillian."

"Yes, of course you are. He's all man and you're all woman. And isn't that a blessing! Sometimes, these days, the differences aren't all that easy to spot!"

Lili had to laugh. From the moment she'd met Gillian, she'd had a feeling of empathy, sensed that they could be good friends. It was too bad they lived on different sides of the world. "Aside from gender, there are other things. Brad comes from great wealth. I come from—well, maybe not poverty, really, but not far up the ladder from it. There isn't supposed to be a class system in America, but there is, and he's in the top category. I assure you, it isn't at all easy to penetrate the upper crust."

"You were a friend of his sister's, so you must know his parents. Did they treat you badly?"

"Oh, no. They were wonderful to me."

"And back then, did Brad look down on you for being poor?"

"No. Not at all."

"So why are you building barriers, girl? If you can get him, grab him, and to hell with the obstacles! He's too good to pass up, Lili. And a good man, nowadays..." Lili joined her in singing the end of the line, "is hard to find!" They laughed, putting their arms around each other, a gesture that was short-lived because of a sudden narrowing of the trail.

"Oh, how I wish I had some of your optimism, Gillian! Can you give me a little? Just a weeny portion? You have plenty to spare."

"And what are you, a pessimist?"

"Yes. Always have been. My mother calls me an expert in the art of 'awfulizing.' I go through all the terrible possibilities long before they happen, or, in many cases, don't happen. I've tried so hard to get over it, but it hangs in there, ready to plunge right in at the first opportunity."

Gillian stopped, the levity gone from her expression. Her voice, when she spoke, was serious in tone. "I'll tell you something, Lili. I honestly believe we create some of our own destiny by our expectations. That may sound strange, but I do believe it. I read a book not long ago where the author asked, 'Would you rather be right, or happy?' I really think most people would rather be right. They'll scuttle their own happiness to that end." She shrugged. "Lots of things *happen* to us that we can't help. But there are a lot of things we shove around a bit, nudge in one direction or another, you know. And the direction you nudge—" she started to walk again "—has a lot to do with which way you *expect* things to go."

They walked along in silence for a while, a silence that was shattered for Lili by a deluge of thoughts that loudly demanded attention in her mind as she got caught up in the terrible habit of "what-ifing," another affliction she'd never managed to overcome. What if she hadn't been so adamant about not telling Brad she was pregnant? What if she hadn't taken herself on such a long mental excursion through every conceivable dreadful scenario, discounting even the off chance that the two of them could work something out? She would never forget the terrible scene with her mother when Louise had threatened to go to the Hollingsworths herself, if Lili refused to tell Brad. Lili had thrown the one full-fledged tantrum of her life. Her mother, frightened for her health, had relented and kept silent.

She had always been headstrong, but in that case her obstinacy had reached new heights. Still, she'd been absolutely sure she was right. Now, all the other thoughts quieted to allow one to be heard—the one Gillian had planted. "Would you rather be right, than happy?" Oh, dear God. Had the possibility for happiness been there, destroyed by her determination to cling to her dire expectations? And now... Was she automatically siding with Chicken Little in his prediction that the sky would fall? Or, was it possible... She shook her head. Too much. You couldn't break the habits of a lifetime in one five-day hike.

When they reached Pompolona Hut, Lili threw out her arms and proclaimed, "That really wasn't bad at all. I feel fine. And look—" she waved a hand to indicate the relative emptiness of the hostel "—we're practically the first ones here!" She felt quite smug and self-satisfied. She'd sold herself short. She grinned happily at Brad. "Maybe the feet inside these boots were made for walking, after all."

"Of course, they were. I could tell right away you were born for the trail by that long, swinging stride. And I'll bet you'll be crazy about white-water rafting, too."

"Don't get carried away. I don't know about you, but I'm going to grab the chance to stake out a good bunk and take a shower before the mob arrives."

"Good idea." He nodded his approval. "I'll see you later. Maybe we can try out the bushes?"

"Boy, are you wishy-washy! I thought we were going to be good little doobees. No bushes. It's no place for platonic friends. Besides, then I'd have to take another shower." It was fun, this flirting. Fun, and dangerous. Of course, danger had its attraction, too.

"Plenty of water in New Zealand."

Lili, brimful of health and the exuberance of accomplishment, went to the women's dorm and plunked down her pack on one of the bunks. She pulled out her slicker and tossed it on the next bunk to save it for Gillian. At least there were no clothing choices to be made. She had shorts, slacks, one shirt, sweater and sneakers for evening wear. Impatient for the feel of hot water, she dug out some clean undies and socks and carried her clothes and toiletries to the bathroom.

The evening that followed was full of animated talk: comparisons of amusing incidents and observations, all the joys of sharing a unique experience. "Did you see the ground orchids? Those pretty little flowers next to the trail?" "Beautiful, wasn't it, that section of tree fuchsias!" "We took off our boots at Prairie Lake and cooled our feet in the water. No, take it back—*froze* our feet in the water!" Camaraderie was in full force and Lili reveled in it. She loved being part of a group, a rare experience in her life. It reminded her of being in that play with Marcy, feeling the closeness that came of involvement in a shared effort.

Brad stayed near all evening, his conversation peppered with "Lili and I's." The sound of the joining of their two names sang through her like a love song. The two sat together, supported by large cushions, on the built-in couch that ran the length of the living room. Soon Lili found herself cradled in the curve of Brad's arm, tucked against his chest, convincing herself there was no harm in it. After all, they were in the midst of a crowd. Safety in numbers. Gillian caught her eye from across the room and gave her a wink and nod of approval. "Grab him, Lili," the look said. Not, Lili mentally agreed, such a bad idea. But the negative twit of a brain cell that patrolled against the intrusion of wandering optimism sharply retorted, "Forget it. It's impossible."

Lili was taking a lot of ribbing about the upcoming ascent of the mountain. Ed, sitting on the other side of her on the couch, patted her arm. "You can do it, Lili. Look how well you did today! We won't have to bury you on the trail, after all." Everyone joined in the laughter, along with Lili.

"Well, in case you do, put something nice on the marker. Something real original. Like, She Died With Her Boots On."

Brad crooked his free arm, flexing a muscle significant enough to show through the layers of his shirt and sweater. "Never. I'll rescue you, girl. I'll sling you over my shoulder atop the backpack and carry you out, like any mountain man worth his salt." Everyone cheered.

Brad made one last in-out movement of his clenched fist, then leaned back, smiling with contentment. He couldn't take his eyes off Lili. She gleamed like one of the water-polished stones in the rivers along the trail. She was having such a good time. He'd almost forgotten what a great sense of humor she had, which included the ability to poke fun at herself. It had drawn them all in; the whole group was charmed by her open confession of "chronic cowardice" and "couch potato-itis." He wondered if they saw through the facade of wispy fragility to the core of strength that ran through her. Solid steel. He'd bet his life on it. She had set one goal after another and met them. And talk about odds! She should be so damned proud of herself. He found his own pride in her spilling over, and he had to mentally shake himself free of the sense of bonding. What in the world was going on? Why, despite all intentions, was he unable to keep his emotions disentangled?

Could he be falling in love with her? The old head-over-heels variety he'd never believed in? Or maybe—was it possible?—he'd been in love with her all along, since that one magic night that had burned itself into his memory and refused to be erased for years? Or more likely, *refused* to be erased, period. God knows, it had sprung to life in full detail the first night he'd seen her in Te Anau. Lili, Lili. He ran his hand across her shoulder and cupped the back of her neck. The smile she sent him created havoc with his peace of mind. Or, more specifically, with his peace of body. His need to stay separate, to avoid taking her in his arms, was close to being obliterated, completely disposed of. Then what?

They were lulled into a temporary somnolence by the heavy meal they both ate, combined with the aftereffects of an eleven-mile walk, a half-hour slide show and an hour of sitting around the fire visiting. By nine, when they did go outside for a breath of air, they were halted in their tracks by a sheet of rain.

"Good Lord!" Lili gasped. "I didn't even hear it coming down."

"Too much noise inside. Damn. And I had such great plans for a nice evening walk."

"Hey. We have a mountain to climb tomorrow."

"But that's tomorrow. A long way off. Tonight has a lifetime of its own." His head was bent toward her upturned face; his eyes, dark secrets in the muted light. His height and muscular frame made Lili's five feet eight inches feel small and extravagantly feminine. He outlined the curve of her cheek with one finger. "You've grown from a very beautiful girl into a very beautiful woman. I wish..." His eyes smoldered in a face shadowed with doubts and unresolved pathos.

"What? What do you wish?"

"That we could say to hell with it. Take the moment and worry about it later. That we were capable of being shallow people with no concern for consequence." Pressures were building between them, as powerful as the pounding rain that imprisoned them on the small porch.

She stood rooted in place, immobilized, incapable of moving away or of heeding the maddened chatter of her mind: "Lili, no. You can't give in to this. You'll jeopardize every part of your life. Run, back off, say no. Now, before it's too late!" It was no use. His dark stare burned into her, causing tingling currents to race through her. His word ricocheted inside her brain, raising havoc with her senses. Could this really be happening, or was it just another of those middle-of-the-night fantasies she'd had for so many years?

He'd always had an animal magnetism that was overwhelming. And now, the combination of his closeness, the strength of the hands holding her shoulders and those incredible eyes searing their way into her soul was disintegrating eleven years of painfully built defenses against the vivid memory of that one night of passion—the only night of passion in her life. How could she quell her raging emotions? How to remember that this wasn't a game, something she could play for five days, then fold up and put away? This was a slice of life larger than life. A slice that could cut away her heart and leave her empty. She had to stop it, but how? Where was the iron-spined pigheadedness her mother said she had? Mush. All mush. Unfamiliar responses were building. A hot flush crept over her skin, a burning hunger to reach out for him, to touch, to hold, to fold herself into his hard masculinity. *Oh, please,* she sent a silent plea to her hard-trekking feet, *walk away!* Instead, they stayed planted like tree trunks.

Brad wrapped her in his arms and buried his face in her hair. "Lord, you smell good. I just need to hold you, to know you're here. I thought about you, worried about you...." He touched his cheek to hers. "We haven't talked about that night, all those years ago, but it haunted me for a very long time."

She stiffened. This was truly dangerous ground, ground she had no intention of treading. *That night.* The night Donny was conceived and her world changed forever. "Brad, please. It's better left alone."

"No, I disagree. I felt so rotten about what happened, Lili. I was a twenty-two-year-old man, and I took advantage of a seventeen-year-old girl. I should have been horsewhipped."

She rested her head on his chest, unable to bear its weight on her neck. "You didn't mean it to happen. I knew that. I was so grateful to you for taking me to the senior prom when I didn't have a date.''

"I hope you didn't give in to me out of gratitude!"

"Of course not. You know that wasn't the way it was. And I didn't 'give in to you,' as you so gallantly put it. I led you on. I wanted you." It was gushing out, unstoppable, a confession that needed to be made. She had no idea he'd felt guilty, and it *wasn't* he who'd done the initiating. She lifted her head to look at him. "Brad, I had such a crush on you. Since that first day I met you, when you barged into Marcy's room and invited us to play tennis."

"Really?"

"Really." She grimaced. "This isn't real good for the ego, but fair is fair. You stirred up feelings I never knew I had, and I did everything I knew to egg you on." She gave a small, self-deprecating shrug. "Which, I admit, wasn't much."

The tiniest trace of a smile curved his lips, then vanished. "Yeah. I have to admit, the way you came on that night, it was a real shocker to find out you were a—" He stopped, flustered.

"A virgin."

"Yes. Lili, if I'd known . . ." He stepped back and hit the side of the building with the flat of his hand. "Hell, it shouldn't have made any difference. My little sister's friend, for crying out loud. What an ass."

Lili laid her hand on his arm, deeply moved by his remorse. "Brad, don't. It was a long time ago."

"I worried about you for months."

"I appreciated your calls to see that I was okay."

"Well, I knew I hadn't used anything, and you obviously wouldn't have known how." He turned back to her and put his arms around her. "It's years too late, but I want to apologize. To let you know how sorry I was." He looked down at her, his face creased with sincerity. "If I hadn't been all but engaged, Lili, I'd have been very serious about you. I want you to know that. I'd never in my life, without exception, wanted anyone that much. And it took a long, long time to set it aside.''

''But you had to.''

''Of course. There was no alternative.''

Everything in Lili was in turmoil—her heart, her stomach, her brain. To know that he'd cared, that he'd carried the memory of that night around, too. Maybe not for as long; certainly without the other, overwhelming, factors. But he'd carried it. How she loved him still! Her fingers crept up to touch his cheek, to stray over to the edge of his mouth. ''I loved you so much.''

''Lili. God, Lili . . .'' He cupped her face in his hands, captivating her in his hypnotic gaze. Lili was falling into the deep-sea-blue eyes, drowning in them, twirling, spinning, dissolving. The wonderful face came closer, the tantalizing lips opened slightly. This was it, the pot at the end of the rainbow, the ninth cloud, the seventh stratum of heaven. All, everything, more.

Brad, his vows of singleness forgotten, bent to her, overcome by a need so demanding that it canceled all others. She was so beautiful, so sweet, so desirable. The memories of that long-ago night flooded his mind, engulfing him.

She raised her face, pushing to her toes to hasten the touch of mouth on mouth, then froze. Her whole body stiffened. ''No!''

''What?'' He stared at her as if she'd gone mad.

''We can't. My God, we must be crazy!''

''Lili, what the hell?''

She pushed away frantically, suddenly so frightened she was close to hysteria. Memories flooded her mind, too, but memories of a far different nature. ''We have to stop. Have to. Oh, God, I can't. I can't go through this again. Not the same thing again!'' With that she tore herself loose, turned away from him and, without a backward glance, dashed down the porch and up the stairs leading to the dorms, leaving Brad feeling, both physically and emotionally, like a casualty of battle. A battle he'd lost.

He stood outside for a long time, hidden from the view of the other hikers, who had begun to filter out of the main building to get to their beds before the ten-fifteen lights-out. His mind was a disaster area. What the devil had happened, anyway? Of course, the whole thing was foolish, letting themselves get so carried away when they'd both sworn not to. It wasn't that he blamed her for stopping. Some faint glimmer of reason must have got to her, after bypassing him entirely. But what she'd said didn't make any sense. Couldn't go through it again? The same thing again? What was that all about?

In a state of deep confusion—and frustration—he headed into the men's dorm, grateful to see the quick flicker of light from Ed's flashlight to guide him to his bunk.

Lili awoke the next morning with a hangover—an emotional hangover, which was worse than anything alcohol could produce. Her head ached and her body was weighted with unresolved anxiety. How could she face Brad? What would she say? Sleep had eluded her for hours, and when it had come, it had been no help. Anything but. It had enveloped her in a dream of erotic sensation. Brad's hands on her breasts, his fingers probing the center of her desire, driving her wild. But the dream was unencumbered by the straitjackets of reality, and it proceeded to the conclusion denied her in the waking hours, arching her body and shaking her awake. She had lain there, stiff with embarrassment, her skin damp and chilled, listening for sounds of wakefulness from the adjoining bunks. And the dream had eased nothing; only further titillated senses still burning with frustration.

As she lay there, she became aware of the pelting rain against the roof. The storm hadn't passed. She was actually going to have to go out there, climb that impossible trail on that torturous mountain, in the rain! If anything could add a full portion of dread to the already heavy load of angst, that was it! She reached to the floor to retrieve her flash-

light, then scooted under the covers to check her watch.
Five-thirty. Damn. If only she could slip back to sleep for
another hour. But the habit of early rising was too well in-
grained. As she lay there, she realized she was almost ill with
homesickness. How she longed to be back in that little house
in Dorchester, getting dressed for work, preparing her son's
lunch, looking forward to the short time they'd have together before she had to dash for the office.

She still had two weeks to spend in New Zealand before
she went home; two weeks that had sounded like a sojourn
in paradise during their planning. But now? Complications
twisted all the connecting wires of home, vacation, reality,
fantasy, wisdom, desire. When Brad took her in his arms
last night she'd entered a prison whose doors would never
open to let her out. A prison of love, of yearning, of need
so powerful it held the threat of driving all reason from her
mind.

How could she stand it? How could she say goodbye to
him in Milford Sound, knowing she'd never see him again,
knowing she couldn't *allow* herself to see him again! Or
could she? The memory of the conversation with Gillian set
a new, tantalizing series of possibilities in motion. What if
she *did* get together with him at home? Met him somewhere between Hartford and Boston. Some nice hotel,
where they could have a private room with a lock on the
door, where they could talk, completely undisturbed. She
could see it in her mind: the two of them, calm and steady.
Reasonable. She had several weeks to compose her story, to
couch it in the best possible terms, to rehearse its presenta-
tion. The truth. Fairly simple, if it was just laid out, bare of
garnishment. You are the father of my son. Just like that.
But the peaceful, artfully arranged picture in her mind, exploded as Brad blew up, shooting bits and pieces of himself
against the four walls, destroying her in the blast.

Lili pulled the covers over her head in a futile effort to
hide out—from the day, the rain, the mountain and the
damnable unalterable facts of her past that looked irre-

deemable in the future. He would never understand. Not in a million years.

The spirits of the trampers were not so ebullient this morning as they prepared to brave the unwelcoming out-of-doors. The temperature had dropped, so it was not only wet but cold. Shorts and sleeveless shirts had given way to long johns, sweaters, slacks and slickers. The prevailing mood was damp even before the first venture outside.

Lili and Brad greeted each other warily, moving around each other as though one brush might ignite an explosion. They ate halfheartedly and stared at their plates, their solemnity infecting their companions, whose sporadic conversation dropped to a muted decibel. When excuses for procrastination ran out, they left the shelter of Pompolona, slickers on, backpacks covered with plastic sheeting. Even the raucous kea birds—who had dictated the necessity of putting everything, smelly boots and all, inside—were gone to shelter.

Traversing the suspension bridge that crossed an avalanche-blasted creek was even more precarious in the driving rain. The width prevented a firm grip on both sides at once, and it was almost impossible to make the crossing clinging to one side, so Lili grabbed first one cable, then the other in a futile effort to achieve a sense of stability. When Brad joined her at the other end, he touched her arm and asked, "You okay?"

She nodded. "Just a little shaky."

"Long walk yesterday. Your legs may be wobbly for a while." Their look exchanged the unspoken qualification, "Among other things."

There was no opportunity for talk as the trail narrowed and grew steadily steeper. Water poured across the track, making some of the sections slippery and hazardous. Brad stepped out in front and told Lili, "Grab onto my jacket, put your feet in my footprints, and don't look down!"

The path leveled and opened on to a lovely plateau where the trees were draped with lichen. Relief, was temporary, however, and they were soon headed sharply upward, feet testing for safe steps, lungs straining to adjust to the increased quest for air. Her legs were still tired from the previous day's exertion, her mind weakened by the previous night's trauma. And the rain, relentless in its onslaught, made the climb a fearsome feat. Even so, Lili was glad of both the exertion and the downpour, because it canceled any possibility of talk. She certainly did not want to discuss last night with Brad. Not yet. Somehow she had to arrange the events into some semblance of order so she could justify, or attempt to justify, her bizarre behavior.

What had she said? She couldn't remember, exactly. But she was afraid she'd said more than she should have. It could have been a repeat performance. If she hadn't been seized by fear, there'd have been no leashing her desire. As for Brad? He had seemed transported, too, into that realm where reason was a stranger. His effect on her was lethal. Never, in any of the dating she'd done since that one night with Brad, had she had any difficulty saying no. But, even given her lack of control, it was perfectly reasonable that she'd finally come to her senses. What was not perfectly reasonable was her panic and headlong flight from the scene. He must think she was crazy.

Just as Lili had decided she was about to breathe her last, the vista disclosed a beautiful lake and, more beautiful still, a rest hut. "Oh, boy, a place to sit out of the rain." Lili's steps quickened. Once under the shelter of the roof, she peeled off her parka. "This thing may keep the rain out, but it also keeps the sweat in. I've got to get this sweater off."

"Be sure to put it right on top of your pack. It could be cold as all hell at the top of the pass," Brad said.

"Cold as all hell. Isn't that an oxymoron?"

"I guess it is, at that." They were both fishing for banalities to gulf the strain between them.

"Actually, I think this whole hike may qualify as an oxymoron. Here we are, doing the healthy outdoor bit, and after today, we'll probably die of pneumonia."

"This is no time to be pessimistic," Brad protested.

"Now you're asking me to go against my basic nature."

"Not go against it, just rise above it."

"Wait until we get to the top of the pass, and I'll have a more secure sense of survival so I can figure it's worth the trouble."

Brad laughed. "You'll make it. You're a lot tougher than you give yourself credit for. Just one foot in front of the other, that's all it takes. Think of yourself as an early pioneer—one of the women out to settle the West, heading for Donner Pass."

"Wasn't that where they ate each other?" Lili shuddered. "If everyone were like me, the entire population would still be huddled together on the East Coast. I do believe that in this entire body is not one single droplet of pioneer blood."

He sat beside her and took her hand in his. She stiffened, then let it stay. "As long as your blood is healthy and red, that's all that matters to me."

"Huh. Be better, where you're concerned, if it were healthy and blue."

"Lili, come on. Surely you don't believe I give a damn about that crap."

She stared out over the expanse of the lake, its surface alive with rebounding raindrops. Lake Mintaro. Quintin Mackinnon had called it Lake Beautiful. Jonathan had told her to keep an eye out, that this was a refuge for waterfowl, but any chance at seeing them was obliterated by the storm. She glanced at Brad, wondering how she'd managed to veer so close to a subject that, to her, was deadly serious. "I'm not sure. However, I *am* sure it isn't the time to discuss it. We still have most of a mountain to climb." She stared dolefully at the wall of water that faced them, then turned around to survey the hut. "Where is everyone?"

"I'm afraid most of them are ahead of us, although—" he squinted to see through the plummeting rain "—here comes someone."

Jan Crater, a young social worker from Rhode Island, and her friend Gale, a veterinarian, made for the shelter. "Oh, wow!" Jan shook herself, scattering water like a dog. "Is it nice to be out of that!" She smiled at Brad and Lili, obviously glad to see other humans. "Are any of us having fun yet?"

Brad grinned sympathetically. "How're your feet?"

"Demolished, toe to heel." Jan had made the mistake of borrowing boots for the hike, and after the first full day on the trail, every inch of her feet was covered with moleskin. "That was the most expensive saving I ever made."

"Not buying your own boots?"

"You've got it." Jan helped Gale take off her backpack. "Wish I'd brought knee pads. I have a feeling that's going to be the method of travel for the last leg of this mother."

Gale started to take off her slicker, then stopped and asked, "Is there a john here?"

"Yes." Brad motioned to one side. "Right out there. You can just see the building."

"Good, be right back."

"Lili, are you ready to get back on the trail?"

She nodded reluctantly. "I guess. You're being an awfully good sport to stick with me. I'm sure you'd like to be doing this at a much faster clip."

He hoisted her pack and held it ready. "Nope. Your pace is just fine." She put on the backpack and turned to face him just in time to catch his sardonic expression and the rise of one eyebrow as he said, "Most of the time."

So, she thought as they said goodbye to Jan and, heads lowered, braved the rain once more, he's been thinking about last night, too. Probably waiting for a good time to bring it up, ask what the hell happened. Oh, Lili. You are, as George Bush would put it, in deep doo-doo.

What followed was a trail of endurance. The zigzags of the trail grew sharper and steeper, and Lili felt more and more like sitting in the middle of the rocky, unforgiving track and bursting into tears. Brad stayed right with her, giving her a hand up some of the tough sections, offering words of encouragement. Lili refused to allow herself a single word of complaint. Though she was tired and wet and each downward glance sent shivers of fear through her, she was determined to see this to the end without one moan, groan or suffering sigh. Maybe she'd never win a prize for being Jock of the Month, but she could take a shot at the "most improvement" category. After all, for a woman who considered an elevator the natural way to get from one level to the next, this was a major leap.

Then the rain slackened and stopped, all within a span of minutes, as though the Great God of Harried Hikers decided enough was enough and turned off the spigot. Lili, lifting her face to the suddenly benevolent sky, yelled, "Hallelujah! And many thanks for large, gigantic, top-of-the-line favors!"

Brad, who was walking ahead of her to check for tricky spots where she might need help, turned and grinned down at her. "Want some more good news?"

"Oh, yes."

"We're almost at the top. One more little hump and we've got it knocked."

When they emerged at the top of the pass, where the memorial cairn stood its stolid watch, several groups of hikers were clustered together, shedding rain gear and chatting enthusiastically about their feat. Gillian spotted them and yelled, "Lili, congratulations! You did it!"

Everyone there laughed and gave her a round of applause, to which she bowed in a grand manner. "Nothing to it, nothing at all. A simple little stroll up a ninety-degree mountain. I could do it in my sleep. I'd *prefer* to do it in my sleep!" She wanted to hug them all to her, to share the exuberance of the moment, but she settled, more than satisfied, for a hug from Brad.

"How's it feel, tiger? Pretty special?"

"*Very* special." Lili, who had been too overwhelmed by the relief of attaining the summit and the pleasure of the welcome given her to take full note of her surroundings, suddenly became aware of the view being disclosed by the opening clouds. "Oh, Brad. Just look! Isn't it magnificent?"

Brad stepped behind Lili, placing his hands on her shoulders, nestling his chin on top of her head. "Wow." Words failed him. The skies were swiftly clearing, and the scene they revealed precluded paltry verbal description. An astonishing panorama encompassed the view: Mount Hart, Mount Mackenzie, Elizabeth Glacier, Staircase Gully. Mount Pillans, Green Valley, Dumpling Hill, Mount Elliot, the Jervois Glacier, Mount Wilmot and Mount Balloon. The sweep and majesty of these glacial giants begged the rhapsodizing of poets. And down the steep rock-faces tumbled hundreds of waterfalls—roaring rivulets of water that were runoffs of the storm just past.

"It's worth it," Lili commented with a sigh.

"What, the climb?"

"Yes. And the rain. We'd have missed seeing the waterfalls if it hadn't been for the rain." The exhaustion of the past hours drained away, leaving only the exhilaration of this splendor and the thrill of conquest. Who would have dreamed, halfway up that torturous path, that this magnificence awaited? Who could have hoped for the rain to stop and the heavens to open to reveal the munificence before them? Lili leaned against Brad's solid chest, drinking it all in with wonder and satisfaction.

"You know, Lili—" Brad's hands tightened on her shoulders "—we'll never lose it. This moment."

Lili's heart was so full that it threatened, like the waterfalls, to overflow. A surplus of happiness lightened her head and made her body buoyant. Taking a deep, breath of what had to be the cleanest air in the world, she borrowed one of Donny's favorite words: "Awesome."

Chapter Six

"Dear heaven," Lili gasped, "look at Ed and Josie! What in the world are they doing, trying to kill themselves?"

The English couple was seated on a rock that hung over what appeared to Lili to be the edge of eternity. Their silhouettes were etched against the cloud-dotted blue sky, and their feet dangled above a drop that would shatter a mountain. Farther along the bluff, Gillian stood, focusing a camera at the grinning pair. "Tip your faces this way to get the sun. That's it! Smile!" *Click.* "Okay, one more for insurance!"

"I hope they have more insurance than that," Lili muttered.

"What a picture that will make," Brad enthused. "Come on, Lili, let's get someone to take a shot of us sitting there."

"Are you kidding? Nobody without wings should be on that perch, and I'm neither bird nor angel!" She squinted at them in disbelief. "Why would anyone want to do such a crazy thing?"

"That's the twelve-second drop I told you about."

Lili stepped out of his embrace and regarded him with skepticism. "Okay, I'll bite. Twelve seconds to where? The next world?"

He laughed, shaking his head. "Nope. If you'll glance over the side, you can spot our next hut. From that rock straight down, it is reputed to take twelve seconds to get there. If one chooses to do it by trail, it's three to five hours, depending on the rate of descent."

Lili leaned down to get her sweater out of her backpack, which lay on the ground beside them. "If they're pushing the twelve-second route, there must be an acute food shortage at Quintin Hut. Besides, I'll take any bets that no one can give firsthand testimony to the time it takes to make the drop."

"I can't argue that point."

"How high are we, anyway?"

"Close to thirty-nine hundred feet. You've come up about twenty-seven hundred feet today."

"I feel every inch of it. And how far is it, that twelve-second drop to Quintin Hut?"

Brad frowned, calculating. "Around nineteen hundred, more or less."

Lili sighed and shook her head. "Strange breed."

"Who?"

"Mountain climbers."

"Careful, love. After this hike, everyone will assume you're one of them."

"Huh!"

Glynne strolled over to them, camera in hand. "As long as I have my photographer's eye adjusted, how about you two sitting on the rock?" Lili's head moved rapidly back and forth. "N.F.W."

"What? What does that mean?"

Her face colored, and she dove into the sweater to hide her embarrassment. "Nothing. Forget it. It just slipped out."

"N.F.W.?" Glynne looked at Brad, mirroring the other man's puzzled expression. Then they both burst out laughing together. "Why, Lili Jamison! What would your mother say?" Brad teased.

"She would say," Lili replied, pushing her arms into the warmth of the wool garment, "to stay away from the edges of cliffs!"

"Ah, Lili." Brad's beautiful pearly-white teeth glinted in the newly emerged sunlight, making his handsome countenance irresistible. "Be a sport. Just think, you can have a blowup of the picture to put on the wall, and years from now you'll still be pointing to it with pride. How many people do you know who have photos of themselves on the twelve-second drop at the top of Mackinnon Pass?"

"Dead women don't point fingers." But despite her very real, very active dread, she gave in to the beguiling persuasion of the man of her dreams, who, in all fairness, could probably talk any woman on the face of the earth—even steep, jutting peaks of it—into anything. Every step toward the precarious placed rock bench was taken with extreme trepidation. "I've heard of seating in the outer lobby. This has to be seating in the outer sphere."

"Stop mumbling, love. If you fall, I promise to go with you," Brad said.

"Oh, thanks. What's the logic of that? Two splats are better than one?" Lili could have sworn she held her breath through the entire picture-taking process, as well as the timidly executed ascent back up to the bluff. "I don't believe I did that," she muttered as they readjusted their packs for the next leg of the hike.

"Honey," Brad said, beaming at her, his dancing gaze offering congratulations, "you have more damn guts than any woman I ever knew."

"Oh, Brad, don't get carried away. I was scared sense-less! Obviously, or I wouldn't have done it."

"That's what I mean. It's easy to do things if you're not scared. It takes real guts to do them when you are. I'm proud of you, girl. Now, I only want one more agreement before we hit the trail."

"There's more?" She screwed up her face, waiting for the suggestion that they ride one of the waterfalls down the side of the mountain to Quintin Hut. "Okay, shoot."

"If'n ah cain't make it out, will y'all carry *me* on *your* back, 'longside your pack—seein's how you've turned out to be such a true 'n' mighty mountain woman?" Brad managed, with some mysterious shifting of his body, to make himself appear bent and crabbed and sickly—no small feat, given his impressive proportions. Lili laughed aloud and readily agreed to the bargain. After all, at that moment she was sure she could do anything.

It was another mile to the lunch hut, where the late-noon meal was eaten amid hoots of gaiety and far more than a modicum of bragging. Everyone there felt, as her mother would say, "full of himself," including Lili. She had done it! She had climbed the mountain to Mackinnon Pass, and in a rainstorm, yet! She looked over at Brad, whose head was thrown back in laughter at one of the many trail stories that were being told and retold, with growing embellish-ment. He was still, without doubt, the most beautiful male she'd ever seen. Her girlhood assessment held. And, more important, his beauty invaded heart and mind, as well. She loved him so much she was afraid she'd pop out all over in hives the shape of hearts. *And what am I to do about it?* she asked herself.

As she watched him, a picture of her son leaped to mind. Donny would look just like him! Not only look like him, but *be* like him. Homesickness shot through her so sharply she gasped. Brad turned to her immediately.

"Lili? What's wrong?"

She shook her head, trying to smile reassuringly. "Nothing. Really. It's just... Well, I was watching you laugh, and it reminded me of Donny. It hit me pretty hard. I really miss him. I can't imagine how I thought I could be gone for such a long time without getting terribly homesick. I haven't thought of it much for the last few days, because..." She looked at Brad and colored. "Well," she said with a laugh, "there's been so much going on."

He leaned forward, full of interest. "Tell me about him. Donny."

Oh, I'd like to, she thought. *Tell you every little detail— how he looks, thinks, acts. All the gestures and mannerisms that are absolute replicas of yours. But then you'd know. And I have to be very, very certain that it's safe before I allow that to happen.* Even the possibility of telling him was still so new that it jarred her to wariness. How much could she safely reveal? Some, certainly. Bits and pieces of the whole that made up that terrific little boy.

"Well, for one thing, as I watched you laughing, it reminded me of him because he does the same thing you do. He gets so tickled about something he looks like he's going to fall right off his chair. In fact—" she grinned, remembering "—sometimes he does."

"Good sense of humor. I like that."

She nodded. He'd like everything about her son. *Their* son. Well, with the possible exception of his occasional lapses into obdurate bullheadedness. Which, she feared, he inherited from her. "Oh, yes, a wonderful sense of humor. Donny really enjoys life. It's such a blessing, especially when I see how negative and unhappy so many kids are today. He seems, well, like he's absolutely sure someone's going to show up at any minute with a wonderful present for him." She laughed. "Now that's a pretty dippy description, wouldn't you say?"

"No, I wouldn't. Just surprising."

"Oh?"

"It's funny, but that reminds me of myself as a kid. That's just how I always felt. Exactly. Mom told me once she and Dad used to worry about me, about how well I'd weather my first real setback." He studied the tips of his fingers, which he was pressing together, another gesture Lili noted with amazement. Donny did the same thing when deep in thought! "I took my share of drubbings and survived them all right. Until the divorce, anyway."

Lili's high-flying mood took a sharp dive. The divorce. It was like the duck coming down, igniting an instant reaction of gloom in Brad. How he hated having failed at his marriage! She felt as though a gauze cover had been drawn over the sunny afternoon. Esther was right here on the track with them, casting a shadow larger than any rain cloud. Was he really free of her, or was that impossible? The question increased the girth of the Caution sign that was positioned so prominently in her mind.

Brad dropped his hands on his knees with a slap. "But let's skip that. I want to hear more about Donny." He frowned. "He's what? Eight?"

"Ele—*Eight!* Yes, that's right." Her heart jumped to a rapid beat. Oh, Lord, that was close. Had he noticed?

Brad was too far into his next thought to have caught her slipup. "I advise you to switch that to Don within a few years. Don't saddle him with a little-boy nickname while he's trying to become a man. Embarrasses the hell out of a kid."

"That's a good idea. I hadn't thought of it. We'll have to be careful, Mom and I, to avoid the pitfalls of bringing up a boy in a female household."

Brad's gaze swung to her, almost pinning her in midsentence. "I don't think that should continue much longer."

"What?"

"The female household."

Lili's eyes darted around as her mind raced. She felt as though she were in the middle of a soap opera. A badly written soap opera, in which the dialogue veered wildly this way and that in a constant attempt to hide facts. The few soaps she'd seen had driven her crazy. She used to say to her mother, "Why don't those people just sit down and tell each other what's going on? It would save all of them so much trouble!" And here she was, in full-color real life, mired in a similar subterfuge.

Brad seemed to be backing away, ever so cautiously, from his adamant stand about staying uninvolved. Gillian's comments about a few well-timed temptations leaped to mind. Was it possible, if she really set out to do it, that she could make him forget vows of singleness entirely? Suddenly there were carrots dangling in her imagination, carrots so lush that any rabbit in its right mind would leap ten feet straight up out of its hole to take a stab at them. And yet she was burrowing deeper and deeper. Well, one thing was certain: she couldn't drop the truth on him now, in this crowded lunch hut on the side of Balloon Mountain, so she may as well continue her feinting and dodging.

"Yes, I suppose you're right. Do you suggest I take out an ad for a male boarder?"

Brad's mouth set as a rush of impatience shot through him. That wasn't exactly what he had in mind. But what the hell *did* he have in mind? He retracted his body, straightening, and moving back in his seat. He wasn't used to this indecision, this vacillation. It was so out of the norm that he had no idea how to cope with it. He'd come to New Zealand to heal, and he felt as though he were opening new wounds for which the woman seated across from him had the only salve. Hell. He couldn't afford this. He wasn't ready.

Glynne and Jonathan had donned their packs and were helping Gillian on with hers. Gillian called out, "Hey, you two, better get a move on. It's a long way yet to the next stop, and we'll want to go see Sutherland Falls when we get there."

Lili, glad of a chance to short-circuit the conversation, jumped up. "She's right. I can't wait to see those falls!"

Actually, the idea of completing the day's hike and turning right around to tack on another hour's walk was appalling, but it made a good exit line.

After a stop at the toilet, where Lili stripped off the long underwear she'd donned that morning, they headed down a path that offered a beautiful view of several small mountain lakes, or tarns. The sun, dispensing warmth as it regained its dominance of the afternoon sky, cast a myriad of stunning beams through the remaining clouds. Dramatic shadows turned the Clinton Valley, far below, into a stage set worthy of a play to be acted out by the gods.

As Brad strode along beside Lili, his mind kept turning over the dilemma building between them. Diverting his mind from the impact she was having on him, he concentrated on Lili. There was a definite mystery in her attitude. Why was she so persistently skittish about any reference to a future that might link her with any man? She was single and—quite the opposite of what he'd assumed—not tied to her late husband by any bonds of affection. A child, particularly one who was from all accounts well adjusted and happy, shouldn't present a huge barrier to a new relationship. And where the two of them were concerned, she had by her own admission, been in love with him once. He didn't think he was misreading her attraction to him now. But the moment his own defenses had begun to crumble last night, she had bolted like a frightened deer.

Come to think of it, what about last night? He still wanted to ask her what she'd meant. Yes, Lili was a walking container of contradictions. He'd better be extra careful—he loved a challenge. He glanced over at her. *Be honest, Bradford. She's more than a challenge. She's been there, tucked away in your memory, all these years. And the woman she's grown into is even more beguiling than the girl you remember. Far more.* He had a lot of questions he wanted to ask. But not now. They had a long, difficult hike ahead of them still—far more difficult, according to a couple who had done the track before, than he'd wanted to tell

Lili. Why dampen her euphoria at having conquered the tough climb with news about how hard the descent would be? In any case, heavy discussions must wait until later, when they could relax and devote their attention to the subject. He frowned. But time was running out, and he was finding the prospect of saying goodbye to Lili at the end of the trail very difficult. Very difficult indeed.

Three hours later, Lili was struggling to put one foot in front of the other. The trail led steadily downward, often steep and always rocky, and the rocks were still slippery from the seeping remnants of the rain runoff. Gillian, just ahead of them, had taken a nasty fall, from which luckily she had recovered with nothing more than a scraped knee. But it had made Lili even more tentative in her steps. Her feet felt like sponges at the end of two long, wobbly strands of cooked spaghetti. In fact, she felt cooked all over. The sun, once it had gotten rid of the rain and the clouds, had decided to show off its heat-giving powers, and she was bathed in sweat. She felt about as ladylike as a member of Hell's Angels on a nonstop cross-country ride.

"This is February," she muttered. "I hate to think what it's like in midsummer."

To her chagrin, Brad was close enough behind her to overhear her mumblings. "This *is* midsummer."

"Oh, yeah. I forgot. Everything's upside down."

"How're you doing?" His voice was coated with concern. She wanted to hit him over the head with her boot—if it would ever come off her foot. It was nothing personal. She wanted to hit everyone over the head.

"Fine. Great. No prob." *Liar, liar, house on fire! Where, out of the depths of some long-lost memory cells, had that come from?*

"Would you like me to carry some of the stuff in your pack?"

It was the third time he'd made the offer. He was so kind she'd like to belt him with both boots. She'd also like him to carry the whole pack, but she couldn't imagine how she'd get it off her shoulders. She was absolutely sure it had sunk into her flesh and melded to her, a permanent load to be carried through life. Besides, she had to think of her pride. It had to be around here somewhere, at least a fragment; some tiny vestige that was salvageable in case she survived this. She fervently hoped Brad couldn't read minds. Hers was a swimming sea of irritability, with nary a kindly thought anywhere for anything, with the possible exception of that shower and bunk at the end of the day's hike. If there *was* an end to the day's hike.

"No. Thanks anyway. I think the weight on my back is the only thing that's keeping me from pitching forward, like Gillian did. As a matter of fact, that's just what happened, isn't it? Glynne took her pack and she fell right on her face. Scary."

Brad shook his head, marveling at the dogged way she kept moving forward. He didn't know what was going on in her head, but she hadn't uttered one word of complaint. She must be dead tired; this wasn't an easy stretch, even for him, and he'd done some pretty strenuous hiking. In addition to the rocky, steep terrain, the heat obviously took its toll on her. Luckily, he'd packed a small towel, which he kept wetting to put over the back of her neck. It was important to keep the heat under control. He grimaced. He'd have to remember that the next time they were alone together in the cool of the night!

When at last Lili sighted the hut, she almost unleashed her tightly held emotions. It took real stamina to hold back the tears of relief. Had she ever been so tired? No. She was sure not. She stopped and turned to Brad. "I have to sneak in and get to the showers without running into anyone."

"Oh? Why?"

"I have a myth to maintain: Lili, the Humorous Though Hesitant Hiker. And there isn't a scrap of humor left in me. None. If anyone so much as says hello, I may bite."

"A bit testy, huh?"

"You've got it."

"Make a beeline for the showers. I'll cover for you."

"You—" she sighed "—are a real pal." With that, Lili took off at a snail's pace—the only one she had left—for the women's dorm, which was blessedly vacant. She dropped her pack on the bunk and sagged against its wooden frame for a moment before gathering enough energy to rummage through her bag for clean undies and evening garb. It took the last ounce of her strength to make it to the shower. But, oh, the effort was worth it! Never in all her life had a stream of hot, running water felt so good! She soaped everything, head to toe, washed off and soaped again, rubbing until her skin squeaked in protest and her scalp tingled in alarm.

When she was dressed and had applied a dab of lipstick and run a comb through her wet hair, she gingerly gathered her soggy garments from the hike and took them to the laundry room, where she threw them in a washer that was waiting for the load to be topped off, put in the detergent, and started their "bath." She could swear she heard her clothes sigh with pleasure. Later, when she was able, she'd come back and hang them up in the heated drying room. Right now, it was off to the bunk to collapse.

Brad caught her at the door to the dorm. He was radiant with cleanliness and good health. And vitality. Under the circumstances, she thought, that vitality was a tacky thing to display. "Good. You're ready."

"Ready?" An overwhelming sense of foreboding enveloped her. "For what?"

"For the walk to Sutherland Falls. There's a whole group out front waiting."

The urge to kill was new to her. "Brad, I can't. I mean, these legs have had it."

"Ah, Lili…" A warning sign shot up in her mind. Hadn't she heard that "Ah, Lili" before? And in just those dulcet tones? "You wouldn't want to miss the falls. It's the fourth-longest drop in the world. Almost two thousand feet!" At this point, she'd be willing to take a twelve-second alternate route.

Gillian poked her head around the corner of the hallway. "Lili, want some tea and cookies?"

"Oh, yes. Yes, I really do." She smiled weakly at Brad. "Tea and cookies. Doesn't that sound like heaven? I mean, if you're not hungry, don't feel obligated. Go on to the falls without me. I promise I won't be upset. It's just, I really *need* some tea and cookies!" She would have sunk to her knees in supplication, but she knew she'd never get up.

His smile never wavered. "That does sound good. I'll tell the others. I bet they'd be willing to take a tea break before going. Be right back!"

Lili stared after him in dumb horror. He was such a brilliant man, why couldn't he pick up the vibes? Was she going to have to come right out and refuse? Drop to the floor in a heap? She made her way, slowly, to Gillian. "Right now I can't stand him. He's all full of energy, which is obscene after today. He actually expects me to go see Sutherland Falls! On my own two feet, or what's left of them!"

Gillian's eyes rounded. "Oh, Lili. You wouldn't want to miss the falls!"

Lili leaned against the wall, defeated. It was a conspiracy of jocks. She could feel their presence, thousands of them, closing in on her, breathing up all the air, threatening her with suffocation. "Where's the tea?" Her voice sounded whiny; it was entitled.

Lili was sure that, in future years, when she looked back on this experience, she'd never be able to recall how she got her feet back into her boots, got those same sponge feet to move, one in front of the other in regular step progression, thirty minutes there to watch that damned torrent of water—as if she hadn't seen enough water—pound its way down the side of yet another mountain—as if she hadn't seen enough mountains. She felt definitely meanspirited. Altogether, nasty. But through it all, she maintained a cheerful demeanor and a winning smile. Phony to the core. She wondered if phoniness and falsehood were becoming epidemic in her. And would being a "good sport" on the outside while grousing and cursing her hardy companions on the inside fall into the same category as other forms of lying? It all seemed muddled, an impossible conundrum of values.

As she slogged along the damp trail, her semihumorous musings grew more serious. Lili was, in her innermost, true-self core, a straight arrow who honored truth and forthrightness and abhorred falsity in all its gradations, including the "little white" variety. In most ways, she'd adhered to her codes of behavior, but there were times when she sugarcoated the truth to make it more palatable, or sidestepped a frank answer to guard the feelings of the questioner. She'd never worried much about those small untruths before, never given them much thought. But now, as she watched Brad stride along in front of her, the larger question of truth versus fabrication loomed like a Balloon Mountain in her mind. The "Big Lie" sat, a rock monolith, in her conscience, begging exposure. She had thought, eleven years ago, that she was protecting him, his family, his wife-to-be. Had she been? Or was that lie, like most, grounded only in fear and self-interest? Fatigue, of a more virulent, vicious strain, crept through her, sapping her tiny reservoirs of strength. God, she was tired. Of so many things!

When they finally returned to Quintin Hut, she stumbled into the dorm and dropped her body on her bunk. There was a precious hour before dinner. Nothing and nobody was going to interfere with a nap. Not even that walking pitfall to womanhood with his "Ah, Lili." Just as she was sinking into blissful oblivion, she felt a hand on her shoulder, a hand that jiggled her.

"Lili?" The voice belonged to Gillian. The hand, too, she supposed. Her eyes wouldn't seem to open, so she couldn't be sure.

"Huh?"

"Want to go for a plane ride?"

"What?" Her eyelids, which had, seconds before, been immobilized, shot open. "A what?"

"A plane ride. There's a tiny little airstrip right alongside the hut, and the supply plane is here. The pilot is giving rides. Brad wants to know—"

"N.F.W." It was the only reply she could think of. And she was beyond shame.

Supper was served to a quieter bunch that night. Lili wasn't the only tired hiker. It had been an exhausting day to most, as well as exhilarating. Lili's Mackinnon Pass euphoria had dissolved, leaving a pall of uneasiness that bordered on depression. The realization that they were one day's hike from the end of the trail, and two days from the time when she and Brad would bid each other goodbye and go their separate ways, had seeped into her consciousness the moment she awakened from the nap.

Brad was the soul of solicitous concern. He hadn't realized how truly exhausted she was, or he'd never have pushed her to walk to the falls. "Do you feel any better after your nap?" He leaned close to her, feeling, illogically, as though he could transfer some of his more than ample energy to her by proximity.

"Yes. Some." She managed a smile of sorts. Even the corners of her mouth had trouble moving very far.

"I'm sorry you missed the plane ride. It was spectacular."

"Are you kidding? I saw that airstrip. It's the size of a suburban driveway. No plane can really take off and land on that."

Brad grinned. "He did, though. Really."

"Huh. How many times can he pull it off without falling over the end of the runway? And did you take good notice of the end of the runway? Talk about a twelve-second drop!"

Just then the guide came out of the kitchen and stood at the front of the room to make an announcement. "I know this offer won't appeal to any of you, you're such an obviously hardy lot." A groan greeted his observation. "But just on the off chance that there are any worn shoulders among you, the weather report for the morning is good, so the pilot is going to stay for the night. That means he can fly your backpacks out tomorrow, for a small fee. Any takers?"

Lili's hand flew up of its own volition, without waiting for a signal from the brain. It was followed by the hands of almost every person there, the exceptions being Glynne and two other men who appeared unscathed by the "stroll" so far. She glanced over at Brad. "What, you're going to put your pack on the plane? You astonish me!"

"I'm not entirely sure I won't need my back free, to sling you over." It was said in jest, but he really wasn't sure how well she would fare the next day. Her entire body had a list to it and showed no sign of straightening in the near future.

The guide wasn't quite finished. "Okay, have your packs out here by eight in the morning. Funny. Haven't had a group yet who've passed up that offer when it came along. Now, on top of that opportunity, if anyone feels unable to make the trek tomorrow, our pilot has room for a few passengers. You can think it over and let him know in the morning."

Brad's eyes shot to Lili's face to check her reaction to that offer. The idea of separating, for the last day on the trail, was terrible. "What think, Lili? Sound too good to pass?" He hoped she'd say no, but there was yes in her eyes.

Lili studied his face, asking herself how she could sacrifice a full day of his company, one of the two she had left, simply to save her life. No. She couldn't do it. "No, I'll walk out. By your side." She laughed weakly. "Or ride out over your shoulder."

"Atta way, Lili. You wouldn't want to miss doing the whole trek."

Like hell I wouldn't! Although the mental retort was instantaneous, she knew, through her aching denial, that he was right. This was a one-of-a-kind experience in every way, and she'd feel terrible later if she hadn't seen it to the bitter end. And at the moment that end looked pretty damned bitter. You can do it, she told herself. You can! You've never been a quitter, and you're not about to start now.

"Lili, are you through with your dinner?" Brad interrupted her thoughts." Could we take a short walk to get some of the evening air?" His hand went up. "I take it back. No walk. Amend that to a stand-around to get some evening air."

They took their dinnerware to the kitchen window, then walked—or in Lili's case, limped—outside. It was a gorgeous night, clear and star-strewn, with a half-moon rising in the sky. The air, intoxicating in its freshness, carried the special green-spiked scent of nature peculiar to high mountains, and the distant hoot of an owl lent an exotic aura to the scene. "It's unbelievably beautiful, isn't it? I've taken a lot of pictures, but I'm sure they won't capture it. How do you get the *feel* on film? I do hope the memory of it stays clear—that I never forget, as long as I live."

Brad put his arm around her shoulders and drew her near, unnerved by the attraction that was growing to dizzying proportions. He'd been so intent on savoring his freedom, letting no entanglements hamper his comings and goings. But Lili had come back into his life, and the mere thought of her leaving it again was becoming unbearable. "Lili, has it occurred to you that we might be around to remind each other? Does that possibility have any appeal?" She made no reply—a fact that formed knots of apprehension in his stomach. "What is it? Why are you so guarded about the idea of having a man in your life? Why should the possibility of something happening between us be unthinkable?"

She hunched her shoulders. "Brad, you laid out a few pretty formidable barriers of your own. I'm no masochist. I'm not about to throw myself at a man who says point-blank that he doesn't intend to get involved. And I'm not geared for a one-hike stand." Her try at a weak smile didn't alter the seriousness of his expression.

"I know what I said, and I meant it, at the time. But it must be obvious that *I'm* waffling. You have to admit we have a good time together. And . . . Well, am I kidding myself that this attraction is mutual?"

She walked away from him and sat on a wooden bench that looked out over the fading silhouettes of the mountains. "I've grown skeptical of dreams, Brad. And this has all the elements of a dream. Thrown together in an exotic place, sharing a unique experience. It's heady stuff. But I'm not sure it's the stuff reality is made of."

He sat beside her. "You used to be brimful of dreams. It was a quality that spilled out of you. What happened to them, Lili? Was the loss of your husband bad enough to erase them all? It seems hard to accept, especially when you tell me the marriage wasn't exactly made in heaven."

She shook her head. "It wasn't just that, it was . . ." Her voice trailed off.

"Tell me something. What did you mean the other night, when you ran away from me? You said you couldn't go through the same thing again. I mean, I know we'd both said all kinds of things about holding the line at friendship, but people change their minds every day, and we appeared to be very much in tune on that. To admit you were in love with me, and then bolt like that. 'The same thing again,' — what does that mean?"

Dear God, he had picked it up. Now how was she going to explain it? She was too damned tired to think straight, let alone inventively. Should she blurt it out, drop it like a meteor from the profusely starred sky, and see how big a crater it would make? Maybe she'd better drop a couple of trial stones first. "That just popped out, Brad. I wasn't sure where it came from myself, till I thought about it later. Then I remembered what it was like, all those years ago, after you and I made love."

She took a deep breath. She'd committed herself to at least a partial truth. Truth felt good, even in bits and pieces. "It was almost a full month before I knew whether I was pregnant or not." True. "My period was late, and I went through the tortures of the damned, trying to figure out what in God's name I'd do if I were. I'll never forget it." True. "Mom was so worried, she didn't know what was wrong with me for a couple of weeks, then, being the sensitive soul she is, she figured it out. She kept telling me I'd have to let you know, if I was pregnant. I kept telling her I couldn't, that you hadn't meant it to happen, that you were about to be married to a girl who was the right sort for you." Still true.

"Lili—"

"No, let me finish." How much could she say? Where must truth end? "Anyway, it was a real fast period of growing up. My childhood, or what tiny bit of it was left, vanished. Or maybe I mean my innocence. Don't say it. I don't mean I began to think of myself as a slut. I mean the kind of innocence that makes you feel invulnerable, the kind only the young have. From then on, consequence was always a part of my life." She stopped herself, tallying the cost of continuing, and finding it too high. "I know it was only a kiss—last night, I mean—but the attraction... Well, you're not wrong about its being there. So, that's what I meant. I was remembering that...month...of anguish, and it spooked me." Her nervous laugh sputtered a couple of times, then died.

"Lili, I'm so sorry." He covered her hand with his. "I knew you must be worried, but I was too young and self-absorbed to have any idea what you'd be going through." He hesitated. "To tell the truth, I don't suppose men ever do, really. It must be an awful feeling, to think you've lost control of your body."

"Yes." Tears came to her eyes, pushed up by painful memories. One night. *One night* had changed her life forever. And even though she wouldn't give up Donny for anything the world had to offer, the fear and anxiety and trauma of that period would never be diminished by time. Brad had put his finger on it. She'd lost control of her own body by that one misguided act. No wonder passion frightened her. In her experience, its cost was awesome. It had erased all her plans for her future. She looked at Brad—at his strong, finely honed face, his intelligent eyes that held such depths of concern, the strand of dark blond hair that perpetually broke loose to stray over his broad forehead, the determined set of his jaw. She looked and, in her mind, saw a smaller version of the same man: Donny. No wonder she loved him so much. And no wonder that love caused such fear!

"But you say your mother insisted you'd have to tell me." His forehead creased in perplexity. "Surely you *would* have?"

Everything in Lili stopped. Blood flow, heartbeat, breath. Her reflexes took over, and she answered the question with a question. "And how would you have felt, if I'd called you up and said, 'By the way, I'm pregnant'?" The question hung between them like a baited hook.

Brad leaned forward, elbows on his knees, hands clasped, studying the ground at his feet. His shoulders rose and fell twice, the prelude to an answer that was slow in forming. Finally, he looked at her and shook his head. "I'm not sure. Obviously, it would have thrown a significant monkey wrench in my plans. Not to mention Esther's." The toe of his moccasin etched a circle in the dirt. "I'm trying to recall what I thought about it then, but I don't remember taking the possibility all that seriously. After all, one night— it didn't seem too likely." The shoulders went up and down again. "But I'm sure I'd have done whatever was necessary."

A spark of anger flickered in her. "And what does that mean? You'd have offered to pay for the abortion?"

He sat up straight and stared. "Hell, no!" His body sagged a little as an expression of uncertainty came over his face. "At least, not unless that's what you insisted on." His hands spread. "How the devil do I second-guess this now, Lili? I'm trying to say what a twenty-two-year-old would have done, and it's all filtering through my thirty-three-year-old mind. There's a big difference, you know. Today, I'd fight like a tiger to save any child of mine. Then? I wish I could give you an honest answer, but—'' His head tilted to one side, and his eyebrows rose. ''Why are we going into all this, anyway? It's something that never happened.''

She laughed. And the sound of it fanned the anger inside her. What the hell was she laughing about? But her lips turned up in a silly smile of conciliation. The habits of a lifetime of holding firm: Don't make waves. Keep it all buttoned up, tamped down, swallowed and buried. The anguish, the anger, the bedeviling uncertainty that had followed her through eleven years. She leaned back, forcing her body into less rigid lines. ''Right. Why go into it?'' But she couldn't leave it quivering on the ground before her. ''In any case, I was right.''

''About what?''

''Not telling you.'' Her hand waved away any importance that held. ''*If*, of course, I had been pregnant.''

Brad's whole body stiffened, and his face followed suit. His voice was flat with suppressed fury. ''What the devil are you saying? You sure as hell wouldn't have been right! I can't believe you'd consider lying to me about something that important! It may have been your body that was involved, but what it might have held would have been half mine!''

''But—'' Lili was thrown off guard. She'd allowed the rise of anger to loosen her tongue, and now she didn't know how to remedy the situation. ''What could you have done, really? I mean,'' she said, groping, wildly, ''your wedding date was all but set, your life was planned.''

''We're talking about two different things. The central issue here is honesty—dealing openly with a mutual problem. That transcends plans and dates and all that stuff.''

''We're talking about a situation as it existed and how it could, or should, have been handled. And that always involves a lot of 'stuff.' ''

"Lili, come on. This situation never existed, so at best it's an exercise in conjecture. The core of it, the one thing that matters today as much as it mattered, or *would have* mattered then, is attitude. Honesty or dishonesty. Openness or concealment. To me, it's one of the most important issues in life."

Lili was floundering. How had this discussion taken such an undesirable twist? Somehow, she had to get it back on track. Back to "conjecture." "But if you try to make black or white, good or bad kinds of judgments, it's, well, it's too simple for real life. You *have* to put in the 'stuff.' That's part of being human. We were talking about something that might have happened, and all the things that went through my mind at the time. And frankly, I just didn't see how I could have told you. *If* it became an issue. You have to remember, I was very young."

"Of course, I remember. And having a baby to care for at that point would have shot hell out of your life. But I don't see how that affects telling me or not telling me."

She threw up her hands. "Because! You had a beautiful, fairy-book life all planned out, and I'd have been the bad witch, throwing everything into a muddle!"

"You must have read too many fairy tales as a kid."

"Probably. But this much is true—there weren't any good solutions!"

Brad leaned toward her, his face looking starched. "There were all kinds of possibilities."

"Oh?" Marriage, between the two of them?

"Esther and I might have taken the baby."

"Come on, Brad! Are you joking? You really think she'd have been willing to do that? You have to remember, this was long before she knew she couldn't have one of her own."

"Yeah, you're right." He had been caught up in the conundrum, and his brain, trained for problem solving, was hard at work. "But my parents undoubtedly would have offered to raise the child. I know how terrified you must

NO COST! NO OBLIGATION TO BUY!
NO PURCHASE NECESSARY!

PLAY "LUCKY 7"
AND GET AS MANY AS SIX FREE GIFTS...

HOW TO PLAY:

1. With a coin, carefully scratch off the silver box at the right. This makes you eligible to receive one or more free books, and possibly other gifts, depending on what is revealed beneath the scratch-off area.

2. You'll receive brand-new Silhouette Special Edition® novels. When you return this card, we'll send you the books and gifts you qualify for *absolutely free!*

3. If we don't hear from you, every month we'll send you 6 additional novels to read and enjoy. You can return them and owe nothing but if you decide to keep them, you'll pay only $2.92* per book, a saving of 33¢ each off the cover price. There is **no** extra charge for postage and handling. There are **no** hidden extras.

4. When you join the Silhouette Reader Service™, you'll get our subscribers'-only newsletter, as well as additional free gifts from time to time, just for being a subscriber.

5. You must be completely satisfied. You may cancel at any time simply by sending us a note or a shipping statement marked ''cancel'' or by returning any shipment to us at our cost.

This lovely Victorian pewter-finish miniature is perfect for displaying a treasured photograph—and it's yours absolutely free—when you accept our no-risk offer.

PLAY "LUCKY 7"

Just scratch off the silver box with a coin.
Then check below to see which gifts you get.

YES! I have scratched off the silver box. Please send me all the gifts for which I qualify. I understand I am under no obligation to purchase any books, as explained on the opposite page.

235 CIS ADES
(U-SIL-SE-10/91)

NAME

ADDRESS   APT.

CITY   STATE   ZIP

7	7	7	WORTH FOUR FREE BOOKS, FREE VICTORIAN PICTURE FRAME AND MYSTERY BONUS
cherries	cherries	cherries	WORTH FOUR FREE BOOKS AND MYSTERY BONUS
coin	coin	coin	WORTH FOUR FREE BOOKS
bell	bell	cherries	WORTH TWO FREE BOOKS

DETACH AND MAIL CARD TODAY

DETACH AND MAIL CARD TODAY

BUSINESS REPLY MAIL
FIRST CLASS MAIL   PERMIT NO. 717   BUFFALO, NY

POSTAGE WILL BE PAID BY ADDRESSEE

SILHOUETTE READER SERVICE
3010 WALDEN AVE
PO BOX 1867
BUFFALO NY 14240-9952

NO POSTAGE
NECESSARY
IF MAILED
IN THE
UNITED STATES

have been, because having that responsibility when you were so young and you and your mom were so hard up, it must have seemed overwhelming. But I can't imagine my folks letting the baby go anywhere else. And later, Esther and I—" He stopped and shook his head, a bemused grin on his face. "God, why are we doing this?" His expression eased instantly and he laughed aloud. "I can't believe we've just shot a big hunk of this gorgeous night arguing over something that never happened! That's not like me."

She felt drained, emptied like a water bottle at the end of a long trail. "I'm sure." Unwillingly, she met his gaze. "But it's like me. I do it all the time. What if? I did it endlessly, back then. Hours and hours of it."

His eyes softened with compassion. "It must have been hell." He touched her cheek with his fingers. "Of course, in all this, I didn't mention what I'd probably have done, after the shock wore off."

"And what's that?"

"Asked you to marry me."

It came too late, after too many other speculations, to do anything but widen the cracks in her heart. He'd have asked—reluctantly, feeling cornered and angry.

"Lucky you didn't have to go to that extreme."

His face darkened as he realized his gaffe. Damn. He'd launched into the hypothetical question, too busy trying to recall his long-ago thoughts and fashion solutions to a non-existent problem, to be sensitive to the fact that she'd wanted him to say he'd have married her right off. She had, the night before, admitted to being in love with him at the time—a big admission for someone as proud as Lili. And now he'd stepped on her pride, and he could hit himself over the head with a two-by-four for being so dense. "Ah, Lili, I'm a real clod. I don't mean that would have been my last alternative. I was trying to think through all the ramifications, in order of their appearance in my mind, my twenty-two-year-old mind. And that's a silly exercise at best. It was a long time ago, and what I would have done or thought at that time is, frankly, beyond me." His smile—wide, white, perfect—glittered in the moonlight. "Or behind me, as the case may be."

"Either way." She stood, glad to find she was able to do so. "As you say, it's silly to speculate about something that never happened."

Chapter Seven

Lili wanted to cry. No—to wail, to keen, to beat her fists on her pillow; to vent the disappointment and hurt of the seventeen-year-old girl who still lived, and loved, inside her. What had she expected? Nothing. The whole conversation had been a surprise. No. Worse than that, a shock. Maybe he was right: she'd read too many fairy tales as a child. She'd wanted the Lochinvar of her dreams to ride out of the past on his white horse and swoop her up and carry her off to Never-Never Land. She wanted him to tell her that of course he'd have married her. Gladly, with no reservations. That, in his heart of hearts, it was what he wanted anyway back then, in that faraway youth. That he was, secretly, as much in love with her as she was with him.

She rolled onto her back and stared at the strapping under the mattress above her. The stillness of the room was broken only by a distant, soft snoring and an occasional sigh or rustle as someone turned over. The scene that had been played out earlier kept replaying in her mind, accompanied by the hurt of hearing the "hypothetical question" dissected and examined so objectively, the solutions offered logically, one by one, with the only one she wanted to hear appearing last. What a fool she was! She hadn't realized, until this evening, that she'd harbored the dream fantasy all these years: that Brad had loved her and, given the "excuse" of her pregnancy, he would have leaped at the chance to marry her instead of Esther.

Then why hadn't she told him? Pretty obvious. That would have put the fantasy to the test of reality, and deep down she'd known, even then, that he was right where he wanted to be, and, more important, where he belonged—with the girl he'd grown up with, from his own class. Lili had been an incident in his life, and everything in her had rebelled at the thought of trapping him into marriage.

Yet here she was, all these years later, crying into her pillow because she'd been right all the time. Oh, Lili, grow up. Tell that silly seventeen-year-old to take a hike! She almost laughed at the thought. She had, unfortunately. She'd come along on this one.

The scene reeled on, once again, then stopped in midroll and backed up. Oh, God. In all her breast-beating over her hurt feelings, she'd skipped the most important part. "What matters is honesty or dishonesty, openness or concealment. It's one of the most important issues in life." Would a man whose attitude was that adamant about honesty be able to forgive a lie as huge as hers? Of course not. His anger would surely erase any feelings he might have for her now. He might consider her unfit to raise a child with solid, unshakable values and attempt to take Donny from her!

Lili now had a full-fledged headache pounding away inside her skull. She fumbled under her bunk for her toiletry bag, picked it up as quietly as possible, and slid out of bed to go to the john. As she stood in the empty women's bathroom, filling a glass with water, taking the aspirin from its case, swallowing, she met her own gaze in the mirror over the washbowl. Met and held it. What a muddle she'd made of her life! All the choices she'd felt so righteous about, so self-sacrificing: were they wrong?

She went outside and sat on the porch bench, gazing at the glory of the night sky ablaze with stars made vividly clear by the pure air. Leaning back against the hard wood, she tried to recall the steps of her decision. Actually, they'd all been rooted in her concept of Brad as the handsome prince, living in the magical kingdom with the good, kindly king and queen and his sister, the princess. A life so perfect, so enviable, it seemed a crime of gross dimension to disrupt it. Talk about a fairy-tale mentality! The idea of dumping such a problem on not only him, but his parents, who had been so unfailingly kind to her, and Marcy, her best friend, had been more than she could cope with. She felt it was her problem, and she had to deal with it.

"Lili? Is that you?"

Her head whipped around. For a split second, she felt exposed, as though the clarity of the air could reveal her thoughts. "Oh. Jan, hi. What're you doing up at this hour?"

Jan hobbled over to sit on the bench beside her. "Nursing my wounds. Or rather, the pain from my wounds. Ant, you know, Anthony...the doctor from Wellington? He gave me a pill to take for the pain, but I was trying to bull it through the night without it." She gave a derisive laugh. "I just came from the loo, where I washed it down. I hope it works fast."

"Your feet must really be in bad shape."

"Ha! That's an understatement! They are sending up threats of strike." She slipped them out of her moccasins, and Lili gasped.

"Good grief! I've never seen so many Band-Aids in my life!"

"Yeah. Ant is also going to cover them with moleskin before we set out tomorrow. Says it's lots better than Band-Aids. Seems my planning for this hike was uniformly bad."

"Do you have a package of wool?"

"What?"

"Sheep's wool. You pack it all around your feet so it softens the pounding against the boots." She looked at Jan's blank expression and said, "I'll give you some in the morning." She shook her head over the sight of the massively injured feet. "One question."

"Yes?"

"Why aren't you flying out tomorrow? Why put yourself through more torture?"

"Pride. Plain stubborn pride. I made some dumb decisions and now I have to live with them. You see, as a social worker, I spend a good deal of time preaching responsibility to the people I work with. Make-your-bed-and-lie-in-it sort of thing. You can't erase the past, so you have to bear with whatever pain necessary to carve out a decent future. So. How can I go home and admit that because I didn't spend enough time to find out how important it was to take the right boots, I quit halfway through? The truth of the matter is, I didn't think I should spend the money on a pair of boots. Dumb, huh?" She stood. "Well, off to bed."

Lili watched her limp away. All because she hadn't bought herself some good boots! She recalled the favorite parting words of a friend at work: "Be good to yourself!" Pride, responsibility, decision, consequence. Where did one end and the other begin? Life held so many contradictions.

Her gaze followed the path of a star that fell across the heavens, and as she watched its sparkling descent, a new question popped into her mind. *And what about you, Lili? When you found out you were pregnant, why didn't you count your own worth higher?* By discounting herself, by taking on the role of sacrificial lamb, she'd not only sabotaged all her plans, but deprived Brad of the right to know and to make his own decision. She had also unwittingly trapped her mother in the consequences of her decision. She had, by ignoring one of the most basic rules—to be true to oneself—mistaken dishonesty for unselfishness. Her eyes squeezed shut in pain. And now there was no turning back, no means of correction. She'd made her bed and she had to lie, and lie, and lie in it! She dropped her head into her hands, then raised it up and gave it a shake. Shape up, Lili. Stop "mewling and puking in the nurse's arms," as old Willie Shakespeare put it. Go back to bed. As Jan said, you have to bear the pain and get on with the future.

"Here she comes, the lovely Lili!" Glynne lifted his glass of orange juice in salute as he slid over to make room.

"Hey, hey, the gang's all here!" Jonathan beamed his approval of the gathering of the group. Brad was sitting beside Gillian, but his move to make room for Lili was a second too late. Actually, she was just as happy to slide in beside Glynne. Her whole psyche felt wounded by the previous night's conversation with Brad, and a bit of distance was not unwelcome.

"How're you feeling?" Jonathan poured her some juice and passed the toast.

"Trashed."

"Oh, boy. Haven't recovered from yesterday's forced march yet, huh?"

Lili paused, searching for the right air of insouciance. "I doubt that I'll ever recover from yesterday." She didn't have to tell them what *part* of yesterday. "My legs are two inches shorter and my hips two inches wider. Which is a clue to what happened to the legs."

They all laughed but Brad, who was regarding her with a mixed expression of puzzlement and concern. "Lili, if you're really tired, you can still take the option of flying out."

She shook her head. "No, I want to finish on my own two feet. If Jan can do it, so can I." She forced a grin. "Besides, you know my sentiments concerning the drop-off factor of the airstrip." There were things in her life she was far from proud of, and she wasn't about to add "quitter" to the list.

"Okay, sport." Brad stood and came over to laughingly hoist her out of her seat. "In that case, you are required to eat a good breakfast. We have thirteen miles to traverse."

"Oh, no," she moaned. "Did you have to say the number?"

"Listen, it should be a lot easier. No packs to carry."

"What'll we do with our lunches and sunscreen and—"

"You see before you a man who is always prepared. I packed a small fanny-pack in my backpack, just in case it was needed."

"My, that's impressive. I bet you were a Boy Scout."

"*Eagle* scout."

Everyone was hustled along through breakfast, cleanup and takeoff. It was to be a long day, so they were encouraged to start early. A degree of wariness hung between Brad and Lili as they set out in the company of Jonathan and Gillian and Glynne, with Ed and Josie close behind. Brad, totally unaware of the impact of his views on honesty on Lili, was still kicking himself for being so insensitive to her pride.

He frowned as he trudged along, his mind racing. He wasn't much good at hypothetical theorizing. All of his training—and inclination—veered sharply toward the concrete, dealing with facts. So, when Lili had asked him what he would have done had things been different, his analytical mind had gone to work on it with the sensible, one-two-three approach he used in balancing recalcitrant budgets, forgetting that Lili actually had gone through the terror of waiting, praying and dreading, while he, in his usual optimistic manner, had pretty much assumed it would turn out okay. It was perfectly normal for her to want to be told, "If it *had* happened, naturally I'd have been happy to marry you "—even if he weren't sure of its truth. *Sometimes,* he chided himself, you get *too* damned wedded to truth.

Funny, in retrospect, which always provided a clearer picture, it might have been the best thing that could have happened to him. At this point, the idea of marrying Lili, having their baby, sounded damned nice. There was no question, even back then, he'd felt something with Lili he didn't feel with Esther. He'd pushed it out of his mind because it had seemed totally inappropriate to his commitments, but— He stopped the ramblings of his mind with a shake of his head. Why was he going over all this? What was, was. And that was that. Lili had gone on to marry someone else and have his son, and now she was a widow. He'd married Esther, had no children and he was divorced. The past was past. But they still had a shot at the future, and he had a growing determination not to miss this chance.

The downward trail quickly became steep and rocky, an unwelcome replay of the day before. Lili's ankles appeared to have lost their bones, and folded with maddening regularity. The boots she had bought were designed more for lightness and comfort than hefty support, so her ankles were in for a flim-flam day. Brad dropped back to her side and asked, "Can you believe they call this hill 'Gentle Annie'?"

Lili raised an eyebrow. "Someone with a *Far Side* sense of humor."

"Obviously." He hesitated, wondering whether to bring up last night's discussion, but decided to drop it. They'd done enough "what-iffing" about the past. Time to get on with the future. "Just think, it's the last day of the hike. Bet you'll be delighted to see Milford Sound."

"You better believe it! But, I'm sure going to miss . . . everyone. When we have to say goodbye."

"So will I. But it doesn't have to be the end of any friendships. New Zealand may be on the other side of the earth, but it is readily accessible by plane. And Jonathan and Glynne and Gillian all live in Auckland, so they'd be fairly handy to visit. And of course, Ed and Josie are in one of the most scenic parts of England."

She glanced over at him. "Maybe they'll be readily accessible to you, fella, but a ticket to New Zealand will probably never be in my budget again. Unless the Australian branch has some more trouble with their purchasing installation, which I doubt. As for England? I'd have to start working on another dream."

Brad opened his mouth, then closed it. No use saying they might make the trips together. Lili still wasn't buying it. After last night, her resistance to such speculation was probably more rigid than before. She'd been through a lot because of him, at an age when trauma of any sort made a big impression. No wonder she was gun-shy where he was concerned. As far as her assertion that this was all too unreal to last? He was hoping, more each day, that she was wrong.

After the stretch of rocky descent, the track reentered the rain forest, providing a blessed relief from the hot sun, which seemed determined to make up for yesterday's defection. When they rejoined the Arthur River in a section called Sandy Flat, the heavy rains had left the sand covered by water; this lessened the ease of the level terrain by making it wet and slippery. Jonathan, always on the alert for birds, held up a hand for them to stop—something Lili was glad to do at the least excuse. "Look over there! That's a rare duck."

Glynne clapped him on the back. "So're you, fella."

Jonathan, pausing just long enough to give his friend a jab in the arm, continued, "It's a blue duck. You don't know how lucky you are to see one of those!"

Lili fell into stride beside Jonathan. "You know, it occurs to me I don't even know what you do for a living. You are etched into my brain as the bird expert."

He grinned. "What's your guess?"

"English professor? Poet? Museum curator?"

"Nope. Mechanical engineer."

"Oh, Jonathan, you're putting me on!"

"Not at all. Damned good one, too, if I may say so. One of the fascinations of birds is their remarkable efficient structure. The engineering of a wing is wonder to behold."

"I have to admit, I'd never have thought of a bird in quite that way. Don't they have a bird here that can't fly?"

"The kiwi?"

"Yes, that's it. Must have been a foul-up in design."

Jonathan laughed. "You bet. Couldn't escape from their predators. It's now a protected species, because there're darn few left."

"That's what you New Zealanders call yourselves, isn't it? Kiwis?"

"Right. National bird. Both feathered and two-legged." They were trudging through Racehorse Flat with breathtaking views of Mount Kepka on the right and Mount Edgar on the left. "There used to be a huge bird called the moa. Couldn't fly either, so now it's extinct. The Maoris ate them—" he grinned at Lili "—along with the rats."

"At least they sound a little more appetizing."

"Look, we've reached the Boatshed. We can have a cuppa."

"Oh, boy. We can also sit down."

After the break, they faced yet another suspension bridge that offered spectacular sights in every direction. Lili doggedly made the crossing without pausing to savor any of them, then had to wait for Brad, who was still exuding fresh enthusiasm for the scenery. "Lili, look at that!" he called from the middle of the bridge. "Did you get a picture?"

"No." A picture? She'd have had to let go of the cable to take a picture. Was he mad? She watched him lift his camera from around his neck, stand with legs straight and strong, holding on to nothing as he focused and shot, then stride on to meet her, adjusting the strap around his neck, still doing the "Look Ma, no hands!" Maybe just a little slipup? A skid or a fall? Nothing serious, just a crack in the perfection? No way. He was safely across, robust with health and vigor.

Soon they were back into the rain forest, with its abundance of beeches heavy with Grandfather's Beard. Grandpa, Lili thought, you need a shave! With each new panoramic vista of mountains sweeping dramatically in front of them, Lili said a silent thank you that she didn't have to climb them. Maybe she'd been an eagle in a previous life, and had got sick of heights.

After crossing the Mackay Creek suspension bridge, they reached Bell Rock, a landmark well noted in the guidebook. From the outside it looked like a grossly overgrown mushroom. Gillian, Jonathan and Glynne crawled through the tight opening and shouted out, "It's true! We can stand up in here!"

Upon their exit, Brad insisted they follow suit, so Lili struggled through to the interior to join him. He turned on the flashlight, shone it around at the bell-shaped interior. Lili shivered. "It's spooky in here."

"Spooky? Lili, for shame! Think of us as Alice and Arnold in Wonderland, exploring the mysteries of the dark tunnel." Just to emphasize the drama, he turned off the light.

"It isn't a tunnel, silly. It's a stone bubble, whose mysteries are extremely limited. And it's spookier in the dark."

"Boy, for a reader of fairy tales, you're a flop at creative fantasizing."

Lili giggled, and the sound echoed around them like a chorus of hyenas. It was a strange sensation, encased as they were in complete darkness, in each other's ambience. Lili's laughter died, and the silence took hold. Enclosed in this womblike rock, sheltered from all contact, it did take on a magical essence, like a place for rebirthing. A place for renewed beginnings. *Please, please,* she entreated, *give us another chance! Somehow, make it all right. I love him so much!*

Suddenly their ears were assaulted by a loud *bong* that vibrated around them like a knell of doom. "Jesus!" Brad's voice joined the echo. "Hey, knock it off!" But the shouted words bounced off the rock walls, causing further auditory distress.

Lili shook her head in an attempt to clear it. "Do you think a message is being sent?"

"Yeah. I get that feeling. What a bunch of soreheads, spoiling our rendezvous."

"Maybe we'd better get out. I'm not sure my ears would survive another little signal."

When they emerged, their friends had disappeared. "Chickens, all of them," Brad remarked. "Must have known I'd clean someone's clock."

"Now, now. No violence."

"Certain things demand harsh measures. After all, they might have been interrupting a kiss, which would call for something drastic. Strangulation in Grandfather's Beard, maybe."

"Sounds like a moss terrible way to go."

Brad groaned and gave her a playful push to propel her back on the trail. As they walked a little farther, three figures came into view. "Okay, you clowns!" Brad shouted. "Which of you did it?"

They stopped and turned, wearing matching expressions of childlike innocence. "What? Who? What's that?" It was a chorus of mock guiltlessness. After a bit of jousting and a good laugh, they all set off again, swinging along with the new ease of pack-free backs.

A set of wooden steps, incongruous in this wilderness, led them steadily toward the rushing-water sound of Mackay Falls, a sight so spectacular it stopped Lili in her tracks. "Oh, my." Brad's arm went around her and she snuggled into its curve. "How beautiful!" Great torrents of foaming water flowed over a series of rock promenades, separating and reuniting in an exuberant deluge. The verdant green of the surrounding rain forest enhanced the aura of lush tropical wonderland. "I think this is prettier than Sutherland Falls."

"You were so pooped, I'm not sure you *saw* Sutherland Falls."

"I saw it. It was long, lean and dramatic. This has more...panache."

"Panache? How can a waterfall have—"

"It can. Trust me."

Despite the continuing magnificence of the scenery, Lili's weariness was accelerating with each step. Her wobbly ankles and spongy feet carried her across another suspension bridge, over a flat, swampy area and a treacherously rocky span, up another steep climb, which seriously threatened her flagging endurance, and, at last, to Giant Gate Falls and the lunch hut, where she barely managed to restrain herself from eating right through the plastic wrap on the sandwiches. They had passed the thirty-mile marker. Only five to go. Maybe, just maybe, she could make it yet!

They ate under the shelter of the hut, then waded out into the river to sit on the rocks that jutted free of the burbling water. There they turned faces up to the warmth of the sun and sank gratefully bared feet into the cold stream. Brad, along with seven or eight of the other men, took off on a side excursion along the riverbank, and Gillian and Lili settled down for a blessed rest, thankful that the breeze and dancing water discouraged the attendance of sand flies.

As Lili watched Brad disappear from sight, she thought of the impending departure she would have to endure tomorrow. They both planned to return to Te Anau. Then she was off to Queenstown while Brad headed back to the U.S. With a start, she realized Gillian had spoken to her, more than once. "What? I'm sorry, I didn't hear you."

"Just wondering what the big sigh is all about."

"Oh." Lili was too tired for false faces, so she didn't even ask her mouth to smile. "Just thinking. Tomorrow Brad and I will say goodbye."

"Well, don't look so glum about it! It's only until you get back home."

"Uh-uh. I'm not going to see him again, Gillian. I can't."

The look of astonishment on Gillian's face would have been comical, if anything about this subject was comical.

"You have to be kidding, girl! What is this? An exercise in self-flagellation?"

"I don't know. Maybe." Lili shrugged hopelessly. "I'm not sure about anything anymore, except that the one most important person in all this is Donny. He can't get hurt. I must make very sure of that."

"Whoa. Wait a minute, back up. You've lost me. Donny. That's your son, right? So what does Donny have to do with your not seeing Brad?"

Too late, Lili realized the slip she'd made. She'd been so engrossed in her thoughts, she'd let them escape without check. "Oh. I mean." She looked into Gillian's kind, sympathetic eyes, and something inside broke loose. Lili leaned toward her and put a hand on her arm. "Gillian, I need a friend. I need someone I can confide in. But I don't want to put the responsibility of secrecy on you unless you're willing, and I'd have to ask you to promise you'd never say anything to anyone."

"Of course, Lili. I'm good at keeping my mouth closed. It's no hardship for me. If you need to talk, talk."

It took Lili a few seconds to garner the courage to break eleven years of silence, but her need to confide, to share the burden with someone, overcame her reluctance. "I told you Donny was eight—that he was born after my husband died." Gillian nodded. "Well..." She took a deep sigh and plunged in. "Donny is over ten years old, and there was no husband. I've never been married."

Gillian's eyes rounded, then narrowed to a squint. "So you had a baby out of wedlock. Big deal. Surely you don't think that's enough to scare off a man like Brad?"

Lili reached down to dangle her fingers in the cold water. "It isn't as simple as that. Gillian, I told you about Brad taking me to the prom because I didn't have a date?"

"Yes."

"Well, things got out of control. I mean, well, things got a little out of control."

Gillian grinned. "You mean you and Brad got it on."

Lili actually felt the heat of a blush rising to her cheeks. Good God, how could she blush now, eleven years after the fact? At the age of twenty-eight? She suppressed an inclination to lean over and dunk her heated head in the water. "You see—" It was hard, this confiding, especially for someone who'd never done it before. Just spit it out, Lili, it'll be such a relief! "It didn't end there, there were...complications." She took a deep breath and let it go. "Brad is Donny's father. And he has no idea."

This time a panorama of expressions marched across Gillian's face in rapid transit: disbelief, amazement, comprehension, chagrin. "Oh, my God."

"Exactly."

"Then you have to tell him, Lili. You *have* to!"

"Gillian, it is so complicated. More than you can imagine." She launched into a full recital of the situation, from its inception eleven years ago to the discussion she and Brad had had the night before. "So, there's no way of knowing what his reaction would be, but anger seems most likely." She ran her hand across her eyes. "If it were just me, Gillian, I'd take the chance in a minute. I mean, how can I lose what I don't have? But, as I said in the first place, Donny's the most important one in this mixed-up mess." Lili flexed her sore toes in the cooling swirls. "My son is, well, how to explain him? He's okay. What I mean by that is, he's *fine.*." Her eyes entreated the other woman to understand. "In today's world, with all the craziness, that's a marvel. In the neighborhood I live in, it's a miracle. He's happy, he's well adjusted, he's productive. I don't mean to make him sound like some kind of paragon, because he's a normal boy, and that means a certain measure of mischief and all that stuff."

"He sounds like a boy who's had a lot of love."

Lili's eyes filled. "Yes. He has. As much as I, and my mother, could give him. We've both *participated,* you know—gone to soccer games and tossed baseballs and helped with homework and attended umpteen thousand meetings, so he wouldn't miss having a father around too much. And—" Off in the distance, she could see the clutch of men returning. "Damn, here they come."

"Yeah. Listen, Lili, isn't it just possible that, after Brad blew his top, he'd settle down to trying to add what he could to his son's life? That's an awful lot, I should think, even if you two didn't get together." She held up her hand. "And don't get me wrong. I'm not all that convinced you wouldn't still get together. I'm just trying to look at all sides."

"Yes, it's possible. But even if Brad adjusted to it, how about my son? Finding out he's had a real, live father all these years." Visions of catastrophe filled Lili's mind. "God. Would *Donny* ever forgive me? Might *he* get so mad at me that if Brad offered to take him to his big, beautiful home with all the marvelous things he'd have to offer, might he want to go? I'd die. I'd simply die if I lost him! Gillian..." Tears were running like miniwaterfalls down her cheeks. "I've made such a mess out of everything!"

"Hey." Gillian leaned over and tried to hug her, which was a clumsy attempt at best, given the precarious nature of their perch. "Lili, you did the best you knew how at the time. For God's sake, you were a seventeen-year-old kid. What were you supposed to have? The wisdom of Socrates? If anyone should have put her foot down, it was your mother. No, hold on, I'm not being critical, really. Sounds like her life hadn't exactly been a smooth ride down a greased slide. We make decisions based on where we are at a given time, what we know and how we feel. Add into that all the emotional factors." She frowned in emphasis. "*At the time!* Don't give yourself hell for not having done what you'd do now. You weren't equipped. It sounds to me like you tried to be, if anything, too good to Brad. Besides—" she kicked at the water "—there's another possibility."

"What's that?"

"Brad can say what he will, but, as you tell me, he readily admits he doesn't really know how he'd have reacted. What if he'd wanted you to get an abortion? What if he'd really pressed you on it?"

Lili stared at her as an unwelcome answer leaped to mind. "Dear God. I probably would have."

"Sure, you would. You were nuts about the guy. Maybe you were protecting a lot more than you even realized, Lili. Tell me something, and be as honest as you possibly can."

"Okay."

"If you could wave a magic wand and change it any way at all, would you *not* have Donny? Wait, don't answer until I finish. Keep everything else the same. You're here, Brad's here, you're free, so is he. No impediments. Would you choose that?"

Her head was moving violently back and forth. "No. Not for a minute. Nothing, Brad included, could make me want to be without my son."

"Then do the best you can, my friend, and quit beating yourself over the head. You've raised a fine boy, and that's one hell of a lot. If you can tell Brad, tell him. He's a very bright guy and a good man. Trust him, Lili. I have a feeling you wouldn't be sorry." She looked up. "Now, you'd better either fall into the water or run for the john and fix your face. The men approacheth."

"I'm off." Lili grabbed her boots and leaned over to kiss Gillian on the cheek. "Thank you."

"My pleasure."

Brad watched Lili dash off as he came out to sit beside Gillian. "Can't be anything I said, because I didn't have time to say anything."

"Maybe she reads minds."

"There's nothing on my mind that should send her running." He grinned. "I hope."

Gillian laid a hand on his arm, dropping every vestige of levity as she said, "Brad, she's a wonderful person. A wonderful, loving person." She appeared to be searching for words, but finally, with a slight shrug, she picked up her boots and waded to shore, leaving a puzzled Brad to stare after her.

* * *

When, at long last, they reached the sign heralding the end of the Milford Track, Lili almost collapsed in relief. She had begun, halfway through the day, to count the posts that marked each mile, and not long after that to marvel at how endless a mile's journey could become. Every once in a while she sent up silent thank-yous for the fine weather that allowed the plane to fly their packs out that morning. If she'd had that weight on her back, she'd probably have sunk right into the sandy bog.

Everyone applied enough Dimp to survive the onslaught of the sand-fly attack while pictures were taken standing by the sign—indisputable evidence that they had, in fact, done the whole thirty-five miles. She and Brad stood together, their arms around each other while photos were snapped with her camera and his. Then they took shots of their friends in return. Lili, as had become her pattern, insisted on at least one picture of herself alone. The more she looked at Brad, observed the striking resemblance between him and her son, the less sure she became about the idea of displaying snapshots of him to any of her friends and, most especially, to Donny.

As soon as they finished their photography, they all made a dash for the screened-in shelter. "Wow!" Gillian yelped, slapping at a hanger-on fly. "I can see where these creatures get their reputation. Ouch!" *Slap!* "Damn it!"

The launch showed up soon after they arrived, and everyone who was there was taken aboard. "You realize, Lili," Jonathan pointed out, "you made the three o'clock boat. The last one doesn't go until four, so you beat some of the others."

She laughed. "Don't think that won't be mentioned—*gloated* about—over and over, when I tell my friends about this hike. In fact, it wouldn't surprise me if it became the *two* o'clock launch, somewhere along the line."

"Why, Lili!" The stern lines in Brad's face twitched from his effort to hold them firmly in place. "Don't tell me you'd *fabricate* a few of the details? Is it possible that, some time in the near future, the idea for sitting on the twelve-second rock will become yours?''

The expression on her face held all the innocence of a professional cardsharper's. ''Why? Wasn't it?'' To the accompaniment of laughter, the motor engaged, and they embarked on the trip across Milford Sound to the hotel.

Brad leaned to whisper in Lili's ear, ''Let's go outside.'' She nodded, and they pulled on their windbreakers as they stepped onto the outer deck.

The air was bitingly crisp and much cooler here on the water than it had been on the trail. They made their way to the front of the boat, where Brad braced himself against the curve of the bow and Lili settled against him as he wrapped his arms around her and clasped his hands at her waist. She leaned her head back against his chest and put her hands over his, surprised anew at the infusion of pleasure afforded by the simple contact of her flesh against his. What a sensation, being in this bucolic setting in Brad's arms! Heaven, she thought. This is heaven. And even if she couldn't take up permanent residence, it was nice to be afforded a brief sojourn in paradise.

Although she thought she'd seen all the scenery she could absorb, this was too much to ignore, and her senses snapped to attention. Mitre Peak, a stark triangle of rock, bisected the blue of the sky as it rose out of the water for almost a mile. This was Fiordland, the only one outside the Scandinavian countries. ''Funny, I was just thinking—these mountains remind me of visiting a granite quarry in Rockport,'' she said to Brad. ''They look like some giant workman tapped away with his tools until a huge piece of granite sheared off, then he shaped it into a proper mountain and dropped it in place.''

''Some giant workman did.''

She twisted her neck around so she could see his face. ''Why Brad Hollingsworth, are those the words of a religious man?''

"Sure." He grinned down at her. "Does that surprise you?"

She leaned her head against his chest again, turning the question over. "Guess I never thought about it before. But it shouldn't surprise me. It fits the pattern."

"Pattern? What pattern?"

"Your family. Your values. You."

"Yeah. I see what you mean. Conventional to the core. I'm a Presbyterian. That fit, too?"

"Oh, yes. It'd have to be that or Episcopalian."

"I hope that's not a snide tone I hear."

She laughed. "Not at all. I have no snide tones where you're concerned."

"That's good to hear. How about you?"

"Me?"

"Are you religious? No, rephrase that. Do you believe in God?"

Her silence, mute testimony to her indecision, troubled her. "Strange. I haven't thought about that, either, for a long time." She watched a sea gull, probably on excursion off the Tasman Sea, swoop over the boat and soar up to ride a wind draft. "I used to be, but I'm so busy now. Church is... Well, it takes up time. Donny goes to Sunday school." She frowned, knowing she was avoiding the question. "You know, I *used* to have such a strong belief. I think, well, I got pretty mad at God."

"Thought he let you down?"

"Yes." She nodded, acknowledging his assessment as much to herself as to him. "Pretty dumb, huh?"

"No. You have a perfect right to your feelings. You got married and pregnant and became a widow in awfully short order. Enough to make anyone mad. God can take a little anger—He's not fragile."

Lili stared out at the fierce blue of the water, and her hands tightened their grip on Brad's. If only she could absorb some of his sureness, his strength, his faith in the general orderliness of life. How different her life might have been if she'd had him beside her, offering his support. "I wish—" She stopped, biting her tongue.

"What? Come on, don't stop there. How am I to really know you unless I'm privy to your wishes?"

"I'm not sure you'd want to really know me, Brad. I'm not sure at all."

His hands moved to her shoulders and turned her sharply to face him. "Hey, stop that! Don't try to tell me there's something dark and ominous about you. I know there isn't—I can feel it. And my instincts are damned reliable."

"Brad..." Hell, she was on the verge of bursting into tears, and how would she explain that?

"Lili, listen to me. We have a chance to get to know each other, all about each other. Whether we end up friends or something more, it'll be worth a lot. And whatever it is you've got squirreled away that bothers you so much, you may as well get ready to spill it, because I'm damned if I'll stand by and watch you suffer from something that'd probably evaporate with a little simple exposure. We should promise to be honest with each other, you and I. Honest and open, so everything can be shared, good and bad."

She contemplated, just briefly, jumping over the side of the boat.

"Now. What are you going to do when we get to the hotel?"

"Huh?" The sudden shift of subject caught her completely off guard. "Where did that come from?"

He grinned. "Just thinking ahead."

She stepped out of his grasp, to help clear her head. There was something about his touch that short-circuited some of her brain cells. "Well, now. Hotel. Okay, this is the plan. I'm going to take a shower and shampoo—"

"What a surprise."

She laughed. "Isn't it? And then, I'll dig some different clothes out of my duffel bag, which I assume will be on hand, as promised, and dump every single garment that went on this hike with me in the washer."

"How do you know they have one?"

"It's in the brochure. Then a nap. A *long* nap. And after that? Spruce up in my finery—" she shrugged "—which means the one dress I brought with me—put on some makeup, curl my hair and appear, in all my splendiferousness, for the group dinner. And you?"

"Well, since you're booked solid, I'll follow step number one and step number two."

"Cleanup and washing?"

"Right. Then take my trusty camera and shoot dozens of pictures of this extraordinary scenery. Maybe a lie-down. Then into *my* finery, which consists of the one set of slacks and shirt and jacket I brought."

"No tie?"

"No tie."

"Heavens. What would your grandfather say?"

"Good for you, kid." Brad took her hand, and his expression sobered. "Lili, later on, after the dinner and the awarding of the certificates and all, we need to talk."

Her heart bumped into her chest wall and stalled. "Why?"

"Don't play dumb. This is not just a 'Hey, kid, see you sometime' encounter, and you know it. Even though we were both determined to avoid serious attachments when this hike started, something's been happening between us—something we need to acknowledge. We're adults now, Lili, and adults don't just turn their backs on what could be the greatest thing in their lives just to hold on to a preset notion."

Yes, she knew he was right. Gillian's quotation—"Would you rather be right, or happy?"—came back to mind. But in this case her clear vote for happiness was thwarted by other considerations too massive to bypass. They'd have to talk, and she'd have to tell him some good reason, or something that at least *sounded* reasonable, for her not seeing him again when she got home. At the thought, the sun seemed to dim, the water to cloud and the air to develop a sudden case of pollution. "Yes, okay. You're right. Where?"

"Where what?"

"Where shall we talk?"

"Your room or mine, take your pick," he replied.

The sea gull made another dive, and Lili figured it would be an appropriate time for him to drop more than a wing. "Isn't that a little dangerous?"

"Yeah, probably. But, hell, do you want to go through life taking no risks?"

"Yes. Absolutely. Straight on through the rest of the journey. Right to the end."

"Impossible." He bent his head and touched his lips to her hair. "But we'll be careful. I promise."

Careful. The only way she could be careful with Brad was not to be with him. And certainly not in a hotel room on the other side of the world from home. Alone. Somehow it sounded like a terrible place to try to say goodbye.

The launch moved swiftly toward its dock at Milford Sound. And the hotel. And the room. Lili sighed. This was the time for her to say "N.F.W." But it stuck in her throat.

Chapter Eight

Lili glanced at her watch as she paused outside the entrance to the bar, where the volume of excited babble indicated that most of the other thirty-six members of her group had already arrived. The moment she stepped inside and saw Brad's eyes focus on her and widen in appreciation, she knew the extra time spent on primping was worth the tardiness. Brad had declared his attraction to her, and no matter the outcome, just knowing his interest rang chimes of joy in her heart. She was suffering a tug-of-war between mind, heart and gut, each feeding different input to her beleaguered brain. He had a right to know he had a son, but she had gargantuan reasons not to tell him; she yearned for him, ached for him, needed him, but he posed the greatest of dangers to her carefully constructed life; she wanted, desperately, to see him again when she returned to the States, but every rationale dictated saying goodbye right here and running for cover.

As she crossed the room, she smiled with appreciation at the comments from some of her fellow hikers.

"Hey, Lili, what a change! Where have you been keeping yourself?"

"You look simply lovely...."

"Here she is, the picture of health, youth, and beauty!"

As she returned greetings, made rejoinders, called hellos, the sweet sorrow of the occasion hit her. These people had all been part of an extraordinary experience, a one-of-a-kind adventure, and saying goodbye was going to put a period on it. The end. As she drew closer to Brad, pulled like metal to a magnet, the sorrow increased and the sweetness diminished. How could she endure a future without him? That ending was more bitter than anyone should be asked to endure. This trip had certainly clarified one mystery in her life. She'd wondered, all these years, why she hadn't been able to fall in love. Although it was true she'd had scant time for dating, she'd certainly done enough of it to have had the opportunity for a love affair; yet no one had interested her enough for her to become involved. Now, like it or not, she knew why. She'd been in love with Brad since she was twelve years old, and all other men had paled in comparison to her memory of him.

"Lili." Brad leaned over to place a restrained kiss on her cheek, managing, with great cost to his self-control, not to pull her into his arms and kiss her properly. Or improperly. "You look beautiful." He reached for her hand, thankful that she allowed it to nestle in his.

"I should hope so. I spent most of the afternoon primping. It was fun, after five days of being nature woman."

"Nature woman or femme fatale, you're a knockout."

"Well, I must say, you look pretty gorgeous yourself."

"I should hope so. I spent the whole afternoon at the hotel beauty parlor, getting the works." He said it with a perfectly straight face.

"At the beauty parlor? But what—" She caught herself and gave him a jab to the arm. "What did you do, really?"

"Just what I'd planned. Shower, general cleanup, short nap, took lots of pictures. Mostly tried to kill time until I could be with you."

"Ah, how romantic." They were both using playful tones, but the message in his eyes said: *This isn't a joke. This is serious.*

From the moment she reached his side, felt his hand enclose hers and inhaled the heady scent of his after-shave, all the events of the evening blurred into one continuous confusion of mixed longings: to stay here forever; to be at home with her son, safe from all probing; to be anywhere at all with Brad *and* Donny, the three of them, a family. Towering above all else was desire. Desire to be in Brad's arms, flesh to flesh, locked together so firmly that nothing could ever separate them again. She leaned against his side, unabashedly savoring their public pairing.

Her leeway for indecision was narrowing to minutes, yet she was still awash in uncertainty, swinging between the overwhelming desire to try anything, take any risk that might provide even the slimmest chance to spend the rest of her life with him, and her conviction that, once they parted, she must never see him again. Such alternatives. Walk through this door, Lili Jamison, to joy and promise and anticipation of a life so bright it dazzles, or this door to hopelessness and absence of passion, and dull endurance. Take your choice, girl. You're running out of time! It was all an exercise in futility. In fact, she'd run out of time eleven years ago, and the choice was already made. Between now and the moment the hotel-room door closed them into a womb of privacy, she must find the strength to tell him this had to be the end.

Lili, you're setting yourself up for failure. You know what's going to happen once that door closes, and it is not going to be a farewell address! Tell him you've got a headache and will see him in the morning, the voice of reason warned. But she knew she couldn't.

As her eyes flicked restlessly around the room, she noticed the glances cast their way, the knowing smiles. It was pretty obvious they were regarded as lovers, or about-to-be lovers. Being so intimately paired with Brad, even in the imagination of others, gave Lili a delicious feeling she was unwilling to relinquish quickly. What she had was the moment, and the moment was rich enough to fill hours of recapitulation. Later she'd get back to stern resolve. Now? Well, now would be her last lapse into the world of fantasy. She moved closer to him, willing the proximity to work magic, to erase obstacles, to cure mistakes.

Brad felt as if he couldn't take his eyes off Lili. God, she was lovely. He twined his fingers through hers, afraid to loosen his grip lest she slip through and away. Her pixielike quality gave credence to his strange fear that she might vanish from sight in a poof of vapor. He could scarcely recall his determination to remain unentangled. Had he ever really forgotten Lili, or had the wisp of a memory lingered all these years, tucked away in a sector of his brain reserved for restricted thoughts? Certainly she had reached something in him, on that long-ago night when they'd made love, which had hitherto gone untouched; had inflamed urges that no one, including his ex-wife, had ever awakened. He could remember, now, the incredible hunger she had aroused in him—a craving that had driven him past his usually reliable self-control. It had taken every ounce of restraint, in the days—no, weeks, even months—that followed, to stay away from her.

Once his memory bank had opened, other recollections moved from that mysteriously unreachable part of the brain to the forefront of his mind. He'd been plagued by doubts after making love to Lili, doubts that hadn't even crossed his mind before. Did he really want to marry Esther? Was it love he felt for her, or only the comfort of familiarity? Funny, he'd grown up assuming they'd marry, and that assumption had been shared by their family and friends. Though he'd certainly sowed a few wild oats, no one else had been a contender for his serious intentions. No one, that is, until Lili. That night with Lili had shaken him badly. But all the carefully laid plans and expectations of his family and, of course, Esther, had short-circuited the newly awakened realization that his sister's friend had become far more important to him than he dared allow.

Now? Brad tightened his grip on her hand. He could scarcely believe his luck. He was being given a second chance, and all his firmly wrought resolutions to remain single and uninvolved had faded away into nothingness.

"Would you like a drink?"

She nodded. "A glass of white wine would taste good. Although it really should be champagne. After all, we had it to toast the beginning of the trail. I suppose we should do as much for the end." The moment the words *the end* left her mouth, she wanted to call them back, cancel them.

"That's perfect. Champagne coming up. I'll get a bottle, so Glynne and Jon and Gillian can join us."

Though they had to separate from time to time as the party progressed, Lili and Brad never allowed much distance to come between them. They sat next to each other at dinner, their chairs wood to wood, then moved like an inseparable unit to the bar where the certificates were to be handed out. They laughed together when Jan, whose first purchase upon reaching the hotel had been a pair of well-padded slippers, sank to her knees and crawled across the floor to receive her certificate, and both became moist-eyed while applauding Ginny, a woman from Iowa who had astounded all of them by surmounting the liabilities of a hip transplant, a bum knee and arthritis to stick it through with her proud husband to the very end. They almost raised blisters clapping for their friends, Jonathan, Gillian and Glynne, who had so enriched the experience.

When Lili's name was called, she felt a rush of enormous pride. She'd done it! Despite the limitations of underexercised muscles, a fear of heights and the emotional upheaval Brad's presence had imposed, she had completed the hike all in one piece! She walked to the center of the room to get the precious certificate, then turned, only to be engulfed in the radiance of Brad's smile and sparkling-eyed admiration. Her heart was full to bursting. Surely the perimeters of possibility had widened, the sphere of "perhaps" and "maybe" broadened.

Shortly after taking her seat, she was approached by one of the waiters, who leaned over to whisper, "Lili Jamison?"

"Yes?"

"There's a phone call for you."

"Really?" It must be Donny. She'd placed the call earlier but been unable to get through. "Can I take it in my room?"

"Sure. Just signal the operator."

With a quick explanation to Brad, she quietly left the charmed circle and hurried down the hall to her door. The light on her phone was blinking, and it took only seconds to make the connection with her son.

"Donny?"

"Hi, Mom! Hey, you sound real close, like you're at the store or something."

What a ninny! She'd barely said hello to her son and the tears were already flowing. "How are you, honey?"

"Great. Well, almost great. I've got a broken arm."

"What!"

"Well, almost broken. A cracked bone. The doc said it'd heal fast, but the coach made me quit baseball practice."

"Donny, my Lord, what happened?" Alarm spread through her like a shot.

"Oh, just that stupid jerk, Steve Gouch. He called me a— Well, you won't let me swear so I can't tell you. Besides, Ma Bell'd probably cut me off. Anyway, I slugged him and he hit me with his baseball bat."

"Oh, no, Donny—"

"Mom, don't have a cow. I'm okay. He has a lousy swing. That's why nobody ever wants him on their team. That and the fact he's a jerk. Did you finish the Milford Track?"

The sudden switch of subject set her brain swirling. "First, you're sure—"

"Yeah, really, I'm fine. The old arm is almost back to pitching form."

"Thank God." She took a deep breath, swallowing the urge to let her instinctive maternal panic loose and bombard him with further questions. Donny hated being treated like a baby. "Yes, I finished it. The whole thing. In fact, I was just given my certificate."

"Way to go, Mom!" Donny had been thoroughly impressed by his mother's plans to do the thirty-five mile hike. Impressed and a little skeptical. "Nobody had to carry you out?" He laughed—that delightful sound she missed so.

"Of course not." She remembered Brad's offer to do just that, and smiled. "I've become a regular mountain woman!"

"Awesome. Did you meet some neat people? Who'd you hike with?"

Lili's smile froze as an image of Brad leaped to mind. *With your father, Donny, who looks just like you and talks just like you and has so many of the same gestures and expressions that anyone watching the two of you together would know.* She swallowed the longing to tell him of the miraculous encounter. "I've met some lovely people. Two men and a woman from Auckland have become good friends, and several from the U.S. I'll tell you all about them when I get back. I've taken lots of pictures. We'll hope they all turn out." The enormity of her omission swamped her, and it took all she had to hold on, to keep her voice cheerful. They chatted awhile longer, and Lili spoke to her mother, then reluctantly replaced the receiver in its cradle.

Her mood of elation had vanished, to be replaced by a heavyheartedness that threatened to engulf her in tears. *Oh, Donny! How I'd love to bring you home the wonderful man*

I hiked with, who just happens to be your father. You'd love him, I know. And he'd be crazy about you. Was she being unbelievably selfish, even now, in not simply laying it all out and letting father and son make their own decisions, even if she was left out of both? She stood and walked to the window. No. This wallowing around in self-recrimination had to stop. The mistake had been made by a very young girl doing the best she could. Now she was a grown woman and a good mother who'd continued to do her best all the years of Donny's life. He was a happy child quickly growing into a fine young man. Any decision to disturb his world must be made with the greatest care, and his welfare must always take utmost priority.

She moved restlessly around the room, which was clean and pleasant if a bit spartan. The walls were a soft blue, the double bed covered with a blue-and-white floral spread. A dresser and nightstand completed the furnishings, all placed on a neutral hotel-beige rug. But the interior decor was superfluous to the view framed by the window: the jutting spire of Mitre Peak bisecting the black pool of Milford Sound—a sight no man-made decoration could hope to equal. She glanced at her watch. Surely the ceremony would be over by now and everyone would be heading for their rooms. That thought instantly spawned another. Brad could be on his way to see her at any minute. Here.

She checked her makeup and brushed her hair, plumped up the pillows and tucked her toiletry bag out of sight in the bathroom, then repeated the makeup check and hair brushing and pillow plumping. She might as well have been preparing to walk onstage for a lead role in a Broadway play, given the state of her nerves! Talking to Donny hadn't helped—in fact, quite the opposite. But in one respect, the conversation had been strengthening. She was not going to give way to her desires, no matter what Brad had in mind. She had a lot of willpower when necessary, and it was necessary now. No matter how much she loved Brad, her concern for Donny must—and would—prevail. The soft knock at the door, despite her mental preparation, sent her insides into a scramble. *Hold on, Lili. Hold on.*

The vision that met her eyes when she opened the door would stay emblazoned on her memory forever. Was it optical illusion, or was there a glow surrounding him? Did he crowd the opening of the door frame, shoulders barely missing the sides, head hovering close to the top, blond hair accentuated by the backlighting from the hall? What a prince! She had always thought of him in fairy-tale terms, yet who could ever invent such a man? Imagination would boggle, crushed beneath the impact of the real thing.

He stepped inside and closed the door behind him. "Hi." His eyes swept the room, lingering for an instant on the double bed before returning to her face. "Was your call from Donny?"

"Yes. We had a good talk. He has a cracked bone in his arm."

"Uh-oh. Was it a fall?"

"No. He got in an argument with another boy who happened to have a baseball bat in his hand." She sucked in her breath, sorry she'd told him. Some of the boys in Donny's school were tough as pit bulls and just as mean. She'd rather Brad didn't know that. Just in case her son's environment ever became an issue. Just in case. God, so many things fell into that category.

To her surprise, Brad laughed. "Boys never change. It's a wonder any of us grow up. I got in a fight in prep school once and the other kid threw me down a full flight of stairs. Luckily I'd learned how to fall from skiing, so I tucked and rolled, then ran back up the stairs and beat the crap out of him!"

"And I thought you'd had such a genteel upbringing."

"Well, I wasn't exactly surrounded by a bunch of hoods, but a few of my classmates over the years had nasty tempers. Some of them don't go away to school out of choice, you know. They're sent to get them out of their parents' way. And they take out their anger on the nearest kid who looks punchable." He glanced around. "Got a couple of chairs in here?"

"Yes." She indicated the far corner of the room, where two small boudoir chairs were separated by a table and lamp. "We can move them in front of the window and enjoy the view." It might be a good idea to put the two of them on display. If only to the night sky and the outline of Mitre Peak.

Brad waited until she was seated, then settled as best he could into the small chair, his body eclipsing it from sight. He ran his fingers through his hair, a gesture that betrayed his rare lapses into uneasiness. "I want to talk to you about something."

Her hands twisted together in her lap. "Okay."

"Well, don't look so serious. It isn't life threatening."

"Oh, good. I thought maybe you wanted me to go bungy jumping with you."

His head cocked to one side, and his right eyebrow lifted. "Well, as a matter of fact—"

Lili laughed. "Brad, quit joking around and tell me what you have on your mind." *Tell me you've had a private investigator at work, and you know about Donny, and it's okay, and you love me and want to marry me and have us all live together happily ever after. Once a believer in fairy tales, always a hopeful ninny.*

"I'd like to share the next four days of your vacation with you."

She stared at him, unable to comprehend what she'd heard. "What did you say?"

"I'd like to stay here, Lili, in New Zealand. With you."

"But—" Her mind was racing, searching corners, peeking behind brain cells, looking for dangers, yearning for opportunities. A thousand reasons for saying no lined up, plugging themselves into place, only to be washed away in a single swoop, by one gigantic wave of hope. "How could you? Don't you have to go back to work?"

"I pretty much set my own schedule, and it's been a long time since I took any lengthy vacations." His anxious eyes were glued to her face. "I want you to be perfectly honest with me about this. I know it's the first vacation you've ever had, and you might want to do it on your own, and I'd understand. It's just . . . I thought it'd give us time to get reacquainted. Or, to get *really* acquainted, as adults."

Lili was stunned into silence. The dangling carrots had been turned to solid gold and moved easily within reach. Four more days. With Brad. This was dream-come-true stuff if she'd ever heard it. Careful. Careful. This particular dream could end with her falling off the edge of the world. "My God."

"Say a few prayers if you like. Just, please, come up with the right answer."

Her mind was awhirl with pictures of the two of them, hand in hand, exploring New Zealand. It beat travels with Benjamin Potter any day. Could she? Dare she? She closed her eyes, willing her brain to stop spinning and settle down to thought formulations. One idea did manage to gather itself, an idea so intriguing it swirled a dance of happy speculation in her head. A reprieve! The ultimate postponement opportunity! Surely, during the next four days, the perfect time would present itself. A full-disclosure moment, when all elements would blend together to say "This is it, tell him." Maybe, just maybe, the permanent goodbye would never be necessary. Maybe she'd find a way to the truth that wouldn't threaten Donny! Four days. Anything could happen in four days, couldn't it? After all, God created the world in only seven!

"Listen, Lili, if you really don't want this, don't hesitate to tell me. I can go ahead and leave."

Lili, giving way to the exuberance of hope, leaned forward, her lifted face one beam of joy. "Want it? Of course I want you with me! Don't even mention the word *leave*. Brad, how wonderful!"

"Wow." He sat back, heaving a sigh of relief. "I was sure you were going to say no. I had all kinds of sales pitches ready."

"Oh, dear. All that preparation for nothing. Want to start over, have me change my answer so you can use them?"

"Hell, no. Never try to upgrade perfection. Now, to a few of the particulars. You were going to Mount Cook from here?"

"Yes."

"I called—" he grinned "—just in case, and got a room at the Hermitage."

Lili laughed. "Right down the hall, by any chance?"

"Well, no. Can't say I did that well. Where are you booked from there?"

"Two days in Queenstown, then on to Rotorua."

"Could we just have one day in Queenstown, then spend the last two days of my part of the stay at Huka Lodge?"

"Huka Lodge! Brad, that place is outrageously expensive! Some of the people in Australia told me about it. They suggested I invest a month's salary in a two-day stay."

"It's not quite that bad. My parents stayed there and said it was pretty special." He reached over to take her hands in his. "Let me spoil you a little, Lili. I'd thoroughly enjoy it."

"But—what would I wear?"

He threw back his head and laughed. "Now we're making progress. You've come to the important considerations. We have a day in Queenstown. We can shop in the morning, before going out to watch the bungy jumpers in the afternoon."

"Bungy jumpers!"

"Ah, Lili, come on. Just watch? It'll be a kick."

She should pay more attention to those warning bells in her head, but how could she concentrate while he was centering the full power of those eyes on her? "Okay, but no coercion. I am *not* taking any crazy leaps off a bridge!"

"Of course not. Now we're all set! Mount Cook, Queenstown, Huka Lodge. Then I'll wing on home and you can pick up your own schedule again." He stood and pulled her to her feet. "Isn't it going to be fun?"

"Yes. Yes, it is." Fun and full of pitfalls. But her life had been full of pitfalls, and fun hadn't always been in plentiful supply. How could she blame herself for wanting to grab this precious span of time with the man she loved? "Brad?"

"Yes?"

"I'm sure, in the midst of all your courses in finance, you must have studied literature from time to time."

"Sure."

"Do you remember a device of writing, called 'suspension of disbelief'?"

"Yes. But what—"

"That's what I'd like to do. As you know, I have some trouble associating what's happening here to real life, so I'd like to stop trying, just for the next four days." Her laugh held the sharp edge of nervousness. "As you pointed out, it's my first real vacation, and I want to relax and have fun and not try to figure out the future. Could we do that?"

"No discussions of where we go from here?"

She nodded. "While we're in New Zealand."

He frowned, turning the idea over in his mind. "Sure. If that's what you want. But—"

"No buts. They're forbidden, too."

His smile held an element of doubt. "All right. Actually, it's probably a good idea. We need to take plenty of time with this."

"This?"

"This. This wonderful something that's pulling us together." He took her in his arms then, gently, slowly, watching her lips open slightly in anticipation of his kiss. When his mouth touched hers, it sealed the pact, verified the promise. Their lips moved together, searching for the perfect fit, finding it. He pulled away before either of them was ready for the parting. "Lili. I can't tell you how happy I am. There's this growing feeling that something very special touched my life and I let it slip away eleven years ago. And to have another chance? It's a privilege most people never get."

Lili could barely speak. Her blood felt suspended in its flow, her heart stopped between beats. This was the answer to a prayer, the fulfillment of a dream. It was also her worst fears elevated to a new position, a danger more lethal, more than ever poised for damage. It didn't matter. She'd been handed a precious gift: four golden days. And nothing could induce her to reject it. "Can you understand if I tell you I'm a little frightened?"

"Of course. Who isn't? I'm falling in love with you, Lili, and it was the last thing in the world I'd planned for, or dreamed possible right now." He touched his lips to her forehead. She could feel the tension in his body, a tension echoed in her own. "I want you so damned much." He looked down at her. "Hey, don't panic, I'm not about to attack. When—no, *if* we make love again, it has to be completely mutual, fully agreed upon."

Lili gave a sardonic laugh. "Brad, it was both those things before."

"Maybe. It was also the wrong time. The time is right, now, and I have such hopes!"

"Brad . . ."

"Ah, come on, Lili, don't burst my bubble with a lot of sensible cautions. We're stepping outside reality, remember? Where absolutely anything is possible?"

"I guess I can't argue with that."

"No, you can't. You set the rules—you have to abide by them." Was that the clang of gates closing around her? "Now. I am about to perform a feat of such inconceivable strength of character and willpower that it promises to shake the universe."

"Good grief? Dare I ask?"

"Go ahead. Dare. If I can pull this off, anything is possible. I am about to leave you alone in this most enticing of all places on earth, and go back to that lonely hole of solitude numbered 205."

"Must you?"

"Yes, I must. Nothing should happen for which we aren't both fully prepared. In every way." A quick kiss and he was gone.

Later, cradled in the soft but lonely hug of her mattress, Lili drifted into a slumber filled with dreams of the two of them, running in slow-motion grace across fields dotted with fleecy sheep. As the languor of sleep deepened, they were joined by a smaller figure, a boy. It was not Benjamin Potter; it was Donny. Donald Bradford Jamison. Donald Bradford . . . Hollingsworth.

Their absorption in each other was briefly broken the next morning when the time came to bid goodbye to their friends. Glynne and Jonathan hugged Lili and pumped Brad's hand. There were promises made to keep in touch, to write, to look them up in case they were in the other's country. When Lili faced Gillian, she couldn't prevent the flow of tears. "Oh, nuts. I was planning to get all through this without blubbering."

"Me, too." Gillian's eyes were brimming. "Lili, take care. And remember what I said."

Lili glanced over her shoulder to make sure Brad was out of earshot. "You'll never guess. Brad has made arrangements to stay with me, for four whole days!"

"Lili, how wonderful!"

"That gives me time, Gillian. Time to really weigh the options."

Gillian laid her hand on Lili's arm. "Tell him. Give both of you a chance. More than that, all three of you."

"Hey, Gillian, you ready? The coach is leaving for the airport!"

Lili gave her a last hug. "I hate to say goodbye. What you said to me did make a difference, Gillian. More, I think, than even I know as yet. I'll tell you one thing, I wish you lived right around the corner from me. It's so hard to finally find a good friend, then have half a world between us."

"Keep in touch, Lili. Promise?"

"I promise."

The two women exchanged a last hug and, reluctantly, parted.

Brad took her hand as they watched the coach depart. "I'll miss those guys."

"Me, too."

He put his arm around her and hugged her close. "Well, my love, on to Mount Cook!"

My love. How much happiness could she contain? And how would it feel to have to say goodbye to it?

Chapter Nine

The plane ride from Queenstown to Mount Cook was a hair-raiser. The small plane bounced about on choppy air, swinging to and fro. From Lili's vantage point, next to the window, it appeared to miss the towering mountains on either side by mere inches. "My God! Does he figure he doesn't *need* that wing?"

"This route must be reserved for pilots with steely nerves."

"They probably train on that runway next to Quintin lodge."

"Now, Lili. That was perfectly safe."

"Yeah, yeah. I suppose you're going to tell me this is, too?"

"Of course. He has a good twenty-foot leeway before he hits those mountains."

Her head whipped around and her mouth dropped open. When she saw the twinkle in Brad's eyes she snorted,

"Damn. I have got to quit being such a straight man for you."

His gaze moved over her body. "Honey, no one would ever accuse you of being a man. Straight or otherwise."

Brad leaned across her to study the terrain, and his nearness caused an inner turbulence that was more than a match for what the plane was flying through. No longer bound by any avowed restrictions, their relationship was changing rapidly. There was no doubt in Lili's mind that during the short stay at the Hermitage lodge in Mount Cook, they would make love. She'd once read an article by a doctor involved in holistic healing that claimed there were cells exactly like those of the brain in every organ of the body; that a "gut feeling" was quite literally a feeling from the gut. And, he also asserted, the feeling was often more reliable, because that cell hadn't learned self-doubt. She fervently hoped that the dictates of the heart were as trustworthy. Her brain was a mine field, with posted signs of Caution, Danger, and Turn Back, stationed at every bend. But she was running with her heart, and there *was* no turning back.

Brad stood on the balcony of his room at the Hermitage, admiring the vista laid out before him. The Maori Indians called Mount Cook "Aoriangi," which meant "the Cloud Piercer," and it certainly was living up to its name. The giant peak, snow-covered still in the middle of the New Zealand summer, protruded through the scattered white wisps, cutting a sharp and majestic silhouette against the blue sky.

He checked his watch, then clasped the iron hand-railing and leaned against it, wondering why the minutes were crawling by so slowly. He felt jittery, like a schoolboy about to go on his first formal date. It reminded him of another scene, long ago but just as incongruous....

His mother, on her way down the upstairs hall, stopped at the open door to his room. "Brad," she said, setting a shopping bag from Lord & Taylor on the floor, "why are you pacing back and forth? I swear, you look nervous as a cat in a dog kennel.''

"Hi, Mom." He grinned—foolishly, he was sure. "You're right. I am nervous, and I haven't the foggiest why. Guess I'm feeling out of character, taking Marcy's little friend out on a date.''

"Marcy's 'little friend' isn't so little anymore. She's become a lovely young woman. Maybe that's why you're edgy. Playing big brother won't be quite so easy.''

He really looked at her then. "Do I hear a message?''

"Yes, you do. Be careful, Brad. The girl has a mighty big crush on you.''

"Mom, what're you talking about? She's been hanging around here since she was a little kid. She's used to me. She hardly notices me.''

At that, his mother laughed aloud. "Oh, dear. Poor Lili has been wearing her heart on her sleeve so long that it's you who doesn't even notice.''

He pushed his fingers through his hair, then pulled a comb out of the pocket of his tuxedo to repair the damage. "She is pretty. Wonder why she didn't have a date? Those guys in her class must be blind.''

"Lili's shy, dear, and that's no asset at her age. It was kind of you to offer to take her to the prom. It would have been such a shame if she'd had to miss it.''

"No problem. Esther didn't mind." At the look on his mother's face he asked, "What's wrong?''

"Sometimes I wonder about that girl.''

"Esther?''

"Yes." She picked up her bag and waved a hand to dismiss the subject. "In any case, have a good time, and give Lili my love.''

"Will do." He'd decided that Lili's prom evening should be extraspecial, an event to remember, and so was taking her to the Ritz-Carlton for dinner before the dance. She'd been

*awestruck at the suggestion, and it became quite evident that
she rarely ate in restaurants, and when she did, it was not at
a place remotely like the Ritz.*

*She was full of starry-eyed wonder when they were ush-
ered into the handsome dining room by the tuxedoed maître
d' and seated at a corner table covered by white linen and
laid with crystal, fine china and fresh flowers. She looked so
beautiful across that elegant table, her face shining with excitement, her rounded eyes moving about the room, taking
it all in. The feeling that came over him as he watched her
should have sounded a warning. If it did, he managed to
ignore it.*

Brad stood a moment longer, gazing out over the scenic
splendor of this foreign land—so far in distance from Boston's Ritz-Carlton, so far in time from Lili's high-school
prom—wondering at the strange workings of fate. He was
about to play escort to the same woman; and he was, once
again, as nervous as a cat in a dog's kennel. He'd made reservations at the gourmet dining room downstairs. In a
strange way, it was a reenactment of that long-ago scene.
And if this evening also ended, as he hoped it would, in
lovemaking, he was determined that it would never be an
occasion that Lili would remember with pain.

Later, as he sat across a white-linen-covered table from
Lili, it struck him that her face wore the same glow of excitement, her eyes moved about the room with the same ac-
quisitive air of taking in, storing. In many ways, she was
almost as naive as the seventeen-year-old girl he remembered.

Brad turned his wineglass around while he gazed at her.
There was so much about her he didn't know, and he wanted
to know it all—every little shading of her character, every
event in her life that had touched her in a significant way.
"Does your ban on reality forbid us from talking about
family? You know, background stuff?"

She considered. "I guess not. Why?"

"I don't know much about your father. Only that he died a year or so before you and Marcy met."

"Yes." She hunched her shoulders.

"Still hurt to remember?"

"Yes. I loved him so much. It was hard to understand, at that age, how someone so vital to your life could just . . . go away."

"How did it happen?"

"Dad ran a small auto-repair shop, and one of his customers invited him to go fishing. I guess the man had a pretty fancy boat, one of those big ones with a . . . flying bridge? Is that what they call it?"

"Right."

"Anyhow, he hardly ever took any time off, and he was dying to go—" She stopped and took a sip of wine.

"Unfortunate choice of words."

"Yes."

"Go on."

"They went down to Cape Cod, out of Buzzards Bay. I remember because I was so jealous. I wanted to go with them. Anyway, there was one of those freak storms that come up all of a sudden. Mom got a call that the Coast Guard had been contacted and they were on their way out to find the boat."

"And?"

"They never did. The . . . bodies were washed ashore some time later. I can't recall just how long."

"How awful."

"I was so scared. I thought Mom was going to die, too, she got so depressed." Lili gave a shudder that spoke of great pain. "But she pulled herself together. She'd gone back to work about a year before. She was a nurse, you know." She shook her head, "No, I guess you wouldn't. Anyway, it was a good thing she had, because Dad owed a lot on his shop, and there was practically no insurance. I guess you don't think much about dying in your thirties."

"No, you don't. I'm sorry, Lili. What a loss." He ate quietly for a while, then put down his fork and said, "No wonder you have trouble believing that a man can be relied on."

Her head shot up and she stared at him. "Where did that come from? Did I say that?"

"No. Not in so many words, but there are more ways than one to communicate."

"Okay." She waved a hand. "But what does my father's death have to do with it?"

"You were so young. Your father's death must have felt like abandonment, like he didn't care enough about you to hang around." Brad gave her an apologetic smile. "A friend of mine lost his mother, and he used to tell me all the stuff his shrink talked to him about."

"So, that was enough to make him distrust women for the rest of his life?"

"No. But for you it didn't stop there. Your father was the first love of your life. Then I come along to seduce you and leave you. Two down. Then, of course, your husband lives just long enough to get you pregnant. Not very confidence-building."

"Brad! It isn't someone's fault if they die!" She paused. "As for what happened between us, well, that was at least as much my own doing—"

"You're talking reason, not feelings, Lili. It's obvious I hurt you badly, no matter how 'fair' you try to be. And as for your father, a kid doesn't feel very reasonable about being deserted by a parent, even if it's through death and not on purpose." He tilted his wineglass, letting a sip of the rich red fluid slide over his lips. "I should think Donny would have some feelings of that sort about his father."

Oh, no. Just when she felt so safe, thought she'd put all troublesome subjects off-limits, he sneaked in the most bothersome one of all. "I don't know. To tell the truth, we've never discussed it from that angle." In her agitation, she dinged her fork against the china plate. ''I hadn't thought of it.''

''Might not be a bad idea to explore it a little.'' He leaned back and gave a contented sigh. ''Now. What about dessert?''

She'd like to order up a time warp, so she could shoot back and handle a lot of things differently, then career forward to rejoin Brad. Would she, in that instance, be looking across the table at her husband? ''Vichyssoise, Caesar salad and rack of lamb. It was wonderful. And filling. There's not an inch of space left for dessert.''

''Coffee?''

''Yes, please.''

As Brad signaled the waiter and placed the order, Lili glanced around the lovely room. Funny, she hadn't eaten in a restaurant this opulent since that night of her prom, when Brad had taken her to the Ritz. What a night that had been, from beginning to end! Like a fairy tale. In fact, if she erased the aftermath, it still glowed with a singular brilliance in her memory, perfect in every detail. He had made her feel important that night, as if she were a beautiful and interesting woman. He'd been unlike the boys in her class, who leered at girls as though they were nothing more than carriers of breasts and other interesting physical formations. The sense of déjà vu followed her as they left the restaurant and she could see women's heads turn, their eyes widening as they looked at Brad. It still filled her with pride to be with him, just as it had then....

Oh, how the other girls in her class stared when Lili and Brad entered the room where the prom was held. It was Lili's first and last experience of being belle of the ball. They all came over to say hello, every last one of them acting as though she were Lili's dearest and closest friend who ''just had'' to meet her date. But despite all the flirting and broad hints, he didn't dance with anyone but her. Though he relinquished her for a few dances with other boys, he watched from the sidelines until he could reclaim her. She pressed close to him as they danced, her forehead against his cheek, covetously cupping the back of his neck with the palm of her left hand, her fingers straying into his hair, the way the other girls did with their steadies. She wanted them all to believe he was hers. Most of all, she wanted to believe it herself—if only for that one evening.

They left the Hermitage dining room and walked through the lobby, hand in hand; then up the stairs to the second floor, down the hall to her door. Without a word, Lili handed him her key, knowing, as he did, she was setting something in motion that couldn't be stopped. Just like that other night....

Debby Hendersen invited them to come to her house after the dance, for an "après" party. Lili knew she'd never have been invited if it hadn't been for her alluring date. Debby Hendersen was the true holder of "most popular girl" status. She was beautiful and rich and lived her life completely outside the perimeters of Lili's world. Brad, with some coaxing, agreed to go. He was charming and urbane and had every girl there wild with longing and every boy ready to kill. But his attention never strayed from Lili, and it filled her with a euphoria that became inflated with reckless abandon. This was her night, the night of her life. She was sure of it. She drank too much of the champagne Debby's parents had provided, and her flirtatiousness toward Brad took on sexual innuendo, gleaned from watching others, from seeing movies and from all the uncharted yearnings of her own young body.

As the time grew very late he asked, "Shouldn't you call your mom? She's probably worried."

"Mother isn't home."

"What?"

"Her sister is very sick. She lives in Connecticut, so Mom drove down to be with her for a couple of days."

"But she was there when we left."

"I know. She wanted to see me all dressed up. She was going to leave right after we did." She moved closer, her

breast pressed against his arm. "She said to ask you to look through the house before you left me."

The expression on his face could only be described as alarm. "God, Lili." His fingers touched her cheek, ran down to trace the outline of her parted lips. "Maybe you should come to our house, stay over with Marcy." His eyes were full of hunger, like someone half-starved. He wanted her—she knew he did—and the knowledge filled her with heady power.

"I can't. I have to be at the house in the morning." At that moment, she couldn't remember why. Everything was sliding from her mind but the image of the man by her side, the rampant cravings racing through every part of her.

"Maybe I'd better get you home." His eyes were smoky blue, the pupils huge. He'd had quite a bit of the champagne, too. She wondered if his head was whirling, as hers was.

"Can we stay just a little longer? Fifteen minutes?" The idea of ending the night, saying goodbye to Brad—a goodbye too final to contemplate without pain—was something to be postponed for as long as possible. Besides, tomorrow she'd be Cinderella again, smudged with ashes.

Brad fitted the key in the lock of her door and swung it open. Moonlight flooded the hotel room, beaming across the double bed like a directional spotlight. They stepped inside and he kicked the door shut with one heel while he reached for her. Any trace of reservation left in her vanished the moment his hand grasped her shoulder. *"Lili."* The hoarsely uttered name was heavily coated with desire, desire that shone from the depths of his blue-black eyes. Deliberately and with great tenderness, he drew her into his arms. "Lili. My God, you're beautiful. Ah, Lili, I want you so much." She arched into the curve of his body while her arms slid around his neck. When their lips met, a sigh of relief heaved through her. Home at last....

Brad pulled up outside Lili's house in the racy white Mustang convertible that had been a twenty-first birthday

*present from his grandfather. He sat, enthralled by the
moonlight tracing the fine bone structure of her face. "Ah,
Lili. You have become a beautiful woman." He reached for
her then, and drew her to him. Lili swiftly closed the gap
between them, going into his embrace without hesitation.
The moment his lips touched hers, Brad knew he was in
trouble. But she'd been provoking a kiss for hours, and his
blood was the temperature of molten lava.*

*Though he tried to pull back, his ardor was too much
aroused to resist the pull of her eager mouth, the twining of
her fingers in his hair. He must have been totally wrong
about Lili. These were not the actions of an innocent girl.
She was throwing herself at him with a wantonness that be-
lied her image of inexperience. And Brad wanted her. His
wanting was a hot, demanding stream racing through his
veins, a wanting beyond anything he'd felt before. God, he
had to stop this! Had to get her safely into that house and
get himself out of here. Fast!*

*He untangled himself and opened the car door in the same
movement. "Come on, Lili. Time to go in."*

*When they reached the back door to her house, she
handed him the key. He took it, stared at it a moment, then
at her, hunching his shoulders, trying to find some relief
from tensed muscles. After a brief pause, he fitted the key
in the lock and swung open the door.*

*She stepped inside and turned. He stood rooted to the
outside landing, his hand flat against the doorjamb, as
though he could prevent himself from stepping over that
threshold.*

*"Brad?" Her face was luminous in the moonlight, her
lovely eyes inviting. Her hand reached toward him. "Are
you going to check the house?"*

*Dazed by desire, he followed her through the rooms of the
house, barely noticing their contents or the possibility of a
lurking form. When he stepped into the second bedroom, he
knew at once it was hers. The traitorous moonlight slid*

through the window, slithered across the floor, climbed across the expanse of the bed... pointing the way.

"Lili..."

"Oh, Brad. Please don't go."

His lips met hers, softly at first. Then the pent-up, dutifully contained hunger gave way, and the kiss deepened into a mutual exchange of desire and need. Lili's arms slid up around his shoulders, her fingers pushing into the thick hair at the nape of his neck, savoring the feel of the coarse, wiry strands that twisted covetously around them, extending the kiss to her fingertips. As Brad withdrew from the kiss, his face a few inches from hers, he raised his hand and ran it over her hair in a gesture tender, sweet, full of affection. His gaze caressed her features, as though to imprint each one forever in his mind. Lili was awed by the magnitude of what was happening to her. Brad was reawakening something that had lain dormant in her for eleven years; but now it was increased, expanded—a sexual craving beyond anything in her experience.

Yesterday and today, now and forever, melded, blended, dissolved into each other as she willingly sank into the swirl of her growing desire. He lowered his face to hers, his lips parting in anticipation, the look in his eyes further heating her. She felt her mouth opening, her feet rising on tiptoe to rush the closing of that tiny space. Oh, how could it feel so exquisitely wonderful, this meeting of mouth to mouth?

Gentleness gave way to an untamed, primitive letting go. His tongue explored, darting and thrusting, finding and disclosing. His hand moved from her hair to her throat, cupping around it. She arched her neck, offering herself in animal-like submission to his possession. His fingers slid down the V neck of her dress, dipping in to lightly press the tops of her breasts. With painstaking, agonizing slowness he unbuttoned each of the small covered buttons that restrained her full breasts. Lili wanted him to rip the garment away, to hurry, hurry. He pushed the dress off her shoulders and down her arms, the movement one long caress that left pinpricks of longing in its wake. His hands met in back, finding the clasp on her bra and finally releasing her. She sighed, impatient for his hands to move around and touch her where she longed to be touched. At last, at last! One palm cupped her breast while the fingertips of the other teased the nipple to a bursting ripeness.

Their clothes seemed to fall away, and their heated bodies found the cool surface of the quilt-covered bed. Lili moaned aloud as her body strained toward him, responding to the touch of his fingers, his lips, his tongue. Her palms tingled as they moved over the smooth tautness of his skin, exploring the ridges of muscle. How she loved him! All the years of waiting accelerated her need to be one with him, to be separate no more. At last, moved beyond endurance, she gasped, "Now. Please, please, now. Come to me, Brad!" With a growl of pleasure, he thrust deeply into her. The glory of their union surpassed the splendor of crashing waterfalls, jutting mountain peaks, and the gleaming moonlight in which they lay.

Then they slept...satiated with pleasure, wrapped in each other's warmth. Brad did not return to his own room that night.

The next day sped by, for time was accelerated by the balm of pure joy. They flew to the top of Mount Cook in a small airplane with skis instead of wheels and landed on the flat surface of the glacier, where they looked out over a mountain range indescribable in its majesty. As they stood on the crusted surface of the snow, Lili took a deep breath of air so bitingly fresh it was a shock to lungs accustomed to years of sorting out pollutants.

"This must be it. Heaven."

Brad squinted his eyes, moving his head slowly to take in the panorama. "You could be right. What do you think? Could you take up permanent residence?"

She laughed. "Do you suppose there's a loo? And hot and cold running water?"

"In heaven? If you need it, it must be there." Suddenly Lili was hit by an onslaught of fear so virulent it shook her entire body. Brad's hand shot out to take hold of her arm. "Lili? What's wrong? Are you okay?"

"I was just remembering a dream."

"Must be some dream, to cause a reaction like that."

"It's one I've had a number of times over the years. You know, the kind that haunts you afterward?"

"So tell me."

"I'm usually running through a field full of flowers— beautiful, like it is here. I feel absolutely free and totally fearless and incredibly happy." The shudder ran through her again and Brad's grip tightened. "Then, some enormous dark form swoops down out of the sky, shutting out the light of the sun, and plucks me out of the field. I never know where it's taking me, but I know I'll never come back to that wonderful place, and that I'll never be that happy again."

He pulled her into his arms and held her. "Honey. You have to learn to trust happiness. It *can* last, you know. Even through the rough spots." He gave a short laugh, derisive in tone. "I guess I'm a fine one to spout that philosophy, with a failed marriage behind me. But my basic optimism keeps beckoning."

Lili looked up at him, silhouetted against the pristine sky, his eyes an echo of its perfect blue, and a sudden need to see her son, to hold him and feel his substance, overcame her. "Brad, when we get to Queenstown, I want to change my ticket. I want to go home when you do."

"Really? I mean, I'd love to have your company on the flight, but you still have a week's vacation here. You've looked forward to it so long."

"I forgot to factor homesickness into my planning." She couldn't stay here after he left, alone with all the worrisome uncertainties of her future. If she told him the tightly guarded secret that had dominated her life, would the great, dark "thing" swoop out of the sky to carry her to some awful perdition? Or was it possible that happiness could last, as Brad believed? At the moment, the only thing she was sure of was her need to be home with her son.

The return flight to Queenstown seemed tame, taken on calm air through a clear sky. Lili's fears were layered over by the sweetness of love and joy that permeated the atmosphere around the two of them. On the following morning, the ticket exchange went smoothly, and the shopping tour was another first for Lili, conducted, as it was at Brad's insistence, with stern orders not to look at price tags.

"Brad, I feel like a kept woman!" she exclaimed as her hands moved covetously over the soft silk of one of the dresses he had helped her select.

"Good. A little decadence is conducive to a balanced outlook. Makes it easier to spot temptation the next time."

"That doesn't make any sense."

"Isn't supposed to. Now quit arguing and try on the clothes."

By one o'clock they were seated across from each other ravenously devouring an unabashedly American meal of hamburgers, French fries and chocolate milk shakes. Lili swallowed a tasty bit of potato and sighed. "Boy, this is good. I have a confession to make. I have a decidedly unhealthy appetite. I love meat and eggs and chocolate and fried foods."

"Uh-oh. The courtship is off."

"Is this a courtship?"

"No. This is all a mirage. A short sojourn in fantasyland, as per your directive. The real courtship begins as soon as we get back to the States."

A chunk of hamburger stuck for a moment in its journey down her throat. She had to make a decision. Had to. A courtship. Everything she'd dreamed about. The dangling carrot was right in front of her nose. She could smell it. And if he did come calling, and met Donny. Oh, no. Not yet, not yet. This *was* a stopover in Never-Never Land, and she was determined to ward off reality just a little longer.

"We'll have to talk about that later, since it's off-limits for the next few days." She smiled at him, hoping to take any edge off her refusal to discuss the future. "Are you still set on seeing the bungy jumpers?"

"I don't want to be arbitrary about it. If you really don't want to—"

"Oh, no. Actually, it'll be fun. Since we've agreed that there's no way I'm having anything to do with it."

"Of course." His smile was just a little bit lopsided.

The location for the bungy jump was about a twenty-mile drive out of Queenstown. As they tooled toward the Kawarau River, Brad hummed happily, tapping a rhythm on the steering wheel. "Well—" Lili scooted over to sit closer "—you're in a good mood."

"And why not? It's a lovely, sunny day in New Zealand, and I'm sharing it with the one woman who can make it all perfect. I'm almost indecently happy. In fact, I feel like shouting it to the world. In fact, I think I *will* shout it to the world." With that, he rolled down the window, stuck his head out and yelled, "I'm falling in love, world!"

She laid her head on his shoulder, wallowing in a suffusion of joy. "Honestly, I'm beginning to fear there's a strain of insanity in your family."

"I certainly hope so. What would life be without it?"

When they arrived, there were already lots of cars parked at the abandoned railroad bridge that spanned the river. Clusters of people, mostly young, lined the cliffed banks of the Kawarau, watching the proceedings. Just as Brad and Lili walked within viewing range, they saw a young man, his ankles bound and a long cord attached, give a piercing scream and hurtle off the edge of the bridge.

"Oh, my God!" Lili gasped.

The jumper reached the end of the line, rebounded into the air, halfway back up to the bridge, down again, and then gradually, little by little, bounced to a stop. A small rubber boat moved out on the river to pick him up. By the time he was let on shore, the next jumper was ready to go.

"They're nuts!" Lili couldn't believe the lineup of potential patrons of this bizarre sport.

"I've *got* to do this." Brad wore an expression of maniacal intent.

"Brad, you've got to be kidding. You might be killed."

"They've never had an accident."

"Maybe. But what's the wear rate on that oversize rubber band?"

Nothing would deter him. Lili watched in helpless horror as Brad strode to the bridge, paid his seventy-five dollars, and was trussed up like the victim of an upside-down hanging. Was this the end? Maybe Brad would never have the chance to know he was a father. The thought was piercingly hurtful—enough to bring the whole, unwanted subject sharply to mind once more. It had to be resolved. Soon.

Brad shot out into the air in a perfect swan dive, emitting a yell of pure glee, bounced safely to a stop and was picked up by the boat. During the procedure, Lili figured she never breathed once. And at the same time, a crazy resolve was forming in her mind. They called this "the leap of faith," a name she'd jeered at when Brad told her. "Faith in what? A long string of rubber?" But now, having watched him soar into the air, arms outstretched, she knew she had to do it. If she could summon the courage for this, maybe it would serve as a warm-up for that final leap of faith. Maybe she'd be able to tell him, trusting that their burgeoning love would carry them through the crisis.

Brad was enthusiastic about her decision. "It's a once-in-a-lifetime experience, Lili! You'll love it! They take a video of each person. Think how impressed Donny will be!"

Once the process was set in motion, she'd have given a year's salary to reverse it, to go back to being a bystander. But bystanding was a role no longer possible for her. The leap must be made—one far more frightening than this. If, she wondered as she approached the bridge, anything could be more frightening than this.

Somehow Lili found the strength to get herself to the small platform they'd built to extend over the water, while a tanned, obnoxiously cheerful young man wrapped a heavy towel around her ankles and attached the bungy cord over it. She was so terrified she couldn't speak. His voice chirped on: "Don't look down, look out. And leap, looking straight over at that next bridge down the river. Hold your arms out like a bird. You want to get the best flight possible."

Lili nodded dumbly, wishing she were Catholic, so she could say a rosary; wishing she hadn't chosen this particular activity for the "warm-up"; wishing she weren't here in the first place. Then she was on her feet on the brink of oblivion with that damn-fool kid counting, "Five, four, three, two, one, *go!*" There was a pause, filled by friendly, good-natured laughter. "Okay, take a deep breath. We'll start again. Five, four, three, two, one..."

Lili sailed out into the air, sure it was the last thing she'd ever do, hoping her son and her mother would forgive her this suicidal foolishness. The cord caught, and she was hurled back up in the air, and suddenly she was filled with the most extraordinary sensation of freedom and invincibility she'd ever experienced. As she bobbed up and down, finally settling to a bottoms-up stillness, a feeling of infinite pride washed over her. "I did it!" she yelled. At that moment in time, hanging upside down over a river in New Zealand, she made a momentous decision. She *would* tell Brad, and she'd do it before they left for home.

As they walked away from the banks of the Kawarau, clutching yet another certificate, this one stating that the bearer had the exceeding bad judgment to risk life and limb by leaping off a bridge, Lili was buoyed by heady triumph. She had risked, she had survived—first the Milford Track, second the bungy jump. She would take the final risk, trusting in the charm of threes. And now she knew where and when she would do it. Tomorrow night. At Huka Lodge.

* * *

Lili looked out the window of an indisputably elegant suite in the Huka Lodge, waiting nervously for Brad to finish dressing so they could go downstairs to dinner. This was it. The big night. Her stomach churned and there was an ominous flutter in her heart, but her determination remained steady. After all, she'd bungied, hadn't she? She could do anything!—she swallowed hard—she hoped.

She glanced down at herself, still stunned to see her own body encased in such softly clinging, exquisitely crafted fabric. And this place! Their room, a cabin-suite set a short distance from the main lodge, gave credence to the fantasy mind-set into which they had both entered. A large, plushly furnished bedroom, a dressing room, a bath equipped with all the jets and whirls and gadgets imaginable, with sliding-glass doors leading down a sloping lawn to the Waikato River. They were about to go to the glamorous lodge for cocktails and canapés, before being seated for what was guaranteed to be the top culinary experience of her life. And Brad had vowed, as soon as they had checked in and toured the facilities, that they'd come back for an extended visit. There was no end to the offerings: golf, tennis, fishing, boating, hiking. She took a long look around. Wow. What money could buy!

They'd flown to the Taupo airport, where a limousine had picked them up and whisked them here for their two-day stay. Then, soon, they'd be on their way. From Taupo to Hawaii, where they had an overnight stay, to San Francisco, and on home, to Boston.

So. Tonight. She'd tell him tonight, after the romantic dinner, here in the privacy of this lovely place. That way, they'd have a full day and night left to walk the grounds, see the falls, and talk.

The phone rang. Startled, Lili went over to answer it. "Hello."

There was a drawn-out silence on the other end, then a man's voice asked, "Is this Brad Hollingsworth's room?"

"Yes. Just a moment, I'll call him." With a puzzled frown, she handed the receiver to Brad, who had just come out of the dressing room.

"Who is it?"

"I have no idea."

"Strange. My secretary's the only one who knows where I am." He took the phone and answered, "Hello."

Lili watched with a growing sense of dismay as he listened, making monosyllabic replies. "Oh?" "Jesus, how bad?" "When?" "God. Where is she?" "Yeah, you're right." Her heart sank when he said, "Sure. Of course. I'll get there as soon as I can."

"What is it?" she asked as soon as he hung up.

He stared off into the distance for only a few seconds, but long enough for her to feel a physical twang of disconnection. His mind had shifted; he was somewhere else entirely.

"It's Esther. She's been in a car accident."

"Is she—"

"They think she'll be okay. But there's some question about one of her legs. She's having trouble getting feeling back in it."

Something leaden sank to the bottom of Lili's stomach. She was afraid it was her heart. He had the telephone receiver in his hand again. "What are you doing?"

"She's been asking for me. I have to go."

"But—"

His eyes moved to her, troubled, distant. "I do still care about her. She's very frightened and she needs me."

She needs me. Lili's blood seemed to have formed ice crystals that ground through her veins, shaking a frigid path. All her carefully laid plans for the evening had been obliterated by one phone call. His ex-wife needed him and he was going. Instinctively, instantly. Without a second thought. She observed through a blue haze as Brad talked to the agent at the airlines, impatiently tracking down an empty seat on one plane to Auckland, a jet to Hawaii, another to San Francisco, another to New York. Yes, yes, he said. First class is fine. Book it.

She shook herself, trying to dislodge the dull anguish permeating her system. She mustn't be small-minded about this. Esther had been badly injured, and she wanted him there. He should go. Should, should, should. All the shoulds and oughts in the world wouldn't stop the hurt careening through her. She watched through a dull ache as he pulled out his duffel bag and started emptying drawers.

"I have to leave as soon as possible. I've got a flight from Taupo to Auckland in two hours. Sorry to leave you, but it's got to be this way. I'll call you next week, after you get home. I'll know more about what's required of me by then. Stay here and relax, put everything on the bill. I'll arrange things at the desk."

Lili fished wildly around in her jumbled mind for a mundane, everyday subject. Something, anything to put all this on a rational level where it could be dealt with. He'd call her. They'd pick up and proceed from there. Wouldn't they?

"Who was that who called? He sounded very surprised to have a woman answer the phone."

"Oh—yeah, he would. That was Esther's brother, Jerry."

"I hope that won't be awkward for you." Her breath stuck in her throat as she waited for him to reassure her, tell her he'd be talking about her anyway.

"Jerry won't mention it. In fact, it may slip his mind by then. He drinks pretty heavily, and things get clouded."

"A drinker? In Esther's family?" She bit her tongue, hoping the tone hadn't sounded acerbic rather than simply surprised.

Totally occupied with his packing, trying to be sure everything was covered, he was filling the dead air with conversation. "Jerry's kind of a sad case. Used to be lots of fun. Bright, creative, a little zany. Then, well, he got tangled up with a girl when he was only about twenty-one. Not the kind of girl anyone'd want to bring home to mother, so to speak. Anyway, she got knocked up and told him it was his. Can't blame her. He was the hottest prospect around. I can't see how she'd ever have proved it, considering the track record she had, but Jerry just caved in. Married her, had another child. Eight years of sheer misery. All the pizzazz went right out of him. He acted like a caged animal and started hitting the bottle. Never has straightened out his life."

The ice crystals solidified, turning Lili into a block of frozen angst. The wrong kind of girl. A ruined life. Oh, God. Was she drawing a parallel that didn't apply? But look at him, hurrying home to Esther, the kind of girl one *would* bring home to mother. He had walked away from her once, eleven years ago, without a backward glance. And what was happening right now looked ominously familiar.

"Does he stay with her because of the kids?"

"He stays with her out of inertia. It's a sad bit of business, all around. Esther's parents saw a lawyer, just to explore what would be involved in getting temporary custody of Christopher and Jenny. I'm not sure what came of it."

He gathered up his gear, hurriedly kissed her goodbye, promised to call although he hadn't asked for her number, and then, just before walking out the door to head downstairs to the waiting taxi, he dropped his valise, pulled out his wallet, took out a large amount of money and laid it on the side table. "This should cover everything. Goodbye, sweetheart." And he was gone.

She stared at the wad of bills. Cover everything. And what did that entail? Services rendered?

She ate a lonely meal. Excellent and intolerably exclusive. She lay awake all night in the king-size bed. She sat alone in the breakfast room where other people sat in pairs or small groups. Then she took a lonely walk by the spectacular rush of the Huka Falls.

Leaning over an iron rail next to the falls, she let her eyes roam down the roiling rapids to the river, where she saw, clear as a full-grown whale, her hopes and dreams rushing downstream and out of sight.

Chapter Ten

Lili stood in the lineup of passengers waiting to disembark from the 747 into the terminal at Logan International Airport. Home at last. She adjusted the carry-on bag, painfully aware of its weight on her shoulder. Every part of her ached from the long hours crammed into a coach seat. Even with an overnight stay in Hawaii, seventeen hours of flying was a lot, especially when the "rest stop" was a miserable, endless, sleepless night filled with nonstop "awfulizing." Her brain was battered, flailed by the unrelenting parade of what-ifs marched through it in the last umpteen hours. All the way home, her only longing had been to get home as fast as she could, straight through to Massachusetts, to Boston, to her mother and child. To safety? Or was there any such thing?

Mile after mile, hour after hour, she'd gone over every possible scenario, each successive replay looking worse than its predecessor. If only she'd come straight home from Australia, forgone the indulgence of a vacation in New

Zealand! *Stop it, stop it, stop it!* This had been talked out ad nauseum before she left. It had been such an exciting prospect, with her enthusiasm cheered on by both her mother and her son.

Besides, it could have been the most important, incredible turning point of her life. Might still be, how did she know? Maybe Brad would call and would say, "Esther's doing fine. Mom and Dad and Marcy are dying to see you again. They were so pleased to hear about our trip together." She winced at the pain that shot through her gut. How could a knot in the stomach shake its head? How could nerve ends titter "Fat chance"?

The passengers in front and in back of her were beginning to mutter about the delay in opening the door. Why was it taking so long? Suppose... Oh, no, don't add disaster to disaster. There'd been so much invented by her agitated brain since that phone call. What if the call had come later, after she'd told Brad? The question had dogged her through the skies over fast-changing hemispheres, answering itself over and over with pictorial displays.

Brad sitting by Esther's bed. "I have a son." Her eyes lighting up, the pallor of injury brightening. "A son? Oh, Brad, that's the answer to all our prayers! How can we get him? How?"

Brad telling his parents: "I met Lili Jamison—had he asked her why she kept her own last name? So many made-up stories to remember—in New Zealand. She had a baby. My baby."

His parents, aghast at her secrecy. "She's raising him in *Dorchester?* A Hollingsworth in Dorchester? What if he gets hurt? It seems very irresponsible of her, not telling us, not letting us help. Perhaps we should get a lawyer."

At last the door opened, and the surge of bodies carried her forward and through customs—an interminable wait behind luggage-laden tourists. And just on the other side of the doors, Donny. Her son. *Her* son! Nobody on the face of the earth would ever take him from her!

The moment Lili entered the waiting area, she heard his voice. "Mom! Mom! Over here!"

And then he was in her arms. She hugged the wiry little body to her with a ferocity born of joy, relief, fear. "Donny. Oh, Donny, it's so good to see you!"

"Hey, Mom, you're smothering me! Lighten up or you'll have a dead kid!"

She laughed and held him away from her, soaking in the sight of this boy she loved so dearly. Deep blue eyes, tousled blond hair, face twinkling with happiness. A miniature Brad. "Well, I certainly don't want a dead kid. Oh, it's so good to see you!"

"You, too, Mom. I've missed you!" He bobbed up and down like a duck in water.

Lili turned to her mother and experienced a powerful surge of comfort as she stepped into her embrace. "Oh, Mom. God, it's good to be home." Tears trickled from her eyes, and Louise patted her lovingly on the cheek and said, "It must be a relief to be here, after such a long trip."

"Yes. You have no idea."

Donny wedged between her and her mother on the front seat during the ride home, rattling off questions like a crazed ticker tape. Lili had to think fast, to delete the presence of Brad from all the answers. "Yes, I did fine on the hike. And don't look so surprised! Your mother turned into a regular mountain woman!"

"Australia was very interesting. But I was so busy while I was there I didn't do a lot of sight-seeing."

"Yes, it's true that the toilets flush in the opposite direction."

"I brought you a mask made by the Maoris. They're the natives who first settled New Zealand."

"Wait, just wait until you see the video I brought. Have you ever heard of a bungy jump?"

How would she ever explain how she, Lili the fainthearted, flew off a bridge with an oversize rubber band attached, without explaining Brad's support? Well, she'd think of something. Right now, it was enough to be here with Donny and her mother. She'd figure the rest out later. She glanced over her shoulder at her suitcases. Thank heavens she'd had the sense to pack their presents separately from her new clothes. There was no way to explain those expensive garments unless she told about Brad. For now, they'd have to be hidden away in her closet.

On her second day back at work—four long, long days of waiting since her return—Brad called. "Hi, Lili."

Warmth whirlpooled through her body at the sound of his voice. He had tracked her down through the Digital system. She should have known he would. "Brad, how are you? How's...everything?"

His voice sounded tentative, tired. "I'm all right. How was your trip home?"

Endless. Lonely. Terrifying. "Fine." Words scattered, having vacated her mind.

"I'm sorry not to have called before. It's been...hectic. Esther's in tough shape."

"Her leg?"

"Oh, that'll be okay. She'll need a short period of physical therapy, but it'll come back to normal." A pause. "She's having a lot of trouble emotionally. I hadn't realized, well, how devastated she is by the divorce. And the accident, coming so soon after. Well, she's in tough shape."

Lili felt sorry for Esther, for the fear and the pain she was going through. It must be terrible, on top of that, to realize you'd lost someone as wonderful as Brad—if she *had* lost him. Lili wanted to be compassionate, but more than anything she wanted Brad. And she could feel him sliding away from her, back to Esther's side. "I'm sorry." Muteness held her captive. But did it matter? What else could she say?

"I told Marcy and the folks about running into you, and about our spending some time together. They were excited to hear about how you're doing and would love to see you."

Hope popped its head up, alert, while everything else stopped. *Could life be sustained without a heartbeat?*

"But—"

There it was, that terrible word.

"I haven't said anything to anyone—about our falling in love, I mean."

Back in your box, I hope.

"It's not that I want to hide anything."

Oh, no, of course not.

"But the timing is bad."

As always.

"I have to stick by Esther through the worst of this, until she's on her feet again."

Physically? Emotionally? Both? Somewhere between a week and forever?

"I need so to see you, to be with you."

But not to tell my parents or my friends or my sister. The kind of girl you wouldn't want to bring home to mother?

Lili knew, in that one, tiny, isolated, innermost part of her mind that was functioning on reason instead of hysteria, that she wasn't processing this well. That information was filtering through all the frightening webs of irrational suppositions she'd spun on the plane ride home. But she couldn't seem to push past the pervasive fear that somehow all this would boomerang, and Donny would be hurt. Or, horror of horrors, Donny would be lost to her.

"How about you? How did your mother take the news that we'd been together?"

She shuffled some papers around on her desk, as though there might be a good answer hidden beneath. "I ... Well, she was surprised."

"I'll bet. So, did you show her and Donny the pictures?"

"What? Oh, yes. At least ... Some. Obviously, I didn't want to show them a lot with you in them. I just told Mom we'd been on the hike together and found we were to be in a few other places at the same time, so met up for dinner and some touring."

"Yeah. Good idea."

Good idea. Don't get anyone's expectations up. It only makes for a harder fall.

"When can we get together?"

"Brad, it's a bad time for me, too." Words, suddenly, were spilling out of her mouth. "I have to spend some time in New Hampshire. A problem they're having there. I'll be gone, oh, I'd guess ten days—two weeks?" She'd been asked to take a trip, but not to New Hampshire. She had begged off. Now she'd go. There was another reason to do so. Another offer she had declined and would now reconsider. "I'm going to take Mom and Donny with me. He's out of school on vacation. They need to get away, and he needs to stay with me." *Oh, Lili, here you go again!*

"Damn. That sounds like a lifetime." Was that disappointment she heard, or relief? Was she capable of telling the difference?

"Well, it'll give you time to get things settled. With Esther." To decide whether that divorce will ever become truly final.

"I know. But still, I'd hoped we could see each other."

"Brad." She sat up straight, hoping it would firm her voice. "Until *everything* is really settled with...your ex-wife, I'd rather we didn't let things go any further."

She could hear the long sigh, and: "Okay. That's fair. Not appealing, but fair. It won't be all that long, in any case. Can I call you?" Not: *everything is final, Lili. I love you, and there is no doubt in my mind about our being together.* Tenuous. He sounded very tenuous.

Somewhere around her midsection, an instinct called out, "Trust him, Lili. He's in a tight spot and doing what he has to do. Go with me, your gut feel, and trust him!" But all her defense systems were on red alert. And her defense systems were numerous, well entrenched and overprepped for action.

"Not really. I'll be in and out, going between several facilities. It would be awkward."

"I understand." There was a long pause. "But damn it, Lili." He sighed. "Okay. Call me when you get back." She took down his office number, wondering if she'd ever use it.

She scarcely remembered the rest of the conversation. She had locked into a course of action, and her mind was already moving full bore ahead.

Lili dropped the pebble in the pond that night at the dinner table.

She watched Donny, chattering, animated, still agog at the sight, via video, of his very own mother leaping off that bridge, asking if some of his friends could come over to see that and her snapshots when they came back from the developer's. She was more sure than ever that she must take any steps necessary to keep him from being pulled apart in a custody suit. A deep core of panic had been alerted by her conversation with Brad. He had certainly sounded like a man whose duty and sense of commitment was with another woman. And Lili didn't have the luxury of waiting around to see, of letting fate take its course. Esther was ill and disturbed, and she would give her soul for a child. Brad's child. And Brad was an honorable man who, despite his divorce, had a basic belief in marriage as a lifetime commitment and fulfilled his obligations.

Her eyes shifted to her mother, and she noted once again the expression of puzzled concern that had been on Louise's face since her return. Her mother had an uncanny ability to spot trouble when it involved Lili, but there was nothing to be done about it at the moment, except to avoid the too-discerning eyes.

As it happened, Donny gave her the perfect opening for what she had to bring up. He tapped the steak bone on his plate with his fork and asked, "Can I save this for Clementine?" Clementine was a dog of mixed ancestry that belonged to a friend down the street.

"Sure."

"She's a neat dog. Billy's taught her how to nod her head when he asks if she wants something. She'll sure nod it for this!" A wistful look crossed his face. "Sure wish the old landlord'd let *us* have a dog!"

Lili took a deep breath and plunged. "Well, there's a chance that you'll be able to, honey. I wanted to talk to both of you about it."

Donny's eyes seemed to shoot sparks when he was excited. "Really? How?"

"I have a wonderful job offer, with the Digital office in Colorado Springs."

Her mother gasped and dropped her knife. "Lili! So that's what you've been stewing over!"

"I didn't want to bring it up until the offer was definite, but they want me to go out to troubleshoot the purchasing system, and also to look over the setup, see if I'd be interested." She paused, sucking in air. "I know it's a long way away, but there'd be a good salary increase, and we could afford a lot better place to live there, since the prices aren't as high." She smiled at Donny, selling the idea. "And I'd make sure you could have a dog." The offer had been made before she left for Australia, and she'd put them off, thinking about her almost-attained college degree and the midyear change of school for Donny. Luckily, she hadn't said a flat no.

"Colorado? Wow. That's way far away." She could see the war inside his head: lost friends and schoolmates versus dog and adventure.

Louise frowned. "My goodness."

"Mom, would you mind awfully? I know you've always lived in New England, but it might be exciting. All the moving expenses would be paid, and we could get out of this neighborhood." That was the one big negative, as far as Lili could see, in her son's environment, and she had the capacity to change that, all by herself.

Louise nodded. They'd both been deeply bothered by the deterioration of the area. The steady encroachment of drugs and guns and gangs. They knew the time to move was here, one way or the other. "I don't know, honey. It might be fun, actually, to do something new. It's not like we have family here. And we can make new friends." She patted Donny's hand. "You'd have new buddies in no time, Donny."

"I wanted to let you both think about it," Lili went on. "I have to go in any case, and if there's a possibility for the move, I'll look around while I'm there. See about schools and all." Run. Escape. Before the sky could fall. She touched her son's arm. "Donny? What think?"

"A dog, huh? My own dog. That'd be awesome."

She smiled. "Sounds like it's safe to at least look."

Lili picked up the photos the next day and screened them in the privacy of her office, taking out all the shots that included Brad and storing them in a locked drawer in her desk. It was a trip over an emotional roller coaster, the highs and lows astounding in their impact. And again that night, with Donny and Louise, show-and-tell; but not all. Not all by a long shot.

She had talked to Brad on Tuesday and thrown up her smoke screen, discussed Colorado with her family on a Thursday. The following Sunday found her, once again, belted into a seat on a plane, heading off into the unknown.

Brad paced his office, too distracted to concentrate on the pile of papers on his desk. God, he was tired—the kind of tired that sent creeping tweezers of nerve pinchers over the flesh at night to keep him from sleeping. His need for Lili consumed him; her image sat in his consciousness like a spring day. He'd been so torn since his return, feeling sorry and, admittedly, guilty about Esther, her pain and her frantic desire to hold on to him. Why, he didn't really understand. They'd shared nothing for such a long time, and she had seemed as relieved as he to end the strain of the marriage. But the accident had set her off on a tangent of regret and turned her into a full-fledged clinging vine.

But the past few days had wrought a change in his attitude. He was beginning to feel manipulated, and he didn't like the feeling one bit. He had finally, just the night before, talked to the doctor in charge, who had appeared surprised at some of Brad's questions. It sounded very much as though the extent of her injuries had been exaggerated, and that the only apparent reason was to bring him running. The marriage had been dead for a very long time, and he needed his complete freedom. He was in love with another woman.

The one conversation he'd had with Lili had bothered him and had been on his mind ever since. He had dwelled too much on his own troubles and hadn't told her how much he loved her and missed her and needed her. And Lili had sounded distant, unsure. Every time he went over the dialogue in his mind, it increased his feeling of unrest. Although he'd tried to call her twice since then, she'd been out of her office and hadn't returned the calls. It had been quite clear she thought they shouldn't see each other until she returned from New Hampshire, to give him time to disentangle himself from Esther's problems. And although he could appreciate her logic, he was angry with himself for not just driving to Dorchester to see her and hold her in his arms and reinforce the love they'd shared in New Zealand. Now she was gone, and he'd just have to wait.

Well, he had to go to Boston on business the next day. One of his Harvard classmates was a vice president at Digital. Maybe he'd just call him up, have lunch or dinner. Silly as it sounded, it would make him feel closer to Lili. He reached for the phone. The secretary had to track him down.

"Brad Hollingsworth! What a surprise!"

"How are you, Jim? It has been a long time." They exchanged the usual updating of information. "I ran into an old friend of my little sister's while I was in New Zealand," Brad said, after a few minutes." As it happens, she works for Digital, and it made me think of you and how overdue a get-together was."

"I'm delighted to hear from you." Yes, he could have lunch. "What's the name of your friend? Lili Jamison? Yes, I have met her. Works for one of my managers." They set a time and place.

Brad and Jim sat across from each other at a table in Locke-Ober's, sipping a glass of wine and catching up on family, friends and careers.

"I'm sorry to hear about your divorce, Brad. And Esther's accident. The 'everything at once' department. Amazing how often that's the case," Jim said sympathetically.

"Isn't it the truth. She'll be fine, though, and we're a lot better off apart than together. We'd become a world-class mutual destruction team. It can be done subtly, you know. Snide little remarks, intentional disinterest, that sort of thing. I never thought I had the instincts of a bastard until these last years of my marriage."

"Yeah, I know what you mean. I've seen some of my friends go through it. Painful business. Oh, speaking of business, I mentioned your running into Lili Jamison to Sam Boyd, her boss. Seems she does a crackerjack job. Been doing a lot of troubleshooting lately, from what he tells me. He's very high on her." Jim grinned. "Says she's quite a looker, too."

Brad returned the smile, resisting the impulse to crowbar more information out of him. "That she is. Also one hell of a fine person. She and Marcy were real chums in their teens."

"Funny, your running into her in New Zealand, of all places. Small-world department. Sam says she's out in Colorado for a couple of weeks."

Brad crackled to attention. "Colorado? Oh, no. I think it's New Hampshire."

The other man shook his head. "Uh-uh. You must have misunderstood. She was doing a lot of work in New Hampshire before her trip to Australia. But it's Colorado Springs now. I'm sure of it. We've offered her a job out there, with a good promotion. She's looking it over." He took a sip of his wine and wiped the corner of his mouth with the white linen napkin. "I guess she's all but accepted the position. Plans are to move her out quite soon. In fact, as soon as arrangements can be made."

Brad stared at the hand holding his glass, aware it hadn't moved an inch during Jim's discourse. Colorado? What the hell was going on? "You're sure of that?"

"Dead sure." A sympathetic twinkle entered his eyes. "Sounds like you may be getting the runaround, old friend. Hard to understand. Guy like you. But there's no accounting for women, sometimes. No matter how much propaganda I'm fed, I still say their minds work differently from yours and mine."

Brad drove down the neat street with the nicely kept houses—an oasis in an area conducive to keeping a watchful eye on the rearview mirror. Coming here had been pure impulse. After lunch, he had canceled the afternoon's appointments, taken his car out of the hotel garage and headed for Dorchester. Luckily, he'd copied her address into his book from the list of Milford Track hikers. He had no plans other than seeing where she lived, driving down the street, trying to get his thoughts together. Obviously Lili had deliberately lied to him. Why? If she wasn't interested in seeing him, why not just say so? But that didn't ring true. Everything they'd shared in New Zealand negated that notion. Lili wasn't devious; she was open and honest and forthright. She couldn't fake the emotions she'd displayed when they were together. That simply wasn't possible for a woman like her.

He spotted the number he was looking for and pulled over to the curb in front of a small, very basic house with gray clapboard siding, set on a cramped lot. Two young boys were playing on the sidewalk in front. Could one of them be Lili's son? No. These boys were too old. Both, he'd guess, were about the age of Esther's nephew, about eleven or so. Without thinking, Brad turned off the car and got out, standing uncertainly by the closed door. The two boys stopped their ball-throwing to watch him with open curiosity. Sensing their discomfort at the appearance of a stranger, he smiled and said, "Hi. I'm looking for the house of an old friend."

"Who?"

Both kids had billed caps pulled down over their faces, so it was hard to make any eye contact, a fact Brad found faintly unnerving. "Jamison. Mrs. Jamison." Miss? Mrs.? Which did she use?

"Oh, yeah?" One of the boys looked pert with interest. "This's the house. Wanna see her?"

Brad stared at him. Could she be at home? Was that possible? "Yes. Sure. I'd like that."

"Come on up. I'll tell her." In a flash he'd disappeared, dashing around the corner of the house, leaving his young friend to stare Brad down. With an uneasy nod, he walked up and waited on the front steps.

When the door opened, it wasn't Lili who stood there but Louise. Of course, he should have guessed that. It was one of the few times in Brad's life he felt tongue-tied. "Mrs. Jamison. I don't know if you remember me from Lili's pictures from the trip. I'm Brad Hollingsworth." It was something of a shock, how much the grown-up Lili resembled her mother. Louise Jamison was still a very good-looking woman—even with that expression of utter shock on her face.

Louise looked as though a ghost had appeared on her doorstep. She couldn't be all that surprised, could she? After all, he and Lili had just been together in New Zealand. It wasn't so farfetched for him to come calling.

"Brad Hollingsworth. My stars." She cast an anxious glance at the boy who had spoken to him on the sidewalk, and who was now back with his buddy, keeping a watchful eye turned in their direction. "Well, come in, Brad." She stepped aside and he crossed in front of her, still mystified by her apparent shock.

"I apologize for just barging in. I was in Boston, and Lili told me she'd be away." His eyes narrowed slightly as he remembered that the whole family was supposed to be in New Hampshire. "I was curious about where she lived, so—" she had led him into a tiny living room made cheerful by its neatness and simple good taste "—I drove out." He gave her the most charming smile he could muster. "It must have been quite a surprise to you, when Lili told you about bumping into me in New Zealand."

"Well, I—" Louise's eyes darted up, down, to one side of him, then the other. "Yes. Uh, it's a surprise, all right." She made an awkward gesture toward the one large overstuffed chair in the room. "Please. Sit down."

He tried to overlook her puzzling reaction. He had enough mysteries to deal with already. He tried for another smile as he sat. "The boy out front, I assume he's one of your neighbors?" Why did she blanch at that? Maybe she didn't like him hanging around. "Anyway, when I asked about Mrs. Jamison, he thought I meant you." Oh, hell, that wasn't very smooth. "I mean, well, Lili obviously was still using her maiden name, but I forgot to ask whether she used Miss or Mrs." *Great, Brad. You've got one foot in your mouth. Like to see if the other fits?* "I understand Lili's off to New Hampshire." As his friend, Jim, would say, "testing the waters" department.

There was no way for her to hide the vivid flush that invaded her face. "New Hampshire. I see. Uh, yes. Lili is...away, on a business trip." Something else was showing up in her face. It looked for all the world like anger.

He pressed on, determined to shake loose some bit of information about Lili's deception. Her mother, from all appearances, was playing it by ear, picking up clues from him and commenting accordingly. Maybe it was time to throw her a curve. "I don't know how much she told you about my divorce and my ex-wife." He was watching her carefully, noting the layers of incomprehension build. She was visibly awash, and suddenly it was all too much for Brad. Too much of a sham. Time for a little good old honesty.

"Mrs. Jamison. I have the feeling Lili didn't tell you anything about meeting me in New Zealand. Am I right?" His eyes held hers, begging truth.

She faltered, dropped her gaze, then looked at him squarely, the anger more prominent in her face. "Yes, you're right. She didn't say a word. And it certainly brings up a lot of questions."

"Yes, it does. Like why she told me she was going to New Hampshire, with you and her son, I might add, instead of to Colorado." Her eyes widened. "I had lunch with an old school buddy. Happens to work at Digital. Happens to know Lili."

"Oh, dear." She ran her hand across her eyes.

"By the way—" Brad looked around "—where is her son? Donny. She said it was vacation week. I assume, inasmuch as the neighbor kids are home, that's true."

The color had drained from her face entirely in the seconds it took him to ask that question. "She told you about Donny?"

"Well, yeah." God, what now? Why this strange behavior? Was there something wrong with the boy? Retarded, maybe? "She told me about her husband getting killed right after she got pregnant. Must have been rough for both of you."

"Yes. It was certainly that." He hadn't felt, until that moment, that her anger was aimed at him. What had he said?

Just then, the door banged open and the neighbor boy barged into the room. They sure let this kid have the run of the place. "Can Craig and I have some of those cookies you baked? Please?"

Louise, with a quick, frightened look at Brad, waved him toward the kitchen. "Yes, go help yourself."

The boy started toward the other room, then swung around to grin at Brad. "If you're an old friend of my grandmother's, then you must know my mom, too?"

Brad stared at him, too startled to process the question. "What?"

"Run along now, dear, and get your cookies." Louise was making frantic get-out-of-here gestures with her hand.

"Wait a minute." Brad slid forward in the chair. "Your grandmother. This is your grandmother?"

"Yes, sir." The boy, as though just remembering some long-ago lesson in etiquette, yanked the cap off his head and stepped forward, at the last minute thrusting his hand forward as if it were an afterthought, then looking over at Louise for a smile of approval. "I'm Donald Jamison. You can call me Donny."

Brad sat bolted to the chair as he looked at the tousled blond hair, the deep blue eyes, lively with interest, staring expectantly at him out of a face that looked startlingly familiar. He managed to get to his feet, to take the hand, to shake. "And I'm Brad Hollingsworth." He cleared his throat. "You look about the size of my nephew. Tell me, Donny, how old are you?"

"Donny—"

Brad shot a look at Louise that hushed any further interruption.

"I'm ten. Almost eleven. I'll be eleven on March the twelfth."

Brad's eyes darted to Louise, colliding with her stunned gaze, then swung back to the handsome, smiling boy standing in front of him. It didn't take a calculator to figure this one out. He was looking at his son. *His son!*

He managed, somehow, to let go of the boy's hand, to stay silent while he left the room, for the thump of the back door closing, before confronting the mesmerized woman. "My God. What the hell is this all about? Why wasn't I told?"

Louise was wringing her hands and moving her head back and forth. "Brad, I think—"

"Damn it, Mrs. Jamison. You owe me an explanation!"

At that, the handwringing stopped and she got to her feet and glared at him. "No. I don't owe you anything, Brad. I have been put in the middle of something, and I refuse to stay here. I will get in touch with Lili and tell her to come home. *She's* the one who must tell you what has to be told— what should have been told a dozen years ago."

Brad felt as if someone had punched him in the stomach. Hard. He swallowed the bile that sat in the back of his throat and nodded. "You're right. This has to be settled between Lili and me." He stared at his dark, neatly polished shoes. They looked like foreign objects. "God almighty. I have a son!" His eyes narrowed as he looked at Louise again. "I'll wait, but you tell Lili something. I don't know what her intentions were about sneaking off to Colorado, but she'd better be sure of one thing. She is to go nowhere with my son. *Nowhere!* And if I have to have a lawyer get an injunction to keep her here, I will!"

Never, in his whole life, had it been so hard to hold himself under control than on the short trip back to his car, walking past Donny, giving a weak smile and a small gesture of goodbye, climbing in, shutting the door, starting the motor and driving away. Away from *his son*.

Chapter Eleven

Lili rushed into the office looking the way she felt—harried and disheveled. "Who is it?"

Carol Kester put her hand over the mouthpiece. "Your mother. This is the third time she's called."

Lili took the receiver, experiencing the instant panic known only to parents. "Mom? What's wrong?"

"Lili, you have to come home. Now."

"Has something happened to Donny?" She groped behind her for the desk chair and sank into it.

"Not yet."

"Not yet? What does that mean?"

"Lilith Jamison, I intend to give you no explanation whatever. Remember the old saying, Turnabout Is Fair Play?"

Lili sat back, her forehead creased in a deep frown. Never, within memory, had she heard such cutting anger in her mother's voice. "I don't understand. What on earth is this all about?" She pushed the hair back off her forehead.

"Mom, I'm knee-deep in work here, and I've got an appointment this evening to see a couple of possible rentals."

Louise cut her off. "Forget the rentals. And I strongly advise you to forget the work and hightail it home. Now."

"Mom?"

"That's all I intend to say over the phone. The rest must be face-to-face. Let me know your flight. I'll pick you up. Goodbye, Lili." The buzz of the dial tone was the most ominous sound Lili had heard in a long time.

Although Lili rarely took advantage of company perks unnecessarily, she decided to take a taxi home from the airport instead of having her mother pick her up. Whatever was bothering Louise was no small matter, and facing a mysteriously angered mother on home ground was at least minimally more attractive than in the strained confines of an automobile.

Getting away had been no problem at all. As soon as she said, "Family crisis," her co-workers had snapped into action, getting her a seat on the first available flight, making arrangements for someone else to bandage the troubled project until she could return.

When at last she sat alone with her mother—Donny was down the street, spending the morning with a friend—the icy silence her mother had held to since Lili's return began to crack, revealing the underlying burning anger.

"All right, now, Lilith. You owe me an explanation."

Lili's brows shot up. "Of what?"

"Why didn't you tell me you spent most of your time in New Zealand with Brad Hollingsworth?"

The blood drained from Lili's face in one full rush. "How—" She had to swallow. "How did you know?"

"He appeared on my doorstep, that's how. Talking about seeing you, and putting me in a position that was terribly uncomfortable and terribly unfair."

"I'm sorry, Mom." Lili's hand made a helpless move, then dropped to her lap. "I thought it was better not to."

"You thought. It seems to me that thought has not been a part of any of this."

"Mom—"

"Can't you even trust *me*, Lili?" Louise got up and paced, too agitated to sit still. "If being mother and daughter isn't enough, doesn't all we've been through together count for anything?"

Lili felt about two inches high. She had wounded her mother deeply. And at this moment the logical, well-conceived reasons for withholding the information had escaped her entirely. What on earth had she been thinking of? "Mom. I really am sorry. And I can't for the life of me remember why I made that decision. It was just that I was so frightened and so confused. I'm afraid secrecy has become too natural to me." She stopped, as the full impact of Brad's visit hit her. "Oh, my God. Did he—"

"Meet Donny? Yes."

"Oh, my God." Lili jumped up and took over the pacing as her mother sat on the edge of the overstuffed chair. "What did he say? Did he guess? What did you tell him?"

"The man is far from stupid, Lili. And a brain-damaged sloth would have a hard time missing the significance of the age of the boy and the fact that he's a carbon copy of his father."

"Oh, Mom." Lili's legs gave out, and she sank into a straight-backed chair. "Was he angry?"

"Angry! Lord God almighty, Lili! He was furious!"

Lili could barely hear her own thoughts over her heartbeat. "Did he say anything to Donny? Does Donny know? Does—"

"No. To all of those. How the man held his silence until Donny was out of the house is beyond me, but he did. *Then* he exploded."

"God. Oh, God. What did you tell him?"

"Exactly what I am about to tell you. That I refuse to be in the middle of this. You and Brad must talk to each other and settle matters between you."

Lili was overcome by a sensation of absolute disintegration, as if all her bodily components were caving in, melting, falling apart. She dropped her head in her hands. "Oh, sweet Lord. What am I going to do?"

"Lili." Louise came over to her and laid a hand on her slumped form. "Listen to me. We both made a mistake almost twelve years ago. Mine was greater, in retrospect, than yours. You were only seventeen. I was a mature woman and should have taken a firmer stand. But in those days I was pretty easily overwhelmed, and I gave in under the force of your tantrum. I have regretted it all these years. But that's past. And I, for one, am finished with penance. You and Brad are intelligent adults, and the last thing you need in the center of this problem is a mother. Now, call him up and talk to him."

Call him up? Just like that? "How did he act. What did he say?"

Louise told her about Brad's knowledge of where she was, and why she was there. "The one thing he did say was that there was no way you were going to sneak off to Colorado or anyplace else with his son. And that he'd get a lawyer to stop you, if that was necessary."

That fell like a hammer blow. "Lawyers. I knew it!" She jumped up and ran into Donny's room, yanking open drawers and pulling out his clothes to stack on the bed.

Louise had followed her and demanded, "What do you think you're doing?"

"I'm—*We're* getting out of here. Donny and me. We'll go someplace. Where they can't find us."

"You'd drag that boy into some underground hell of an existence?" Louise stamped her foot. "Lili, stop it!"

Lili's hands hovered for a moment above an open drawer, then dropped. She backed up and sank onto the edge of the bed. "Oh, Mom, what am I doing?"

"Going a little crazy, from all appearances." She sat on the bed beside her daughter. "For heaven's sake, girl. This isn't some monster you're dealing with. Brad is a fine, honest, kind man with good instincts. He deserves better from you.''

''But he's so angry.''

''Of course, he is. Wouldn't you be? But he's not guilt-less in this, Lili. I'm sure he'll realize that.''

''He already does. He feels very badly about that night. He apologized to me, several times.''

''And well he should. You were still a naive girl, and he was a grown man. The responsibility lay far more with him. But that, too, is in the past, and deserves very little rehash-ing. What has to be dealt with is the present situation.''

''What if he tries to take Donny away from me?''

''Lili. After the anger cools, he'll come to the same place that you must reach. Far above consideration for either of you is the good of the boy. Both you and Brad have got to keep that uppermost in your minds.'' She fixed Lili with a meaningful stare. ''Both of you.''

''Meaning, I gather, you don't think I have done so.''

''You want to keep hold of him, Lili. It's understand-able, but impossible. Donny doesn't belong to you. He be-longs to himself. And if his life can be enriched, as I think it can, by learning the truth about his birth and getting to know his father, then that's what needs to happen.''

Lili closed her eyes, searching for some thread of order in the shambles of her mind. ''Oh, Mom. That's the real bot-tom line, isn't it? That's what terrifies me more than any-thing else. How am I going to tell Donny? How?''

''There's no way on God's green earth to make it easy. But he has to be told.''

''Will you help me?''

''Of course. He'll need all the support he can get. And I will do anything in my power to make it easier for him.'' She laid a hand on Lili's knee. ''But first, call Brad. The mother and the father must plan this out together.'' Then, after a long moment's silence, Louise asked, ''Lili, what hap-pened in New Zealand?''

Tears, absent until now, filled her eyes. "We became lovers again. Oh, Mom. I've never stopped loving him. And I've made such a mess of the whole thing. If we ever had a chance, I've probably blown it, once again."

"Lili, dear girl. Things have always been so black/white, either/or with you. Chicken Little could be your patron saint; the sky is always in imminent danger of falling. There is a vast area of gray in life, between the black and the white. And a lot of perhapses and maybes between either/or. Give Brad—no, give *life* the benefit of the doubt. Things may yet work out." She patted her hand. "And if they don't fall into place for you and Brad, Donny will have a father and you will endure. And the sky will stay put."

"Brad?"
"Yes?"
"It's Lili."
"Yes."
Her hand shook so badly she could hardly hold the phone. "I'm back."

"Good. When can we meet?" The frost snaked through the lines to bite her ear.

Today was Wednesday. Was it really possible that just last Sunday she'd flown to Colorado to look for a new life? Now she was back, to attempt to salvage the old one. "I can get away whenever I have to."

"Then I'll be there this evening. We need a place to talk where we won't be interrupted and we'll have privacy. The Boston branch of the bank has a suite on the top floor. I'll give you the address and phone number. You can call from the pay phone downstairs, and I'll come down to let you in."

She hung up the receiver, filled with the dread of a condemned felon about to be meted out her sentence. There was no escape. The peaks were gone, the valleys flattened, the rivers dried. This was the desert: arid and unforgiving.

He stood across the wide sitting room of the office suite, which formed an extended barrier of luxury between them.

Lili was acutely aware that Brad *belonged* here, that he was a top officer of this impressive institution of banking. She felt like a wayward check-bouncer with a massive over-draft.

Beyond the most rudimentary of salutations, they hadn't spoken during the meeting at the door, the ride up in the elevator, or the positioning of their bodies in this oppressive space. Brad turned away from the huge window overlooking Boston and faced her. "How the hell could you do that, Lili?"

What? Which accusation am I to answer first? "Are you talking about not telling you in the first place?"

"Of course, that's what I'm talking about!" His voice rose to a shout, and he took a deep breath and pulled down the volume. "At least for openers."

"You were getting married, Brad. You had your life all planned."

"Didn't it even occur to you I might have changed those plans?"

"I didn't think you would then, and I still don't."

"And just how did you work all that out?"

"I asked, if you recall, on the Milford Track. You weren't sure, in retrospect, what you'd've done. Back then, when I had to make the decision, I was almost certain you wouldn't—at least not willingly. And the idea of forcing you to marry me was repugnant."

"I should have been told."

"Probably."

Brad was shaking with emotion, and he wasn't entirely sure which one. Anger? Frustration? A sense of betrayal? All? It was the first time he'd seen Lili since their return, and he had to fight the desire to go to her, pull her into his arms, cover her with kisses. He had to keep reminding himself she had lied to him, evaded him and cheated him out of eleven years of fatherhood. He had to keep reminding himself how furious he was. Far too furious to give way to a puny emotion like love.

"Do you have any idea what it was like? To look into that boy's face and see myself there? To know that all these years that I've longed for a son, I *had* one, and hadn't been told? I wanted to grab him and hug him and say 'I'm your father!' I can't even begin to describe the feeling, driving away from him—" He stopped. He was running on, sharing his feelings. He'd done that, and what a mistake it had been! All the time he'd been professing his love and getting extremely positive feedback, she'd been looking him straight in the eye and lying to him!

Lili tucked her hands beneath her thighs and wedged her heels against the sofa on which she sat, a physical safeguard against running to him, throwing her arms around him, trying to smooth the anguish from his face. He was the antagonist. She must remember that. He wanted her son, and she wasn't sure to what *extent* he wanted him. But, oh, she loved Brad so! She had to push memories out of her mind of laughing, talking, anticipating, sharing. Making love. *Brad, Brad,* her heart cried, *I need you so!* She waited until she could speak in a level, controlled tone.

"I understand what you're saying. But you must remember, Brad, I was only seventeen, and I was scared out of my mind. Mom tried to make me tell you. In fact she threatened to go to your parents if I refused, but I threw such a scene that she backed down." Lili's foot moved forward and back on the thick carpet. "She told me, yesterday, that she's felt guilty all these years about giving in, and is done with penance." Lili lifted her head to look at him. "She also reminded me that the most important person in this...saga...is Donny."

Some of the bombast went out of Brad, and it took an effort to gather it back in. "She's right, of course. But there are still a lot of answers I need. Like, okay, I can understand, if not agree with, the original decision. But how could you be with me in New Zealand, tell me you loved me, make plans, and still keep this from me?"

She didn't know. Not now. All the agonizing was such a hazed memory, all the rationale so garbled by event on top of event. Honesty is the best policy? Yes? No? At times? She realized her head was moving back and forth, mimicking her thoughts. "I almost did, so many times. But seeing you after all these years was such a shock, realizing that my feelings—" She stopped, frowned, reassessed. "Anyway, that night at dinner in Te Anau? You told me you were divorced and I felt such hope. Then you told me the reason. That Esther couldn't have a child. That if she had been able to, the marriage might have been all right. You were far from happy about the divorce, about ending your marriage. God, the thoughts that went through my mind! 'If he knew, would he try to mend the marriage using his son?'"

"I told you the marriage was over."

"But you didn't sound all that sure about it, Brad." She got up and crossed to the window. "Then, all the time on the hike, when I thought you'd be going back right afterward, I wanted so much to tell you. But I thought, even if I did, it should wait until we were back home. I couldn't stand the idea of your being here, knowing about Donny, with me away."

"That still leaves four days, Lili. Days—and nights—that were, may I remind you, pretty damned significant."

"I wanted the time to be beautiful, and I had no idea whether there could be any harmony left between us after you knew. I had planned to tell you, Brad. I was all set to tell you that first night at the Huka Lodge, after dinner, when we were back in our room. The night you got the call."

"I don't know if I believe you."

Could she blame him? Probably not. Lies built on lies. She tried to garner some of her mother's resolution. All that was past. They had to deal with the present situation. "I don't blame you. But that's the way it was, nevertheless." She turned back to stare at the lights of the city.

He couldn't seem to keep his mind running in any sort of logical progression. He'd never faced anything in his life so

mammoth in scope, so befuddling, so resistant to method-
ical logic. He wanted his son. He wanted Lili. He loved her.
But he was furious with her, felt he couldn't trust her,
though inside, deep down, he did anyway. Why couldn't he
get his brain organized? "Now the big one. Why the runaround *here?* Telling me you're off to New Hampshire instead of Colorado, making plans to sneak off with my son—
and you expect me to believe you planned to let me know?"
Now the anger was unleashed. His body was rigid, his back
ramrod straight, his tone strident.

Lili whirled. "Believe what you want! What was I to
think? Once again, you were rushing off to Esther's side,
telling me, even when I talked to you after I got home, that
you had to stick by her." Her hand waved. "Okay, okay.
She was hurt, she was upset, she needed you. She is also
from the right side of the tracks, and the sort of girl you'd
bring home to mother." Lili put her hand over her mouth.
Where had that come from?

"What! What the hell does that mean?"

She sat down heavily on one of the silk-covered chairs.
"Don't you remember? The story you told me that last
night, while you were packing? About Esther's brother,
having his life ruined by a girl who got herself pregnant?
'The poor bastard never pulled himself together,' I think
that's how you put it."

"Lili, for God's sake—"

"All these terrible things ran through my mind, that long,
long time at Huka Lodge, the interminable trip home.
"What if he reconciles with Esther? They have all the money
in the world. They can get a topflight lawyer. They might be
able to get my son." She wrung her hands together, seeking
succor from the friction. "Or even part-time custody." Her
anguished eyes sought his. "How could I tell Donny that not
only does he have a living father, but a stepmother, and he'd
have to live with these strangers part of the time?" She flung
her hands up hopelessly. "All my old feelings about your
being in a different class, you and Esther. I just couldn't

control it—all the awful, awful possibilities. There's no fancy, well-thought-out excuse for running off to Colorado. I panicked, Brad, and that's that."

Lili, Lili. He wanted to go to her, hold her, comfort her. But eleven years of deception stood between them, and he didn't know if he could ever forget, or forgive, that. "Lili, that woman, the one Esther's brother married—dear Lord, she's in another world from you. We're talking promiscuity, drugs, booze. It has nothing to do with class. At least, not the kind you're talking about."

Lili had run out of words. She simply shrugged her shoulders, hopelessly overcome by uncontrollable emotions.

He sat on a chair next to hers—as close as he dared get. "All right, let's let the past go, for the time being. There are things to get straight, right now. My marriage is over. Literally, legally, emotionally. Esther is putting the house on the market and moving to Philadelphia to be near her parents. Change is hard for anyone, and she had a hard time seeing that final date approach. But she knows it's over. As far as I'm concerned? Lili, I'd never have made love to you, talked about the future, if I hadn't been sure."

She closed her eyes, wondering why she'd been unable to listen to that little voice that told her to trust her instincts. To trust Brad. "Why didn't you tell me that, Brad? Why couldn't you have taken enough time between all your calls to the airlines to reassure me? Have you any idea what went through my mind when you tossed that money on the table and said it should cover everything?" She looked at him then, the anger and hurt and fear fighting for dominance in her eyes.

"Good God, Lili." He stared at her, feeling her pain. "That sort of thing never crossed my mind." He slammed his right fist into his left palm. "Judas priest, and why the hell should it? That's so damned farfetched it's insulting! What kind of a heel do you think I am?"

Her hands shot up in surrender. "I know, I know. I told myself all that on the way home. But when you did call, you still sounded like a man who had returned to the side of his . . . his *wife,* and was trying to let the other woman down gracefully!"

Brad shook his head, wishing all the mangled thoughts would right themselves, sort themselves out. He recalled, through the maze of the muddle, his own concern that he hadn't handled that phone conversation at all well. But that didn't excuse the rest. "You're right, I should have said a lot of things I didn't say. But damn it all, that doesn't wipe out—" He stopped and slapped the palms of his hands on his knees. "This is all just leading us around in one big circle, and that's pretty fruitless at the moment. So we come to the main issue here, which, as your mother so wisely pointed out, is Donny's welfare. This is going to be a shock to him."

Lili's eyes filled with tears the instant his words were out. What an understatement!

"I have to get to know my son. Have to have a part in his life. There is no way I can *not* do that."

"I know."

"So. Question number one. How are we going to tell him?"

If Lili thought she'd experienced panic before, it was a mirage next to this staggering imminence. "I can't. It's impossible. Totally, completely beyond endurance." She ran her hand over her eyes, then sat slumped in silence, which Brad did not disturb. Finally, she sat up straight and nodded. "But it has to be done. And I have to do it."

"Yes." He got up, started toward her, veered off to the magnet of the distracting window. "He'll need to absorb the shock before meeting me." As an afterthought, he added, "I'll also have to tell Mom and Dad. And Marcy."

"Yes. That's right." Was there no end? A sudden thought brought Lili to her feet. "Oh, dear heaven!"

"What's the matter?" Without thinking, he went to her, hands out, ready to comfort. He noticed them, hovering, and dropped them to his side.

"Donny's birthday. It's almost his birthday!" She laughed a harsh, ironic exclamation. "Happy Birthday, son. Do I have a present for you!"

He couldn't stand it then, standing aloof from her, watching such pain. He stepped forward, took her shoulders, squeezed them with as much reassurance as he could, or would, convey. "I'll be a good father to him, Lili. I will."

She nodded and looked into his sapphire eyes. Eyes just like those she would soon be pleading with to understand the unimaginable. "I know."

Brad waited awhile after Lili's departure, then left the building and started to walk, his hands jammed into his pockets, his head lowered. He was staying at the Ritz. He'd stop in the bar and have a drink. He needed one. He crossed streets, dodged cars, ignored signals, too absorbed to notice his surroundings. Then he found himself on Newbury Street, standing in front of F.A.O. Schwartz. His eyes moved hungrily over the display of toys. What a wonderful array! He'd have bought that huge lion for his tiny son. And that set of trains, when he was old enough to work them. And jeez, look at those puzzles! What fun to help him put one of those together. Suddenly he was in imminent danger of crying. With an angry turn away from the window, he stepped off the curb, ran across the street and headed for the Ritz.

The very next day Brad called Lili. "I thought you should know, I told the folks."

She was in her office, sitting at her desk, engaged in being totally ineffective. She pressed the receiver closer to her ear. "How did they take it?" She could just picture it. Those two lovely, stalwart people, so accustomed to the conventional, listening to their son saying, "Mom, Dad, guess what?"

"Well, obviously, they're stunned."

"At least."

There was a new lilt to his tone, different from yesterday's sober edginess. "Somehow, I doubt it'll take them long to adjust to the idea." He actually laughed! "Dad's already planning on how to get him registered at Harvard."

"Oh, my." Donny's life was about to change. Would he want his life changed? She remembered his willingness to consider a move to Colorado and heartened, then considered the vast difference between a relocation and a discovered father—and disheartened.

"Mom entered his name in the family Bible. She wants to know what his middle name is."

"Bradford."

The silence was protracted, poignant. "You named him after me?"

"Yes."

"Thank you."

All the animosity had disappeared, and a softer, warmer tone replaced it. "When are you going to tell Donny?" She could hear the apology in his voice. He was trying not to push her too hard, but he couldn't wait to claim his son.

"Tonight. I'm going to try to tell him tonight."

"Call me? Let me know how it went? I'll be at the folks'." He gave her the number. "And, Lili?"

"Yes."

"Good luck."

Lili burst into the house that evening in a phony show of animation. "Hey, you guys! How about dinner at McDonald's?"

Donny leaped up from the dinette table, where he was doing his homework. "Really?" Lili's determination to keep her son from becoming a fast-food junkie made such a proposition a rare treat.

"Really. Get your jacket. Mom?" Her eyes pleaded for support. She'd called Louise earlier, told her the plan.

Louise nodded and went to the coat closet. "Sounds like a dandy idea."

The tension was so thick and the cheeriness so false that only a youngster besotted with hamburger fervor could have missed it. Mother and daughter maintained the charade through the interminable munching of burgers, fries and gulping down of shakes, through the trip home. The moment they were back inside the house, Lili, exhausted by pretense, shed it.

"Donny?"

"Ah, Mom, come on, just let me watch this one show, it's only a half hour. I can still finish my math before I go to bed. I'm almost through, anyhow." His eyes were already glued to the tube, which he had quickly turned on to one of his favorite shows.

"Honey, you'll have to shut off the TV. I have something I have to talk to you about."

"Can't it wait just a half hour?"

"Donny. Turn it off." Lili caught her mother's warning look. This was no time to get harsh with him. What was about to be spewed all over his life was in no way his fault.

Donny, alerted to the tension in Lili's voice, snapped off the TV and, with a long-suffering look, turned to face her. "Okay, what've I done?"

The urge to laugh came but was quickly done. The normal, natural child's response to an upset parent. "In this case, Donny, it's the other way around."

"What d'you mean?"

This was a new twist. She'd caught his attention. Lili was experiencing a sensation she'd had only once before, when she was taken to the maternity ward, racked with labor pains: the knowledge that no matter how much she wanted to escape, there was none; she had to go through with it.

"I mean that the mistake was mine." Now she had his undivided concentration, which, with Donny, was an intentness that could be somewhat daunting. Whatever was said now would be sucked into that retentive brain and lodged—in this case, she was sure, forever. Where did she find the words? "Sometimes, Donny, people do things they're sorry for later." She fumbled with the hem of her skirt. "And sometimes our mistakes are very, very big, and cause pain to the people we most love and want to protect in the whole world."

A line appeared in his starch-smooth forehead. "You rented a house where they won't allow a dog!"

"What?" The statement was so far afield it brought Lili to a dead halt.

"Well, call 'em up and tell 'em you don't want it. You changed your mind. You can do that, can't you?"

Louise rose from her seat on the couch, where she'd tucked herself out of the way and pulled out one of the wooden dinette chairs, to sit beside her grandson. "This has nothing to do with Colorado, dear. It's more important than that. And it's very difficult for your mother to tell you."

Donny, awash in a confusing situation that was foreign to him, looked up at his grandmother, then over at Lili and lifted his hands. "Why not just spit it out?"

To the degree possible, it cracked some of the ice around her heart. It was one of her own frequent admonitions to her son—"Stop beating around the bush and spit it out!"

"All right, honey. There's no easy way to tell you, so I'll just get on with it. You know I told you that your father died before you were born?"

His small body stiffened with alertness. "Yeah?"

"That wasn't true."

He didn't say a word. The only visible reaction was a slight narrowing of the eyes, as though he were inwardly bracing for a blow.

"The truth is—" the inhaling of air had become a mammoth effort "—I was never married."

His head tilted and his eyes widened. "You mean you were one of those teenage unwed mothers?"

"Yes."

"Boy." He sat back, puzzling it out. "Then I was a bastard. Boy."

Louise reared back. "Donny, where did you hear that? I didn't think the word was even used anymore. In that context."

"A kid called Allan Sparks said that, and got a bloody nose for it." Donny smiled in some mystical boyhood form of satisfaction. "Served him right. If he calls me that, I'll give him one, too."

Lili rubbed the sore spot between her eyes. She should feel somewhat eased. One hurdle had been crossed, Donny knew part of it. But nothing was changed but a concept. Donny hadn't known a father, so he hadn't lost anything real, and being a bastard appeared to have given him something interesting to contemplate. How could she present the real news in a way that emphasized the gain? That made it sound like a special, incredible gift? But any change was hard, and this change, dear Lord, was unfathomable.

Donny's mind, as she should have anticipated, was adding two and two and arriving at an obvious equation. He scooted so far forward on his chair that the back legs lifted free of the floor. "Hey. Then my real father isn't dead?"

Lili sent a pleading glance to her mother, who said, "Just tell him."

"No, Donny. He isn't dead."

Donny leaped from the seat, and it overturned and banged against the hardwood floor. "Why didn't he want me? Why'd he want nothing to do with me?"

Lili and Louise both stood, uprighted by an instinct of danger. "He didn't know anything about you. I never told him." The expression that came to his face made Lili feel like an executioner.

"Why?"

"It's a long story...." He wasn't going to stand still for a long story. "I... He was about to be married to someone else. I was scared. I thought I was doing the right thing."

"I could've had a father? And you didn't even tell him?" His gaze swung around the room, looking for a logic they didn't find. "He doesn't even know I've alive?" He kicked backward at the chair. Missed. *"Hell!"*

Lili's mouth opened and closed. There'd been dozens of confrontations about swearing. All those words were in the general vocabulary at his school, but he'd agreed to a ban. Now he was hurling one of them at her, because it was the only weapon at hand. She didn't blame him. He had an arsenal at his command. She wondered how many he'd use before this was over.

Having no sort of rationale to offer, she just said, "He does now."

The air in the room stopped moving. Everything hung in suspension. "Now?" He looked like a cornered animal, not knowing which way to run. "What's that mean?"

"Donny, your father found out about you just the other day, when he came here. And he's terribly angry at me, too, just as you are. And he does want you. Very much." Lili's legs would no longer sustain her weight, and she folded into the chair behind her, consumed by remorse and guilt and the threat of a loss too immense to imagine.

Louise tried to put her hand on Donny's arm, but he shook it off. He looked like a wild thing, trapped and endangered. "That guy? He came to see Grandma? The tall guy with the blond hair?" He kept looking from one to the other of them, seeing the affirmation in their eyes, the slight nod of Louise's head. "He's my *father?*" Again, Louise nodded. "And he never even knew about me?" His face, usually so bright and full of cheer, was dark with disbelief. *"Goddamn son of a bitch!"* He whirled around, gave the prostrate chair a vicious kick and ran out of the house, banging the door behind him.

Lili jumped up and started to follow, but her mother grabbed her arm. "Leave him be, for a while. Donny won't run. He'll think. And he has to let it sink in."

"But, Mom."

"Lili, the child's wounded, and the last one who can minister to him right now is you. I'll go after him in just a few minutes."

The dam broke then, and more tears than Lili felt she could hold poured out, a burst dam of regret. Her mother folded her into her arms, murmuring comforting-mother words: "Now, now. It's all right. Calm down." But there was no comfort, really. Not anywhere. And Lili couldn't imagine how the tears would ever stop.

Chapter Twelve

Louise's foray outside was successful in finding Donny, but not in communicating with him. He wanted to be left alone.

"Where is he, Mom?" asked Lili.

Sitting in that old tire swing that we never got around to taking down."

"Was he crying?"

"No. He looked very dazed—off in his own world. He didn't sound mad, though. Just very thoughtful. I told him we both loved him very much."

"What did he say?"

"He looked at me like I was crazy and said, 'What has that got to do with it?' I couldn't come up with a good reply."

"Oh, Mom."

"Let's give him some more time."

When Donny did come inside, his carriage bespoke the bearing of newly accumulated weight. He went directly to his room and closed the door. Lili and Louise, relieved at least to have him within the confines of the house, sat around in paralyzed silence, staring sightlessly at a book, a newspaper, a magazine, at each other, at Donny's closed door. At nine-thirty, just as Louise put on water for tea, they heard the door open and, with breath held, waited.

He walked out slowly, his hair rumpled, his eyes heavy-lidded and went over to sit beside Lili on the couch. "That man—his name was Brad."

"Yes." She wanted so to reach out, draw him into her arms, but felt the hands-off warnings he emitted. "Brad Hollingsworth."

"Is that short for Bradford?"

"Yes."

"That's why it's my middle name?"

"That's right."

"You must have liked him, if you named me after him."

"I loved him, Donny."

He was struggling so hard with all this startling input that the effort was palpable. "Well, he got you pregnant, so why didn't you make him marry you?"

Lili stared at him, astounded once again by the knowledge of life a child his age had garnered. It came too fast, most of it. "It would take me a while to explain."

"Okay."

She talked, interrupted frequently by his questions, for over an hour, then sat quietly for a few minutes while Donny stared at his feet. Lili could feel the beat of her heart all the way through her body. It was agony, this silence, but she knew it must be broken by him. Donny was an exceptionally bright youngster, and she had learned to leave space for his musings. Even allowing for his intelligence, this must be incredibly hard for him to grasp.

"I have a real father."

For the first time, she felt a stirring of hope. "That's right."

"Did you say he wants to get to know me?"

"Very, very much. He said it was the hardest thing he ever did in his whole life, to drive away from you that day without saying anything. He's been terribly anxious to get together with you, Donny, but he understands what a shock this would be. That you'd need time."

"Is he nice?"

"Exceptionally so."

"Do you still like him?"

"Very much." Then she told him about meeting Brad in New Zealand, about sharing the hike and some of the trip, eliminating all mention, of course, of traveling together or of falling in love again. She even attempted to explain her reasons for talking of a move to Colorado, which meant exposing still more of her fears to him.

He turned a puzzled gaze on her, studying her face like a new and intricate picture. "Boy. You get scared of things, too. Just like I do."

"Of course I do, honey. Being a grown-up doesn't keep you from being scared." Now she did touch him, laying her hand on his arm, and he let it lie there undisturbed. "You are the most important thing in my life, Donny. If I've handled things badly, it's because I was trying to keep you as safe as possible. And sometimes, I'm afraid, I made the wrong decisions."

"Mom. I'm sorry I swore at you. I was really mad."

"You had good reason."

"Even for swearing?"

She smiled, amazed her lips still curved upward. "Well, this once, maybe. But don't push your luck."

"This man—" he was still distancing himself from the concept of father "—he's getting a divorce?"

"He *is* divorced."

Donny's eyes brightened. "Maybe you should marry him then, and we could all live in the same house?" He waved a hand toward Louise. "With Grandma, too."

Lili closed her eyes, garnering calm. "I can't prophesy the future, honey."

"Yeah. Anyway, I better see if I like him first." He yawned. "I guess if he's my father, we'd better get acquainted."

The night skies split and the sun shone through and the heavy late-winter air was filled with the light scent of spring. "That's a good idea." She and Louise exchanged a look of pure relief.

Donny stood. "I'm really sleepy." He leaned over and kissed her on the cheek. "Night, Mom." After giving his grandmother a hug and kiss, he headed for his room, yawning.

The two women stared at each other in stupefied exhaustion for a long pause, then Louise gasped, "Oh, my goodness! The tea water must be boiled away!" She returned a moment later with the kettle, smoking and blackened.

With a laugh that was only slightly tinged with hysteria, Lili said, "Throw it away, Mom. We'll live it up and buy a new one." They both had tears running down their cheeks, but neither bothered to wipe them away.

Lili waited just long enough to be sure her son was asleep, then went to the kitchen phone to call Brad.

There was much consultation among the adults about the best format for Donny's first get-together with Brad. With Lili, without Lili; at the house, on neutral ground. After listening to some of the speculations, Donny announced that anyone else, including mother, would interfere with the process of his getting to know "that man." He also decided that dinner out, like, say, at McDonald's, was a good beginning.

Brad showed up at the door five minutes early, dressed in almost aggressively casual clothes, looking more apprehensive and unsure of himself than Lili could have imagined possible for the only son of such an august lineage. He stepped inside and got no farther than the tiny foyer before Donny appeared, looking in far better possession of himself than either of his parents.

Brad gave him a hopeful smile. "Hi, Donny."

"Hello, Mr.—uh . . ." For a moment, the assumed cockiness wavered. "I don't know what to call you."

Brad nodded, relieved by the boy's openness. "That's understandable. How about Brad? You comfortable with that?"

"Sure." Donny gave Lili and Louise, both of whom hovered nervously, a quick kiss. "See ya." With that, he was through the door.

Casting one glance at Lili—a look that begged a few helpful prayers—Brad followed.

That short evening was one of the longest in memory for both women. They glued themselves to their seats through the sounds of the car pulling up outside, the door opening, mumbled exchanges between man and boy. Lili's insides were giving what felt like a demonstration of a blender, and her mother, who never chewed her nails, was chewing her nails.

Donny walked in and said, "Hi."

In a voice that screamed "forced casualness," Lili croaked, "How did it go?"

"Okay. I had a Big Mac."

"What did you do after that?"

"Went to Boston and walked around Quincy Market. It's neat."

"Did you, uh, enjoy yourself?"

"Sure. Pretty nice guy. Grandma, are there any of those cookies left?"

"Why, yes." Louise looked stunned, as though cookies were a substance from another world.

"Think I'll have a couple while I get ready for bed. I have a dumb math test tomorrow." And that was the end of his description of his first father-son encounter.

The next couple of weeks were lived between updrafts of hopefulness and downslides of despair, with the radical swings maneuvered with bated breath. Lili's concern over Donny's adjustment to seminightly and weekend sojourns spent with his newly-found father submerged, at least partially, her apprehensions about Brad and herself, with all the ramifications that question held for her own life. Brad was consumed by his acquired fatherhood, and conversations with her were distracted and distant. Both man and boy seemed unwilling to share the details of their time together, and Lili and her mother did everything but sew Velcro on their lips to keep the questions from pouring out. Donny veered from euphoric excitement to deep, furrowed-brow doldrums, with no willingness to discuss either. It obviously wasn't easy, this immense adjustment.

For the first time since Lili attained adulthood, time dragged like a sluggardly turtle with a limp. She lost keys; she forgot appointments; she sent letters to the wrong people. Luckily, her boss and co-workers had been apprised of her situation, and were not only sympathetic, but anxiety-ridden as well, on her behalf.

One evening, with Donny out with Brad and Louise having dinner and going to a movie with a lady friend, Lili was trying to concentrate on a book when the phone rang. Since it was the third call of the evening, and the previous two had been a stock salesman and a woman promoting storm windows, Lili answered with a testy tone. "Hello?"

"Lili?"

She drew in her breath. Could it be? "Marcy?"

"God, you knew my voice after all these years? How are you?"

"Fine. Well, almost fine." Lili sat down on the stool by the phone table, wondering what was about to be said. How angry was Marcy with her? "You sound good. It's wonderful to hear your voice."

"It's good to hear yours."

That probably exhausted the subject of voices.

Lili hesitated, then blurted, "I'm surprised you'd want to. You must be pretty ticked off at me."

"Well, I *was*, that's for sure. I thought you'd just had enough of me and sailed off into the sunset. I felt so betrayed! But now, God, Lili, what a time you had! I wish you had told me so I could've helped. At least by holding your hand or something.''

''Marcy, he was your brother.''

''Yeah, I know. But I still wish you'd said something. He'd probably have married you, instead of old starch-face.''

Lili was, to her surprise, smiling. They'd already dropped back into the old camaraderie. ''Does that mean you don't like Esther? I never heard you say anything about her.''

''I figured I'd like her when I got to know her. After all, she was older, and I didn't have all that much to do with her. But she is not an easy person to know, at least not for me. It was a definite case of losing a brother rather than gaining a sister. I mean, she's *all right,* and all, but—'' Marcy cut herself off with a laugh. ''Hey, I'm talking to my old buddy, right? Actually, Esther is a pain in the grazot.''

Lili's tautly held body relaxed a little. The reference to ''my old buddy'' made her weak with nostalgia. ''I was so surprised when Brad told me you got married and dropped out of college.''

Marcy laughed. The old familiar ripple of glee filled Lili with a forgotten response of joy. ''Pretty astonishing, huh? Me, the original career-woman-to-be? No husband, no kids, just a life devoted to animals?''

''And now you're the mother of three? What happened to your passion for animals? Do you even have a cat?''

''You kidding? We live on a sort of suburban farm. Veddy upper, you know—'' she giggled ''—and so much fun! We have four cats, three dogs, sheep, horses, a goat and chickens. Oh, and two steers and a cow.''

''Good God.''

Marcy laughed in delight at Lili's response. Lili had always been a bit squeamish about getting too involved with the messier aspects of the upkeep of four-footed creatures.

''Who takes care of all of them? You?''

"Well, I can't say I do it all. We have help. But I still love mucking around in stables and caretaking critters. It's just, well, motherhood does take up a lot of time. Which reminds me, how *could* you not tell me about my one and only nephew? I'm dying to meet him! He'll love the farm, and he and the kids should enjoy each other, even though he's a few years older. He can do the big-brother bit."

"Oh, Marcy, how I'd love to see you!"

"Me, too. And we certainly will—see each other, that is. The only question is how soon. What's the deal between you and Brad?"

"What do you mean?" Had Brad said anything about how he felt about her? She pushed hope, still trying to struggle free, back into its box. She couldn't afford to turn it loose. Not yet.

"I've only talked to him on the phone, but there was something in his voice when he mentioned your name. I asked him, and he told me to mind my own business, which is a sure sign of sore emotional muscles. I wish you guys'd get it together, so we could have a wedding. Just think, Lili. You'd be back in the family!"

Back in the family! What a wonderful thing to say. She was too choked up for a moment to reply, and luckily Marcy bubbled on. "Did Brad tell you about Carl? My husband? You'll love him. He's a real gem. Actually, he's a lot like you. Smart, loves to read. Always in the middle of at least one book and two projects. Remember how ticked off I got at you when you had your nose in a book and wouldn't talk to me? Now I yell at him, instead, and he just smiles and ignores me, like you used to do. I've been forced to become a reader myself, out of desperation."

"My, my. Will wonders never cease!"

Marcy's voice suddenly went soft and sober. "I guess not. Oh, Lili, it *is* good to talk to you! What a lot we have to catch up on! Did Brad tell you we live in California? Right on the ocean in a place called Hope Ranch in Santa Barbara. The place belonged to Carl's grandparents and he spent lots of his summers here. Then he inherited it, and we moved here as fast as we could pack up! You'll just love it!''

In spite of all her well-positioned defenses, hope and anticipation and joy were vying for release in Lili. Marcy had, through the years of their friendship, treated her like the sister she didn't have and always wanted, and now she was blissfully assuming Lili was about to become an integral part of her life once again. More than anything she could imagine, Lili wanted the same thing. To be Marcy's sister, through marriage.

Just a few minutes after Lili hung up the phone, she heard the key turn in the lock and the door swing open. She walked into the hallway to welcome her son and was surprised by the sight of Brad, close behind. "Well. Hello." They had seen each other only in quick glances, coming and going, since that last encounter at Brad's bank. He looked tanned and healthy and unbearably attractive. She stared at the two of them, father and son, standing side by side. The resemblance was uncanny. Donny seemed taller and more mature than he had mere days ago, and he exuded an augmented air of self-confidence and well-being. Having a father was obviously sitting comfortably with him.

"Hi, Mom! Guess what? We sat right behind the Red Sox bull pen! And some of the players *know* Brad, and they *talked* to us!" Donny's whole body was agitated, like a grasshopper with a flea. "It was neat! And we had hot dogs and sodas for dinner, and stopped on the way home for a giant hot-fudge sundae!"

"Brad…" Lili's stern look didn't even penetrate the sheer pleasure of the tall man with one hand on the boy's shoulder.

"Ah, c'mon, Mom, don't hassle him. He's trying to win me over."

Brad and Lili both burst out laughing, and Brad asked, "How'm I doing?"

"Okay. Keep up the good work!" Donny glanced at the clock on the mantel. "I have to get to Andy's house. All the other guys'll be there already." His friend down the street was having a sleepover, then all the boys were going on a hike with Andy's father.

"All your things are packed in the duffel on your bed. Oh, and I borrowed a sleeping bag from someone at work."

"Thanks, Mom."

Lili and Brad stood silently until Donny had gathered his bag, given his mother a kiss and said goodbye to Brad and rushed out the door, banging it shut behind him.

As soon as he was gone, Brad said, "I need to talk to you."

"All right." Lili, full of the apprehension that had lain just beneath the surface of everything lately, led Brad into the living room. An edginess sat between them, distancing one from the other. "You and Donny seem to be hitting it off very well."

"Yes. I think we are. He's a terrific boy, Lili. You've done a good job raising him." There was no missing the grudging tone in which the compliment was housed. They sat down, she on the overstuffed chair, he on the sofa. "My parents, naturally, are anxious to meet him. I've put them off, because I didn't want to throw too much at him at once. But now... Well, Donny is willing."

It was such a confusing, fragmenting period. She wanted Donny not only to accept Brad, but to grow to love him, to be introduced to the magical world of the Hollingsworths. But with each inch of progression in that direction, she suffered a terrible inner sense of rending. Her hold on her son was slipping. The world they'd shared was broadening, changing and becoming populated with new people who would, probably, be as important to him as she. And she was beginning to suffer that old inveigling sense of being an outsider. Donny was, by birthright, a part of their world. And she wasn't. And might never be.

"I see." She pulled her hands apart to stop their nervous tangling. "All right. When—" her throat was dry as dust "—did you have in mind?" *Oh, God, Donny. If you love them like I did, if you feel as welcome there—and why wouldn't you?—it will become such a magnet.* Her gaze moved around the room, mentally comparing its plainness with the commodious charm of the Hollingsworths' tasteful living room.

"The folks thought it would be easier on Donny if you and your mother came with him. They want me to invite all three of you to dinner on Sunday evening. I have my slides from the trip, and we figured those would be fun to see. Maybe you could bring your pictures, too, and that video you got, from the bungy jump." At the mention of that, their eyes met in recollection. Brad dropped his gaze and rubbed the center of his forehead with his fingers. "Lili. I'm so damned confused right now. It's all so—" His hand made a motion that spoke of inexpressible emotions. "Having Donny in my life is the most incredible gift I've ever had. And I'm grateful, and happy." He glanced at her. "To a point. But I'm having a lot of trouble with the anger. I'm so damned mad at you for all those lost years." When he raised his eyes again, they were full of blazing light that held no warmth. "So far, I can't separate one from the other."

She nodded, knowing this was something words couldn't help. She had her own anger, but had also had over eleven years in which to deal with it. This was all new to Brad, and she could understand the inner war he must be going through. "I guess..." She sighed, wishing she could simply stand and walk outside and away from all the problems that had to be sorted out. And away from this awful, tearing need she felt every time Brad was near her. There had to be a lot of rage pent up inside him; and although anger had always alarmed her, in this circumstance its release might offer some easing to all the tightly controlled tension that vibrated through the atmosphere like a gathering earthquake. But they were both so civilized. Maybe too much so for their own good. She took a deep breath and started over. "Tell your parents we accept. It's very gracious of them."

"All right. About five?"

"Fine."

They both stood, rooted in memory, anger, need. One at war with the next and the next. Suddenly, Brad banished the space between them with two steps, grabbed her by the shoulders and pulled her to him, his mouth covering hers with a savage ferocity. Lili was too stunned to respond in one way or the other for a moment; then all the shut-in need burst free, and her arms went around his neck while her mouth responded hungrily to his. Their bodies pressed together tightly in a head-to-toe embrace made up more of desperation than tenderness. His lips, ferocious in their demand, ground on hers with punishing rigor. The violence of his ardor was met in kind by Lili. Gentleness had no place here, in this wild embrace.

His tongue plunged into her mouth, circling, thrusting. Lili opened to him, all of her body crying out for total, turbulent immersion into the fury of this craving. She offered no resistance when his hands moved under her sweater, released the clasp of her bra. She uttered small groans when his fingers moved across her nipples and his palms cupped her breasts.

"Lili." It was a growl, significant in its conflicting mixture of lust, love and bitterness.

He kissed her eyes, her cheeks her throat, the pulsing spot behind each ear. His hands laid claim to her flesh, undoing the zipper of her slacks, sliding down over the curve of her buttocks. The two of them, still wrapped in each other's arms, moved inexorably to the couch, sinking onto its spongy surface. Brad was struggling with the buckle on his belt, impatiently yanking at the recalcitrant mechanism of restraint. Then he stopped, the cessation of movement jarring in its suddenness. He pulled back from their kiss, his eyes full of anguish, fury, desperation. With one quick movement he was on his feet, tucking in his shirt, adjusting his slacks.

He stared at her, his expression full of dismay and frustration. "Damn it, Lili." For an instant, she wasn't sure whether he was going to return to the couch, to her, or leave. "Damn it all to hell." He pivoted and strode out of the house, barely stopping the door from slamming with a last-moment move of his hand, leaving Lili, disheveled in both body and spirit, alone in the desolate room.

Brad raged down the steps and across the walk to his car, his entire body invaded by an indefinable sickness different from anything in his experience. His need for Lili was tearing him apart. But could he ever forgive her, or trust her? He didn't know. He just didn't know.

When they made the turn between the two brick gateposts that stood at the entry to the Hollingsworth driveway, Donny, who had been glued to the window issuing exclamations of wonderment over the impressive houses in the impressive neighborhood, breathed, "Wow! Is this where they live?"

"This is it." Lili slowed to a crawl. "On my first visit here, it took me a long time to get up the courage to ring the bell."

"What was your friend's name? Margie?"

"Marcy. And my friend is your aunt. And she called me the other night to say she's dying to meet you."

"Really? That's neat."

Louise looked over at Lili. "You didn't tell me you'd heard from Marcy."

"Didn't I? I can't believe how forgetful I've been lately! Oh. It was the same night Brad came in and invited us here." Her mother's expression bespoke her understanding. "Anyway, Marcy sounds sublimely happy. She has three children and a husband she adores and lives on what she called a 'veddy upper' farm in Hope Ranch in Santa Barbara."

"Where's that?" Donny asked.

"California?"

"Wow! Can we go visit sometime?"

"I'm sure you will, honey. They have all kinds of animals, and it's right on the ocean bluff." The imposing Hollingsworth house was just coming into view. Lili tried to tamp down the rise of apprehension. How could she keep a sanguine face at her meeting with Brad, after what had happened the other night? And that was only one of her concerns. Donny would come here to spend time with his newfound grandparents, and go to California to visit Marcy, and to Connecticut to be with Brad. And that didn't even take into consideration the possibility, at some point, of boarding school. Following in his father's footsteps. It was bound to come up. The future was so uncertain—and so frightening.

Brad, who had been pacing just inside the front door, heard the approach of Lili's car and was ready to swing the door open the second after the doorbell rang. His mother and father, easily as nervous as he, hovered close behind him in the large, marble-floored entrance hall. Lili and Louise held back as Brad gave his son an affectionate greeting and led him inside. The moment the door closed behind them, Mrs. Hollingsworth went to Lili and swept her into a loving embrace.

"Lili, my dear. I can't begin to tell you how pleased I am to see you. My, we've missed you!" She pulled back to give her a good look-over. "Beautiful, still beautiful. Oh, dear, I may cry!"

Brad watched Lili's eyes fill with tears as she greeted his mother and father, and steeled his heart against a wave of sympathy. He was angry at himself for his loss of control at Lili's house. It had been akin to surrendering to the enemy. In many ways, she did seem like the enemy—someone who had held his very flesh and blood hostage to her own fears. He couldn't look at Lili and retain such angry thoughts, so he turned his eyes to his son.

His parents had been looking forward to this day, not only to meet their new grandson, but to renew a relationship with Lili that had meant a great deal to them. Brad shifted from one foot to the other as he watched the warm reunion, feeling out of contact and out of sorts. He wanted to be an integral part of this mutual exchange, not a bystander. It felt wrong to be standing here, hands shoved in his pockets, while his mother and father lavished affection on this woman he ached so to have in his arms at the same time that he still fostered resentment of her.

His parents then turned their full attention to Donny. Mr. Hollingsworth put out his hand and Donny shook it. "So, young man, you are my grandson. What a marvelous gift, and it isn't even my birthday!"

Donny shuffled his feet, suddenly looking very young and very unsure. "So, does that mean you're glad?"

"Glad!" Mr. Hollingsworth gave a bellow of joy. "Why, this is Christmas and New Year's and Thanksgiving, all at once." He beamed at the boy. "As well as my birthday. Welcome to our family, Don. Or, rather, to *your* family."

Donny, clearly overwhelmed by the effusion of acceptance, went gamely through a similar welcoming from his new grandmother, whose face shone with happiness. She kept shaking her head in wonder. "You are the spitting image of your father. The absolute image!"

Brad's eyes met Lili's. She seemed unnerved, behind that smile. No wonder. This must be harder for her than it was for him. Donny had been her son, exclusively, until very recently. Now he was being swept into the Hollingsworth clan. She couldn't help but feel a frightening degree of loss. He pushed his feet harder against the marble floor to keep them from going over to her, held his arms tightly against his sides to prevent their reaching out. Conflicting emotions still fought it out in his mind, keeping him from the very thing he wanted so badly. He hadn't yet forgiven Lili, and wasn't sure he ever could.

The Hollingsworths gave Donny a complete tour of the house and the grounds, knowing, by instinct, that he'd be full of curiosity. Of course the rest of them followed, caught up in the unfolding drama. Brad stayed close to Donny's side, eager to share the boy's wonder, so like his mother's as a youngster. It still amazed him, the degree of love he felt for this child—a child he hadn't even been aware of mere weeks before. Donny did look just like him and have a lot of the same characteristics. But there was a great deal of Lili in the boy: mannerisms and attitudes and that intense curiosity that had charmed Brad when he first encountered it in his sister's young friend.

A strange duel of phenomena had been taking place. As he and Donny spent more and more time together, Brad developed a sense of completeness beyond anything he'd ever known, an enrichment of a sort nothing else had ever provided. Yet, at the same time, each day or evening with his son, with *Lili's* son, also created a greater void—an awareness that something vital was missing. His gaze kept moving to Lili, so lovely, so vulnerable. *Damn it, Lili,* he thought, *don't keep looking at me as though I were about to spirit Donny away from you!* He resented her lack of trust at the same time he realized he'd given her scant reason to trust him. Trust. Something to be earned, yes. But, at a certain point, something to be freely given.

The last stop was the barn, where two horses were stalled. Mr. Hollingsworth, who seemed mesmerized by this addition to his family, stuck close to his grandson. This grandson who should, by rights, bear his name. "Don, do you like to ride?"

"I don't know. I never have."

"Like to try sometime?"

"Sure."

"It's a date." After introducing, with great ceremony, the two stallions, he led the way to a little room to the rear of the stable. "Now. I understand you've recently had a birthday, and your grandmother and I would like to give you a gift."

Donny's eyes lighted up, as any child's do at such a prospect. "Another member of our family has given birth, and we thought you might like to adopt one of her offspring." In the corner of the room, cozy in a large, well-padded box, lay a liver-spotted springer spaniel with six adorable puppies.

Donny was struck dumb. He stood glued to the floor, his eyes big as billiard balls, his mouth hanging open. Then the corners of the mouth swept upward in a smile that threatened to split his face. "Puppies! Oh, Mom, look!" He dashed to the box, stopping himself in a huge show of restraint as he remembered not to rile the mother. Then, approaching with caution, he stuck out an exploratory hand to the dog. "What's her name?"

"Cindy."

"Hi, Cindy. Hi. You're awfully pretty. Good dog." Cindy licked his hand and thumped her tail. Donny looked over his shoulder. "Can I pick one of them up?"

"Go ahead. She won't mind."

They watched entranced as, one at a time, he picked them up, cuddled and petted and rubbed his chin over the down-soft fur of the adorable, wiggly puppies. "Awesome." It was murmured in the hushed tone of prayer. His eyes, full of entreaty, sought Lili's. "Mom. Can I? Can I?"

Brad wanted to step forward, to join in the decision, but decided to stay out of it for the time being. He had a feeling that nothing on the face of the earth could keep Donny from owning one of those tiny dogs.

Mrs. Hollingsworth cleared her throat. "If there's a problem where you live, you can keep it here for as long as needs be. You'll be visiting often anyway—at least we certainly hope so." She cast a hopeful glance at Lili. "And Brad hopes you might be moving soon. You could make sure they'd allow a dog." So, just like that, it was settled. They left Donny, who was obviously not about to move away from the box, to make his choice, while the adults went inside for a drink.

All in all, the evening was very pleasant. Louise struck up a rapport with Mrs. Hollingsworth that promised easy association in the future. Donny appeared, sometime later, with his pick, a little squirming bundle of brown and white fur that kept licking his chin and nipping at his proffered fingers. "It's a girl. I think." After an inspection, the opinion was confirmed. "I'm going to call her Libby, so her name starts with the same letter as Mom's and Grandma's."

After Donny was provided with a thick layer of toweling to keep under his new pet, they all watched the slides from New Zealand, then banished the puppy back to its mother long enough to eat a sumptuous dinner, served by the maid. At the end of the evening, Donny had to say goodbye to his puppy, who was too young, in any case, to leave her mother. He was effusive in his thanks to the Hollingsworths for the dinner and all, but mostly for the puppy. It was, he assured them, the best present he could imagine. When he hugged them goodbye, Brad spotted tears in both grandparents' eyes.

Brad walked them to the car, his hand on his son's shoulder. They had become a team. Man and boy. Father and son. When they reached the automobile, Donny said, "You know, I think it'd be good if you'd all call me Don, like my grandfather did." Brad smiled. It had been a success, Donny—or *Don*—had walked right into his place in the family.

Brad nodded. "Fine with me, son."

Don beamed up at him, full of the bliss of his own parenthood. He was now the full-fledged father of a dog! "Thanks, Dad."

Brad was shaken to the soles of his feet by that one word. *Dad. Dad.* It rang in his mind like a chorus of chimes. He swallowed the lump that rose to his throat. Somehow it didn't seem the right time for a grown man to cry. He just nodded and tightened his grip on the boy's shoulder before letting go and watching him climb into the backseat of the car.

Lili, giving him a glance full of unreadable messages, hesitated a moment before getting behind the wheel and starting the motor. Brad held the door for Louise, smiling, nodding, his mind a bog of irresolution. He felt paralyzed with indecision and helplessness. He didn't want them to go. Either of them. His son or his— God. The word that had popped to mind was *wife.*

Donny wiggled around in his seat, then tapped his mother on the shoulder. "Hey, we going home or what?"

As they drove down the long driveway, away from the man she loved so desperately, Lili thought back to their encounter of a few nights before. The thrill of being held in his arms had been too short-lived, too overlaid with angry emotions to savor, but the memory of his touch still lingered on her skin. Her own fragmented feelings constantly had to be subjugated to second place, behind the drama involving Donny.

She glanced in the rearview mirror at her ebullient son. She wondered how long she'd maintain the upper hold on his allegiance. In truth, it wasn't just the benefit of riches that the Hollingsworths offered. The wealth extended into areas that would be far more seductive to Donny. She shook her head. Don. He had, literally, merely entered the foyer of the Hollingsworth clan. Not only was there Marcy, who offered a California farm, but three cousins. There were great-grandparents, two full sets, one in Maine and one in New York State. And multiple relatives who gathered in massive groups for holidays, weddings, funerals and special occasions of all manner.

And soon there would be one of those gatherings—the introduction of the next-generation Hollingsworth. Donald Bradford. And where would she be? At home, waiting to hear how it went?

It was a busy morning at work. Lili had succeeded in immersing herself in the project at hand, thus shutting out, for a blessed period, all the tangles of her personal life. When the phone rang, she picked it up, muttering a distracted "Hello?"

"Lili?"

Her pencil came to an immediate halt and her attention snapped to alert. "Yes. Hi, Brad."

"I thought the visit with the folks went well, didn't you?"

"Oh, yes. Wonderfully well. Donny—" She paused. "*Don* has been walking three feet off the ground ever since. He keeps talking about the puppy and his new grandparents, and the house, and the puppy, and the horses he's going to have a chance to ride." She laughed. "And the puppy. I really think he's afraid he'll wake up!"

"Yeah. I've had a little of the same fear myself lately. Although, in some ways, I wish I would." There was an uneasy pause. "I'm . . . sorry about the other night . . . at your house."

"Yes. So am I." That experience had been followed by more tears, more hours of introspection, more of the endless, mind-deadening questions. She was, frankly, sick of all of it.

"Listen, Lili. We need to talk." Why did those words strike terror in her heart? "There are a lot of things concerning Don's future that we should discuss."

"Yes. I suppose that's so."

"I thought it would be nice to have dinner together. Maybe at the Ritz? I'm staying here, you know."

The Ritz? Memories flooded her mind. "No, I didn't know."

"Is that okay?"

"Yes. . . Yes, it's fine." Could she handle it, sitting in that lovely room again, looking across the table at the man who was Donny's father?

"Listen, how about wearing that dress, the one you got in New Zealand? Sort of a light purple. What do they call that color?"

"Mauve."

"Yes, that's it. I never got to see you wear it."

Was that wistfulness in his voice, or did he figure, since he'd paid for it, he should at least see it modeled?

"All right. What time should I meet you?"

"Seven okay?"

"Fine."

Lili was awash in déjà vu as the tuxedoed maître d' escorted her to the corner table where Brad stood waiting until she was seated. His gaze moved over her appreciatively. "You look lovely."

"Thank you."

A smiling waiter quickly appeared beside the table. "Good evening, Mr. Hollingsworth." He nodded to her. "Ma'am. May I get you a drink?"

"Lili? Champagne?"

"Yes. I love champagne—" her eyes met his "—as you know." Her pulse had quickened. What was happening here? This was not the setting for the confrontational encounter she'd expected. Had he decided to soft-pedal the changes he'd want made in his son's life?

"Bruce, we'll have the Chandon Moet, please."

"Right away, sir."

She glanced around. "This is such a beautiful room."

"Isn't it? One of my favorite dining spots." He sat back as Bruce reappeared and uncorked the bottle, allowing only a soft pop. He made a ceremony of placing the fluted glasses, pouring the bubbly liquid, waiting expectantly for the assurance that the vintage was satisfactory. As soon as he had left, Brad lifted his glass. "Before we talk about anything else, let's drink a toast. To Don. To our son."

Lili's fingers shook as she raised the glass to her lips, watching Brad over the rim as they both took a deep swallow. What now?

Brad set down the crystal glass, gazing at it with fixed intensity for a few seconds, before raising his eyes to meet hers. "He's a great kid, Lili. He's already brought so much to my life. The whole future feels different. More exciting, more important. More complete." He snapped the glass with his fingernail, causing a sonorous but rather pronounced *ding*. "In many ways."

"I'm glad. I'm glad the two of you have each other. And I'm sorry—" She stopped, dropping her head, then sat up straighter with an unwavering gaze. "I *am* sorry, Brad, for the lost years. But that is the end of the apologizing and the breast-beating. No more mea culpas. Like my mother, I'm through with penance."

"Sounds like a change of attitude."

"Yes, it is." She breathed in a lungful of air and let it out slowly. This declaration was the result of hours of thought: agonizing, tearful, then resolute. "I've gone through hell these past weeks, and I'm fully prepared to take responsibility for the mistakes I've made. But enough is enough. It was all set in motion by a scared seventeen-year-old kid in no way prepared to cope with decisions of the magnitude that suddenly faced her. I thought, wrong or right, I was protecting you. And recently? I can't offer any other explanation than one. I was terrified of losing my son. I've devoted my adult life to raising him, to trying to make up to him for not having a father." She sighed. "To not having *you*. All the usual mother-tiger instincts are, I'm sure, distorted by my sense of total responsibility." Just the hint of wetness came to her eyes and was instantly banished. "I've done the best I could."

"Lili." He leaned forward, his face full of compassion. And something else. Something so warm, so inveigling, that it sparked an answering surge of heated hope inside her. Was there to be a truce? Could they at least be friends, so the raising of Don would be a mutual enterprise, without rancor? His voice was soft, thoughtful. "God, I've been so muddled and unfair. I've gone over and over all the things you've told me, and I can understand why you'd panic. I really can."

"Brad, do you mean that?"

"Yes, of course I do. Now that I know Don, now that he's become such a . . . *precious* part of my life. God, I'd probably kill to keep anything from separating us. And if I feel that way after a few weeks, I can imagine how you felt."

She swallowed hard, determined not to embarrass herself in this sumptuous setting by bursting into tears. All her carefully built bombast had just been decimated by his tender assertion of understanding. "That means a lot to me, Brad. More than I can say." Her mouth closed tightly as she fought for control. "I've been so damned scared."

"You've been scared for far too long, Lili. It's long past time for it to stop. And I'm delighted to hear that you're through with self-condemnation. Guilt trips should be short, if they take place at all. And you have no reason to feel guilty. As we've already discussed, the original mistake was mutual, and we could argue ad infinitum about who owned more of it. So, if you're willing, let's both say goodbye to that one."

She nodded, unable to speak.

"Ah, Lili . . ."

She stiffened a moment, alerted by that familiar tone of entreaty, a tone that had led her to the twelve-second drop and the Sutherland Falls. Maybe he'd request something simple of her, like throwing the champagne bottle out the window and being hauled off to jail.

"Please forgive me for taking so long to work through all my anger. I just didn't know how to handle it."

Something rose up in her in an embrace of wonder. He had forgiven her! "You had a perfect right to be angry."

"Maybe. But then, so did you. I just— Well, it was a lot to deal with all at once. A son!" He turned his head to look out at the darkening sky. "Then I started thinking it all through, all the things *you* had to face. One of which was the unforgivably cloddish way I ran out on you at Huka Falls." She didn't say anything, because in this case, she agreed with him. "I didn't want to be sucked back into Esther's affairs, but I felt duty-bound to go. I didn't stop to realize you had no way of knowing how I felt, when I didn't bother to tell you." His gaze came back to her. "Say you'll forgive me?"

She could feel the Huka Falls gathering behind her eyes. "I'd forgive you anything."

"Careful. You may regret that someday."

"I don't care. Right now I simply can't care about somedays." She could see Bruce out of the corner of her eye, keeping a discreet watch on them. She'd heard that was one of the things that made this restaurant so famous and so fine. The waiters were professionals who could sense when their customers required privacy. It was, at the moment, deeply appreciated. This was something precious, what was passing between the two of them. Forgiveness, understanding. Precious and all too unique.

Brad reached across the table to take her hand in his. "I love you, Lili. I love you so damned much. Every corner of my life feels need of you. Even when I'm with Don, I miss you. I want to love you and be with you and share the rest of my life with you."

Could she believe what her ears were hearing, her eyes seeing? Yes. She could and would. She'd had enough of mistrusting her senses. This was it. The real thing. This was cloud nine, nirvana, heaven, all. "And I love you. Oh, dear Lord, how I love you! I've never stopped loving you since I was twelve years old!"

"Lili. My darling Lili." He tightened his hold on her hand. "Damn, I need to kiss you, but I suppose the other customers might think that was a little out of place."

She laughed—a sound that was, after the past weeks, strange to her own ears. "Who cares?"

He let go of her hand and lifted his champagne glass. "Okay. Time for another toast. To Don's parents. To us, you and me."

"Oh. I'll drink to that."

As soon as the toast was drunk, Brad asked, "Lili, will you marry me?"

Would she? Would she! She looked around the room, at the dazzling chandeliers, the brilliance of white linen and sparkling crystal, the handsome blend of white and blue, the profusion of fresh flowers. Beauty surrounded her, invaded her. Beauty and a profound joy so deep as to feel bottomless. Her gaze moved back to Brad. "Yes. Oh, yes!"

"Thank God. Lili, I'm so damned happy."

"Me, too. Do you think they can tell? All these people? Do you think they can see the bubbles coming up out of our heads?"

"No, they're blinded by our light."

The waiter, evidently sensing a lull in the emotional exchange, approached the table. "Are you ready to order?"

Brad looked up at him and grinned. "Good news, Bruce. We just became engaged."

The man seemed genuinely pleased. "Well, congratulations. Just a moment, sir. I'll be right back." In short order, he had returned, his smile still in place. "The management would like you to consider the champagne a gift, Mr. Hollingsworth, with their best wishes to you and your fiancée."

"That's very kind. And my fiancée and I accept. Now. I think the next order of business is to choose a properly delicious supper for this auspicious occasion."

"Yes, sir, I quite agree."

When they left the restaurant, full of succulent food and aglow with happiness, the maître d' presented Lili with a bouquet of red roses and dainty baby's breath. "We'd like to wish you both the very best of luck."

"Oh. Gosh! Thank you!"

Brad could see that the stiffly proper maître d' was as charmed by Lili's unabashed delight as he was. They both took the elevator up to his room, with no discussion whatever of Lili's going home. A quick call to her mother to explain her absence was all that was necessary.

Later, when they lay in each other's arms, cuddled in the embrace of spent passion and monumental joy, Brad said, "Tomorrow we'll go choose your engagement ring. And there's only one restriction."

"What's that?"

"You can't ask the price."

"I don't think I'll ever ask the price again in my whole life." They both knew she wasn't talking about things like rings.

Nature had cleaned house for the wedding. The Hollingsworths' gardens had never looked lovelier. It had rained the night before, leaving everything with that green smell of freshness that only trees and grass and flowers can provide. The sky had swept itself clear of clouds, and the sun was a blazing brilliance. Marcy, who was Lili's matron of honor, went first, down the path between the row of chairs set on the lawn. Lili, clutching her bouquet with one hand and her about to be father-in-law's arm with the other, smiled at some of the familiar faces raised in her direction.

There were Ed and Josie, come all the way from England. And—oh, Lord, she mustn't start to cry!—there were their three buddies, Glynne, Jonathan and Gillian, flown over on tickets supplied by Brad. "How can we be married without them here, Lili?" he'd asked. "It'd be so incomplete!" The innumerable Hollingsworth relatives were there, smiling their approval. And there, in the second row on the aisle, per Lili's instructions, was the Benjamin Potter book, *A Boy, a Dog, and 20,000 Sheep,* occupying a place of honor.

She smiled at her mother, who was still flushed with excitement over Lili's happiness and her own admission into college to get her advanced degree in nursing.

And then, there he was. Brad. With his son standing beside him as best man, beaming like a high-wattage bulb. Lili was glad that one's body somehow adapted, reformed itself to contain monumental amounts of happiness, or she'd never make this short trek without exploding into a thousand pieces of bliss.

She stood beside Brad, bathed in sun and warm breezes and the scent of early-June blossoms. When the minister said, ''I now pronounce you man and wife,'' Lili knew that now, and only now, had she truly reached the top of the mountain.

*   *   *   *   *

Silhouette Special Edition

COMING NEXT MONTH

#703 SOMEONE TO TALK TO—Marie Ferrarella
Lawyer Brendan Connery was dreading the long-overdue reunion
with his ailing father. But then nurse Shelby Tyree appeared by
Brendan's side, offering to help him heal the wounds of the past....

#704 ABOVE THE CLOUDS—Bevlyn Marshall
Renowned scientist discovers abominable snowman.... Was it genius
or madness? Laura Prescott sought to save her father's reputation;
newspaperman Steve Slater sensed a story. On their Himalayan hunt
for truth, would they find love instead?

#705 THE ICE PRINCESS—Lorraine Carroll
To DeShea Ballard, family meant pain; to Nick Couvillion, it meant a
full house and kisses on both cheeks. An orphaned nephew united
them, but could one man's fire melt an ice princess?

#706 HOME COURT ADVANTAGE—Andrea Edwards
Girls' basketball coach Jenna Lauren dropped her defenses once
boys' coach Rob Fagan came a-courting... again. Familiar hallways
harkened back to high school romance, but this time, love wasn't just
child's play....

#707 REBEL TO THE RESCUE—Kayla Daniels
Investigator Slade Marshall was supposed to discover why
Tory Clayton's French Quarter guest house lay smoldering in ashes.
Instead, he fanned the flames... of her heart.

#708 BABY, IT'S YOU—Celeste Hamilton
Policeman Andy Baskin and accountant Meg Hathaway shirked
tradition. They got married, divorced, then, ten years later, had a
child. But one tradition prevailed—everlasting love—beckoning
them home.

AVAILABLE THIS MONTH:

#697 NAVY BABY
Debbie Macomber

#698 SLOW LARKIN'S REVENGE
Christine Rimmer

#699 TOP OF THE MOUNTAIN
Mary Curtis

#700 ROMANCING RACHEL
Natalie Bishop

#701 THE MAN SHE MARRIED
Tracy Sinclair

#702 CHILD OF THE STORM
Diana Whitney

SILHOUETTE®
OFFICIAL SWEEPSTAKES RULES

NO PURCHASE NECESSARY

1. To enter, complete an Official Entry Form or 3" × 5" index card by hand-printing, in plain block letters, your complete name, address, phone number and age, and mailing it to: Silhouette Fashion A Whole New You Sweepstakes, P.O. Box 9056, Buffalo, NY 14269-9056.

   No responsibility is assumed for lost, late or misdirected mail. Entries must be sent separately with first class postage affixed, and be received no later than December 31, 1991 for eligibility.

2. Winners will be selected by D.L. Blair, Inc., an independent judging organization whose decisions are final, in random drawings to be held on January 30, 1992 in Blair, NE at 10:00 a.m. from among all eligible entries received.

3. The prizes to be awarded and their approximate retail values are as follows: Grand Prize — A brand-new Ford Explorer 4×4 plus a trip for two (2) to Hawaii, including round-trip air transportation, six (6) nights hotel accommodation, a $1,400 meal/spending money stipend and $2,000 cash toward a new fashion wardrobe (approximate value: $28,000) or $15,000 cash; two (2) Second Prizes — A trip to Hawaii, including round-trip air transportation, six (6) nights hotel accommodation, a $1,400 meal/spending money stipend and $2,000 cash toward a new fashion wardrobe (approximate value: $11,000) or $5,000 cash; three (3) Third Prizes — $2,000 cash toward a new fashion wardrobe. All prizes are valued in U.S. currency. Travel award air transportation is from the commercial airport nearest winner's home. Travel is subject to space and accommodation availability, and must be completed by June 30, 1993. Sweepstakes offer is open to residents of the U.S. and Canada who are 21 years of age or older as of December 31, 1991, except residents of Puerto Rico, employees and immediate family members of Torstar Corp., its affiliates, subsidiaries, and all agencies, entities and persons connected with the use, marketing, or conduct of this sweepstakes. All federal, state, provincial, municipal and local laws apply. Offer void wherever prohibited by law. Taxes and/or duties, applicable registration and licensing fees, are the sole responsibility of the winners. Any litigation within the province of Quebec respecting the conduct and awarding of a prize may be submitted to the Régie des loteries et courses du Québec. All prizes will be awarded; winners will be notified by mail. No substitution of prizes is permitted.

4. Potential winners must sign and return any required Affidavit of Eligibility/Release of Liability within 30 days of notification. In the event of noncompliance within this time period, the prize may be awarded to an alternate winner. Any prize or prize notification returned as undeliverable may result in the awarding of that prize to an alternate winner. By acceptance of their prize, winners consent to use of their names, photographs or their likenesses for purposes of advertising, trade and promotion on behalf of Torstar Corp. without further compensation. Canadian winners must correctly answer a time-limited arithmetical question in order to be awarded a prize.

5. For a list of winners (available after 3/31/92), send a separate stamped, self-addressed envelope to: Silhouette Fashion A Whole New You Sweepstakes, P.O. Box 4665, Blair, NE 68009.

PREMIUM OFFER TERMS

To receive your gift, complete the Offer Certificate according to directions. Be certain to enclose the required number of "Fashion A Whole New You" proofs of product purchase (which are found on the last page of every specially marked "Fashion A Whole New You" Silhouette or Harlequin romance novel). Requests must be received no later than December 31, 1991. Limit: four (4) gifts per name, family, group, organization or address. Items depicted are for illustrative purposes only and may not be exactly as shown. Please allow 6 to 8 weeks for receipt of order. Offer good while quantities of gifts last. In the event an ordered gift is no longer available, you will receive a free, previously unpublished Silhouette or Harlequin book for every proof of purchase you have submitted with your request, plus a refund of the postage and handling charge you have included. Offer good in the U.S. and Canada only.

SLFW - SWPR

SILHOUETTE® OFFICIAL SWEEPSTAKES ENTRY FORM

4-FWSES-3

Complete and return this Entry Form immediately – the more entries you submit, the better your chances of winning!

- Entries must be received by **December 31, 1991.**
- A Random draw will take place on **January 30, 1992.**
- No purchase necessary.

Yes, I want to win a FASHION A WHOLE NEW YOU Sensuous and Adventurous prize from Silhouette:

Name _____ Telephone _____ Age _____

Address _____

City _____ State _____ Zip _____

Return Entries to: **Silhouette FASHION A WHOLE NEW YOU,**
P.O. Box 9056, Buffalo, NY 14269-9056   © 1991 Harlequin Enterprises Limited

PREMIUM OFFER

To receive your free gift, send us the required number of proofs-of-purchase from any specially marked FASHION A WHOLE NEW YOU Silhouette or Harlequin Book with the Offer Certificate properly completed, plus a check or money order (do not send cash) to cover postage and handling payable to Silhouette FASHION A WHOLE NEW YOU Offer. We will send you the specified gift.

OFFER CERTIFICATE

Item	A. SENSUAL DESIGNER VANITY BOX COLLECTION (set of 4) (Suggested Retail Price $60.00)	B. ADVENTUROUS TRAVEL COSMETIC CASE SET (set of 3) (Suggested Retail Price $25.00)
# of proofs-of-purchase	18	12
Postage and Handling	$3.50	$2.95
Check one	☐	☐

Name _____

Address _____

City _____ State _____ Zip _____

Mail this certificate, designated number of proofs-of-purchase and check or money order for postage and handling to: **Silhouette FASHION A WHOLE NEW YOU Gift Offer,** P.O. Box 9057, Buffalo, NY 14269-9057. Requests must be received by December 31, 1991.

ONE PROOF-OF-PURCHASE

4-FWSEP-3

To collect your fabulous free gift you must include the necessary number of proofs-of-purchase with a properly completed Offer Certificate.

© 1991 Harlequin Enterprises Limited

See previous page for details.